Dreaming Annapurna

First Edition Design Publishing

Dreaming Annapurna
Copyright ©2013 Leon David Dunn
ISBN 978-1506-912-20-2 PRINT
ISBN 978-1622-873-18-0 EBOOK

LCCN 2013939430

May 2013

Published and Distributed by
First Edition Design Publishing, Inc.
Sarasota, FL
www.firsteditiondesignpublishing.com

Author's Note

On February 13, 1996, the Communist Party of Nepal began what they dubbed their 'People's War'. Their objective was to overthrow the Nepalese monarchy, which had presided over the country since its unification in 1768. After this declaration of war, tourism in Nepal plummeted, along with the number of trekkers visiting the Annapurna region. In 2006, after ten years of conflict, the Comprehensive Peace Accord was signed. The King was stripped of political rights and the monarchy's property was nationalized.

The legendary Annapurna Circuit Trek came into being after the opening of the Manang area of Nepal to tourists in 1977. Since the trek's inception, the government of Nepal has added two roads to the circuit. One has been used for years, although it is not completely accessible for much of the trek. The other is far more industrial and, as of the time of this publication, is nearing completion. Whether or not the addition of this newer road to the trek will be truly beneficial to the people of Nepal remains to be seen. However, I do strongly encourage anyone capable of doing so to complete the entire three week trek without the comfort of roads. Staying and eating in the many guesthouses will directly contribute to the villagers of the region.

Part I

Chapter 1

Not many people were flying into the kingdom in the clouds with me that day. My fellow passengers were scattered about the fuselage, separating themselves as much as the seats allowed. Four flight-sized bottles of red wine lay abandoned on the empty seat next to mine. I hate flying. I wearily looked out the window and watched the scraggly white and black peaks drift by below, lines of green dragging along their edges like a painter's pallet. I was in Nepal.

The plane landed smoothly at dusk, and my enthusiasm for new surroundings awakened my senses, leading to an early sense of elation and a tingling in my toes. But when I grabbed my overhead luggage and followed the other passengers with my small day-pack, I was quite aware of my lone white face drawing most people's attention. After time spent at customs explaining that I was entering the country to do volunteer work, some misshaped stamps were added to the plethora of others in my worn-out passport and I was released into the country.

Disinterested but armed patrolmen stood idly about in a cluster near the one currency exchange that remained open, forcing me to walk around the group to reach the window. Under the gaze of one soldier looking my way I exchanged some money, then somewhat contentedly, headed for the large automatic doors that opened up to Kathmandu.

"Where you go?" asked the lone taxi driver smoking a cigarette, leaning against a rusted hatch-back.

"Thamel," I answered, then showed him a printout of the hotel I had researched from London.

He eyed the paper queerly and then looked up at me. A thin line of hair sprouted from his upper lip, and a scab formed a corner of his mouth. He picked at it, his cigarette nearly burning his nose. I stood looking at him wondering if there was a problem. Consciously nervous, I eventually smiled, to which he sighed and flicked his cigarette butt out into the night. His hand gestured behind him as he turned and walked around the car towards the driver's seat. I did not feel comfortable. It wasn't the wine.

The mad rush of all things Asian I had been expecting did not come. Looking out the window I saw my own reflection pasted onto streets lacking activity. Hesitant to ask the angst driver anything, I kept silent and watched a rather lackluster scene of small shop-fronts mostly in closing.

It didn't take long before the taxi stopped in front of a narrow alleyway. The driver put his hand up and over the backrest but said nothing. I took two one-hundred rupee notes out from my pocket and handed it to him. He crumpled them in his hand and then pointed over towards the alleyway. I didn't argue for change. Stepping out of the taxi, I then followed his directions.

"Namaste," said a voice from behind the counter, a face appearing a few seconds later.

"Namaste."

"Oh, good hello to you," said the young man who had obviously been sleeping. "You stay night?"

I assumed from his strange intonation this was a question, so I replied, "Two nights, please."

"No problem." He grabbed a set of keys from under the table with one hand, and rubbed his sleepy eyes with the other.

Ascending the ancient staircase that sighed wearily with each step, we traversed a dark hallway before stopping in front of an unmarked door. The hotel seemed eerily quiet, and the lightless halls had me thinking of a hospital at midnight.

"Here you are, sir," he said, handing me the keys. "I go bed again now. Tomorrow we do papers, OK?" He turned and walked away, leaving me alone without having paid.

The two years I had just spent working through Europe were exciting, but this was Asia. Determined to see what was going on, this new world awaiting me, I tossed my bag on the bed and immediately headed back out into the near-deserted streets. Being Kathmandu, and surrounded by the Himalayas, the sun had already disappeared. The sky above me now faded from a dark blue to a deep black. A smattering of stars shone brightly in the east. Not having consumed anything since those tiny bottles of red on the plane I wandered the streets in search of something to eat, eventually pushing past the curtains of the first alleyway restaurant I came across that was open. The entrance was low, and I leaned forward so as not to whack my head on the wooden beam. Inside, a narrow passageway led to a small kitchen on my right, and another curtain in the doorway to my left led to a small dining area. The restaurant was large enough for four plastic patio tables and not much else. They stood on a floor of mostly dirt, as the cement had been dug up in many spots. Four sleepy-looking patrons sat at one of the tables in front of me, and a large portrait of what I presumed to be the King hung on a vibrant yellow wall of bricks painted at the back of the room. The eclectic cafes and smoke-filled pubs of Europe this was not. Unsure of whether I should seat myself but too hungry to really care, I sat down in one of the plastic chairs at the other end of the restaurant.

A woman entered from behind the curtain with a tray of food, setting it down in front of the drowsy patrons. Grabbing a dirt-smudged menu from their table, she stretched over and handed it to me. She then asked if I 'want drink.'

"What are those guys drinking?" I asked, nodding my head to indicate the only other occupied table.

"Tongba."

"Oh," I replied. A few seconds passed before I asked, "Sorry, and what is that, exactly?" The men at the other table were pouring hot water over what looked to be rice.

"Is Tibetan beer. Is millet with hot water."

I'd never had Tibetan beer. "I would like one of those, please."

She returned with a large wooden mug of millet and a large container of boiling water. Following her instructions, I poured the boiling water over the millet until the mug was full, which I then pushed around with a metal straw that was pinched at one end to prevent any grain from being sucked up. I waited a few minutes while the millet fermented. When the water turned cloudy, I sucked heavily through the straw and a warm, sharp wine slowly filled my mouth. A man from the other table smiled at me.

I ordered a thukpa, which I discovered was basically vegetable soup with egg noodles. I also ordered a cup of Khukuri rum, rum being the only thing on the menu I knew.

"Why you here?" asked the smiley patron across the room as I sipped my rum. His friends had slowly trickled out starting about a half hour earlier. His eyes were glazed, his lips moist with tongba.

"Um..." I said, my own tongba and rum causing me confusion. "I'm volunteering," I spat out after a moment.

The waitress pushed past the curtain and stepped into the room. She looked to me first, and then to the man who had asked me a question. After a moment's hesitation she smiled, then bowed politely and left the room.

"Where?" asked the man, his voice slow, his eyes still staring at the empty doorway.

"Myagdi?" I answered, struggling for correct pronunciation.

He turned to look at me, the redness of his eyes clearly visible. "Why?" He asked taking a cigarette out of a pack that lay on his table. He lit it with his head tilted sideways, and I had a strange feeling that my answer had startled him. He then exhaled heavily, and a large plume of smoke slowly drifted towards me.

Why? Good question. I had made the decision in London four months previous. An ex-girlfriend at the time (though so brief was this relationship that the term girlfriend could be argued) said it would be best for me. She said I wasn't grounded. I liked her. I believed her. Plus my U.K visa was going to expire.

"Just think it's the right thing to do, I guess." I felt stupid, and slightly deserted, I couldn't think of the words she had used. "Why is it so quiet?" I asked, thinking about my short introduction to the country.

The man stood up slowly, staring at the picture behind me. "Curfew," he said. He then pulled from his jeans an identification card that he held in the air. "I can move around at night." He tapped it twice and then finished his drink in one final gulp. "Most locals can't," he added after a hiccup. Then with a wet rumbling cough he pushed his unfinished cigarette into the ashtray and left the restaurant without another look in my direction.

I turned and studied the portrait behind me. Royalty, I was now sure of, stared blankly out to the empty room. Had this man I had just met, my first real contact with a Nepali implied something? A lone silence filled the small room and the initial rush of being in a new place, in a new country and culture faded. I was alone. Wanting to leave and wanting my bed, I paid my bill then was back outside walking the strange and lonely streets of Kathmandu. Passing the few people still outside at that hour - mostly very intoxicated soldiers, an uneasiness filled me from within. Above me, zigzagging the narrow streets of Thamel, hung low, loose electric wires. Across which hundreds of advertisements selling outdoor and camping gear pushed weathered prayer flags to the outer edges, and dangerously close to the electric supplies. Soldiers stared as I slowly found my way back to the hotel. But no one asked where I was going.

Chapter 2

I awoke late in the morning to a deep, wall-reverberating sound. I stood up, stretched, and walked to the window. Pulling the curtains open, I stuck my head out and saw helicopters hovering above, low enough to see soldiers pointing their guns towards the ground. Below, the customers of the few local shops went about their daily business as though there were nothing out of the ordinary going on.

Leaving the hotel after a simple breakfast, I headed for the volunteer organization's headquarters. With printed map in hand I walked out of Thamel towards the south east of the city. The tourist district was easy to maneuver as it was short of people. Shop owners touted for my business, 'you buy, sir', 'good product for you, sir', they said, their pronunciation monotone. They were not as aggressive as I thought they would be. But the difference between tourist Kathmandu and the rest of the city became shockingly apparent after a ten minute walk. Outside of Thamel nobody cared about me. I was not a customer, nor even a curiosity to them. Neither was the crippled man dragging all his worldly possessions behind him on a three wheeled cart. Or the ashen sadhu with sunken cheeks and thick dreadlocks that fell to his waist I thought I saw dying to my left. And nobody cared about the angry, shouting shirtless old man kicking a statue that appeared to me to be a thousand years old. Now in the day's full sun, the people of Nepal went about their business, shuffling here and scurrying there. They came and went, passing before me, behind me, maneuvering around me, products were bought and sold. Tiny hole in the wall shops sold more colorful spices then I had ever seen, but these towering mounds still had difficulty masking the stench of urine, wet cement and decaying wood, one moment thick, the next palpable. Even with a map the labyrinthine streets and dizzying alleys took it out of me. Too shy to ask for directions, I lost hope and I flagged a taxi.

At just past midday I arrived at what I assumed was the office; the address was correct and the sign over the door might have announced it as such, but I couldn't read it. The writings itself I could see were originally in more than one language, English included, but weathered beyond detail. Walking the stairs, I rang the antique doorbell and waited. Nothing happened. Just when I moved to ring it again, the door opened a crack.

"Hello?" I called, peering down a long hallway.

"Yes, yes, come in, come in," came a hurried voice from somewhere behind the door. The owner of the voice suddenly appeared, causing me to jump, and not just because the man who opened the door appeared to be a dwarf.

"Joseph, is it?" he asked, ushering me in and shutting the door behind us.

"Yes, sir, that's me. Sorry I was a little jumpy there. Didn't realize anyone was standing behind the door."

"That's OK. I wasn't expecting anyone to ring the bell. This is an office building. Please, right this way, Joseph."

The walls of the hallway were adorned with pictures of people who had previously volunteered with the organization, but I didn't get a chance to stop and read the captions underneath. For a dwarf, this guy could really hustle.

When we reached his office, he finally introduced himself. "I'm Elam," he said, stretching his whole body over a desk to shake hands.

"Hello, Elam. Joseph." I shook his small hand in my own clammy one.

"I'm sure you were expecting someone else," he said, smiling. "You were expecting David, were you not?"

"Yes, David," I said, relieved. "He's the person who has been corresponding with me, yes," I added, embarrassed.

"David is out today. Actually, he's always away on Wednesdays doing his rounds for the website. He runs one that details the goings-on here in Nepal. He moves about to the UN offices, the WFP offices, Oxfam, The Nepal Children's Society, and quite a few smaller ones that most people have never heard of, chronicling any violence towards civilians, food shortages, natural disasters, stuff like that. It's his project, really. I only help him out with the typing, but he generally makes the rounds himself."

"You must both be pretty busy, then."

"Yes and no," he said, leaning back in his chair, not offering any further explanation. "I have some things for you here, Joseph." He reached across the desk toward me and grabbed a brown envelope from atop a mess of papers. I could have reached it from where I sat, and felt kind of foolish watching him struggle from his side of the desk. "David has left this package for you. You already have most of the information with you, correct?" He tossed the package onto the desk and it came to a halt, stopping just in front of me.

"Yes, sir. I brought it with me."

"Good. I personally can't tell you much about what's going on in Takam. I wish I could, and I wish David were here because he could tell you all about it. He's been out that way a few times, but I myself have never been there. When you get there you should ask to see someone by the name of Debu Rawal. He's the headmaster at the village school, and he's the one who will be showing you around the village. All of this information is in there too, of course," he said, pointing to the envelope.

I was disappointed David wasn't around. I had been hoping to get a personal account from someone who had actually been to the village, someone who I had already been in contact with.

"I can assure you that everything is OK now," Elam continued. "You know, regarding the People's War and all. You must understand that for all intents and purposes it is safe, but there is always a risk when you're around such things."

War? I wasn't sure I had heard him right. "Sorry ... what did you just say?"

"You know, the People's War," he said, adjusting his seating position. I noticed a large book underneath him. "You'll be fine, though. You did know about the trouble in the country?"

I stared at this man who was sitting on a book discussing a war. He waited as my mind ticked over. This took what seemed like hours.

"The Myagdi area is still OK, Joseph," he said after I failed to speak.

The dead streets, the soldiers, the curfew and identification cards now all made sense. Why had nobody told me this before? I hadn't read anything in the news-papers, nor seen anything on TV. My ex-girlfriend certainly didn't bring it up, thank you very much.

"Listen,' said Elam, his voice now concerned, "A positive attitude is good. We have had a number of people out there who have returned well before they said they would, and, unfortunately, a few who have just up and left. Now, I don't mean disappeared," he added hastily, as if he knew he had chosen the wrong words. "Don't get me wrong. I meant to say that they just left the country without telling us."

Elam and I spoke for over an hour. And in this time he convinced me I would be fine. There was no evidence that anything had happened to any of the country's hundreds of volunteers. All those who had left, and those who were still out there had been accounted for. And after our rather cold introductions I wasn't sure how I was going to take to him, but he turned out to be a very nice man. He had worked for the Red Cross for most of his adult life in Cincinnati, until his wife of fifteen years had suddenly passed away. After that tragedy he had bounced around from job to job for a few years before returning home to Israel. Following a brief stay with his family, he decided to get back into 'the business of helping people', as he put it. Since that time, he had worked with volunteer organizations in some of the poorest African and Asian nations.

Just before leaving, I told Elam I'd come around the next day to see David. And at the last minute, I remembered to ask him what I should be doing about my visa situation.

"Just head out there to Takam first. If you decide to stick around, you can send your passport back to us. I know mail is only a once-a-month thing, but trust me, those boys are very reliable. We can sort the papers out here ourselves and get it back to you after. On the other hand, and you didn't hear this from me, if you 'accidentally' overstay your visa it wouldn't take much to get out of the country." He smiled as if both of us knew what he was talking about, which I did not.

This was most definitely not Europe.

Chapter 3

An afternoon shower started soon after I left. Dripping wet and sitting in a restaurant near the volunteer office, I pulled the papers out from under my shirt where I had put them to keep them dry. I lay the file on the table and ordered a chai. The manila envelope contained everything I needed to know and even included some pictures of the villagers I would soon be meeting. Everyone seemed so happy and friendly, not one smile missing from a single shot. The small village, too, was beautiful and very rustic in every sense of the word.

Putting the trouble in the country on my mental backburner, I left the restaurant on a slight high and, with my afternoon to kill, I thought a visit to the one orphanage I had researched before coming to Nepal was in order. On my map I had scribbled the names of the people who ran it. This map was now heavily creased, but still readable.

The sun had broken through the dark clouds, so I decided to brave the walk. Not entirely sure where I was going, I stuttered 'Gonggabu bus' to a passing stranger who nodded confirmation that the bus depot was in fact in the direction I was headed. A short while later I stood outside of what looked to be an abandoned building. Three young boys kicking an old patched soccer ball around the side of it offered the only proof that it was actually occupied. The building was big, very old, and definitely in need of some repair. It stood two stories high with a small fenced-in courtyard where the boys were playing. There was no number on it to indicate an address as far as I could see, but it sat on a corner where the road ended. I found myself smiling as I watched the boys playing and laughing. They were shoeless and caked in mud, but I could hear them teasing each other playfully. Looking around I didn't see anyone else nearby, and the boys ignored me, which I thought was a bit odd seeing as this was nowhere near the tourist part of town. I took the steps up to the front door and gave the bell a ring. I didn't hear anything.

"Hello!" I yelled to the boys. The one nearest to the steps turned to look at me just as his friend was passing to him. The ball's trajectory was slightly higher than normal, and I watched as the ball slammed into the back of the little one's head. A thump echoed off the wall and the other two fell to the ground in hysterics. I couldn't help but smile either. Must have stung, though.

"Hello," I tried again. "Is anyone here? You know, inside?" I jerked my thumb at the door, hoping they would understand. The little one nodded as he rubbed the back of his head. Then he motioned to push the door open.

I mimicked his gesture and said, "Push." He nodded again, still rubbing the sore spot.

I decided to try the bell one more time before marching in like a soldier of the Royal Nepalese Army. 'Don't want to get shot just yet,' I said to myself, rocking back and forth on my heels and suppressing a smile as the poor little kid clutched his injured head and ran back to join in the game. I tried the doorbell again; still nothing. 'Screw it,' I thought. I opened the door a crack to see if any light emanated from inside. I pushed a bit more, enough to put my head through. "Hello," I half whispered.

At the sound of my voice, I heard movement coming from another room. I stepped into the entrance hall, where I had a chance to look around. To the right was a staircase leading to the next floor, and to the left of the landing a long hall ran the length of the building. A number of doors lined the hall, leading towards the back of the house. A woman appeared at the end of it, walking slowly towards me. Carrying a baby against her hip, she held a finger to her pursed lips with her free hand, nodding slightly at the sleeping child. The sight of her put me immediately at ease for some reason, and I found myself slowly easing the door shut behind me. The woman was short and wore a white t-shirt that was a couple of sizes too large and covered in stains, some of which looked old and some of which had clearly come into existence that morning. Underneath, she wore a long, beige skirt made of corduroy, also stained, probably by the sticky fingers of countless children clutching at it.

"Hello," she whispered, barely mouthing the word. East Asian in appearance, her greeting surprised me; not a trace of an accent.

"Hello," I replied softly. "Is this the orphanage?"

"Yes, welcome," she nodded, pointing to a chair next to the door. She motioned to the baby then back towards the hallway. She put one finger up telling me to wait a minute. I nodded and she smiled. She had a lovely smile.

I sat down and took a closer look at my surroundings. For an orphanage, it seemed really quiet. The walls were bare, notwithstanding a few noticeable cracks and the paint peeling off in many places. All the doors down the length of the hall were closed, and there didn't seem to be much going on upstairs either. Eventually I heard a door shut, then the sound of her corduroy skirt rustling towards me.

"Hello," she said again, this time at a normal volume, as she extended her hand to me.

"Hello," I repeated, "My name's Joseph."

"Nice to meet you, Joseph. I'm Hien."

"Nice to meet you Hien. Are you...Nepalese?"

"No, no," she said, looking at me like my question was an odd one. "I'm American. Well, Vietnamese-American. I was born in Vietnam, but moved to the States when I was three. Would you like some tea?" she asked.

"Yeah, sure. I'd love some." I followed her through the hall towards the back of the house.

Two stoves, three refrigerators, and one extremely large rice cooker filled the kitchen. Having only seen the three boys outside and the baby she had been carrying when I first arrived, I asked why there were so many appliances.

"Oh, well, today most of the kids are at the market with my husband. Every week the shopping has to be done, and it's a day out for them. Most of them actually want to go, but we make sure everyone gets a turn. The three out back were a little mischievous over the weekend so we kept them back. Although, judging by their laughter, I probably should have had them study instead." She looked out one of the rear windows. "Next time," she added, lighting the stove under the window. "Please, Joseph, take a seat."

"Thanks very much."

"So, what brings you here?" she asked, sitting across from me at the large picnic table in the center of the kitchen.

"Well, I was curious as to the different possibilities of volunteering. I stumbled upon your website during my research. I knew roughly where you were located, so I thought I'd come and have a look."

"We don't actually take any volunteers here. It's just my husband and me. We take donations, but we've never had any volunteers."

"Yeah, I noticed that on your site. I'm actually heading out to Takam." I looked around, not really sure what to say, eventually blurting out, "What brings you here anyway, Hien?"

"My husband and I first came here years ago. We're both avid mountaineers so, naturally, we just fell in love with Nepal. After a few return trips, we decided to start our own business here." She paused for a second, as if she was going to say something else, but then didn't continue.

"What type of business?" I asked, hoping I wasn't being too intrusive.

"Guided tours were our gig. We still do them, mind you, now and again." She stood up as the water began to boil and continued, "We did that for the better part of fifteen years, and then one day we just decided that it was time to stop. Having been away for so long and having witnessed the poverty and the injustices to children and the poor here, we decided that we had to help out. We sold the business for a pretty hefty sum, came to Kathmandu and started this." She pointed to the ceiling. "Sugar?"

"Yes, please." She handed me a cup. I was surprised by the aroma of piping hot Earl Grey.

"Simple luxuries are still needed," she said with a knowing smile, taking a slow sip from her own cup.

After tea, Hien gave me a tour of the house. Upstairs were four identical bedrooms, each with six bunk beds. As we walked back down the staircase, Hien's husband returned with the kids. He was about six feet tall and definitely looked the part of a mountaineer. Taking the last step to the landing, I shook his hand as he came in.

"Hello. My name's Joseph."

"Hello there, Joseph," he said, squeezing my hand as the little ones ran between his legs. "What brings you here?"

With my hand behind my back, moving my fingers to get the blood flowing again, I answered, "Well, as I was telling Hien earlier, I saw your website and decided to come over and say hello."

"That's great," he responded, but I could tell he wasn't really listening. He was pretending not to notice the little girl who had jumped on his back. He walked in circles pretending to scratch an itch, the way a dog would chase its tail. The little girl made eye contact with me and held a mischievous finger to her lips.

Suppressing a grin, I continued, "I'm heading out to the Myagdi area. Going to volunteer out there."

"That's fantastic, Joseph. Good for you." He reached behind suddenly, grabbed the child with one arm, then swung her around his waist, much to the delight of the little one.

"You're staying for dinner, I imagine?"

"Hadn't really planned on it, but yeah, I would love to."

"Excellent. It'll give us some more time to talk." He put the little girl down and whispered something to her in Nepali. She ran off towards the kitchen, slapping my leg as she passed me. "I'm just gonna wash up. But feel free to look around, you know, play with the kids, talk to them and whatnot. Most of them don't speak much English, if any, but there's always ways to communicate."

"Thanks. Uh, sorry, I never did get your name."

"It's Blair."

I spent some time outside with the children, most of whom, surprisingly, left me alone. I had been expecting a mad rush of everything little and snotty, but found I had to instigate conversation in order to get any attention. One little girl, however, did take to me, and after I had learned her name, Achala, she grabbed hold of my hand and followed me everywhere I went. Hien came to the back door a few times and I looked up at her, smiling. I played a few games of soccer with the boys and jumped rope with some of the girls. I was outside for barely an hour before Hien came to the door again and shouted something in Nepali. Before she had finished, most of the kids had already rushed to the back door.

"They're washing up now, Joseph. We'll be eating in a little while."

I followed the kids upstairs and washed up in the boys' washroom. One long metal sink ran the length of the room with various soap dishes attached to the walls and four taps emptying straight into the basin. It reminded me of an elongated urinal, and I had actually come to the conclusion that it was one until Blair later informed me that he had made the sink himself and that he thought it was the easiest way for twenty-odd young boys to wash up quickly.

"Many of the children had never used running water until they came to the orphanage," he added.

I came downstairs to find Hien and Blair in the kitchen with a few of the older boys. As I came through the doorway a tall young lad with close-cropped hair shoved past me on his way out. "Excuse me," he said, somehow coming across as both apologetic and annoyed.

Blair looked up from the table. "Don't mind him, Joseph. He's OK. He's just upset that he won't be going home this weekend. He doesn't live far off, but his grandparents are too old to take care of him. He's a good kid, and his English is pretty sharp."

Hien, who was plating some chapattis, added, "He's been with us for almost seven years now, and he's almost finished school. Blair and I are having a bit of a problem figuring out what we're going to do with him."

"You said he can't go home?"

"No. We received a message from his grandparents this morning. They just don't have the energy or the money right now for him to get home and back."

"What happened to his parents?" I asked before my head told me not to ask such intimate questions. I quickly added, "Maybe I shouldn't be asking."

"No, no, it's OK. Unfortunately, they both passed away some time ago. They lived in the country and didn't have a lot of money, so when they got sick they couldn't afford treatment. I don't remember what they had."

"Tuberculosis." Blair said, keeping a supervisory eye on two of the kids as they doled rice onto plates.

"Is there anything I can do to help? With dinner, I mean?" I asked, wanting to change the subject. I was feeling uncomfortable, but Hien and Blair seemed fine. They must have heard countless similar tragic stories. I could hear the children running around upstairs, their little feet a herd of miniature elephants on the creaky wooden floorboards.

Dinner was served in two rooms due to the sheer population of the household. The large picnic table in the kitchen held almost twenty of us, and one of the rooms off the long corridor housed the rest of the kids. The littlest ones were split into two groups and were looked after by a few of the older kids. In the next room, they all ate seated on the floor with their metal plates resting in front of them, placed there by that day's 'helpers'.

"Everyone takes turns," Blair informed me as some of the children dished out the rice and vegetables. "We have a set routine for who does what, when, where, and how."

I ate my meal next to Dipak, who sat on my left. Achala, my new partner in crime, sat to my right. She was a beautiful little girl with jewel-like eyes and short, dark hair that fell in front of them. I couldn't help noticing she had a cute little hop in her step when she walked. Knowing I could grab something to eat on the way home, it didn't seem right to take their food, even though Blair and Hien had offered. I let on that I wasn't hungry and let Dipak eat most of my meal. Blair and Hien looked up at me, smiling. After dinner, most of the children went back upstairs, some to do various chores and the rest to wash up before bed.

"Half of them bathe one day, the others the next," Blair explained as he and I sat on the porch. Hien joined us later with a beer in each hand.

"Here you go. Now, Joseph, I don't want you to think we keep alcohol in the fridge within the kids' reach. We keep it well hidden and allow ourselves just a little bit now and then. Not exactly the rules some international organizations would want, but hey, we do this for the kids and we do it by ourselves. No one around here seems to mind." She pointed to the dark, empty street.

"Thanks very much. Don't worry, I won't tell anyone," I said with an appreciative smile.

"Well, it was nice meeting you, Joseph. I have to go back in and make sure everyone's all right. You know, doing their jobs and washing behind their ears. But I hope to see you again soon. Thanks for all your help today. It's greatly appreciated."

"It was nothing," I protested. "No, really, I did nothing. Thank you for showing me around. What you're doing is truly amazing. Thank you again, Hien." I raised my beer to her.

I asked Blair about the kids' schooling situation, partly out of honest curiosity and partly to quell the awkward silence that had set in after

Hien had gone back inside. "Most of the kids are in school during the day, so it's not that busy," he told me. "It's just weekends and holidays that are hectic." He looked about as he spoke, not meeting my gaze. "We make sure they go to school; that is a must. Hien and I have been here long enough that we can communicate with them, so we don't speak English all the time. There's no point for them to be learning that too, at the same time they're adjusting to living here. Once they're established here and in school, then we bring out the English."

"How do you normally receive the kids? How do you find out about them?"

"Unfortunately, most of the kids are displaced due to conflict. And I don't just mean the whole People's War thing. There is a lot going on in Nepal that has disrupted many families. There's a shitload of stuff going down on the Terai, has been for years. Mainly the Majhis situation. They've been unhappy with the lack of representation they get in Kathmandu and have been known to attack the homes and businesses of anyone who is not their own, mainly anyone from the north, but they don't stop there. We've had about twenty-odd kids come to us from that conflict. We also have four Tibetans with us who managed to escape with their grandparents. The rest are mainly from small villages scattered across the country. Many communities know of us just from word of mouth. We have the website up and we're registered with a few national organizations that help fund us, but for the most part we run it the way we want." He held up his beer as if to emphasize their independence.

"How old are they when they eventually leave?"

"That depends, really. We don't just kick them out onto the street at a certain age. We make sure they know what they're doing. Most of them, unfortunately, just head right back to the villages where they came from. We have sent a few off to university, though, and one little girl was adopted by an American couple. We still stay in touch with her."

I looked out into the still night and took a swig of my beer. "At what point did you decide you wanted to do this, Blair? I mean, when did you say to yourself, 'this is what I should be doing with my life'?"

"I'm not sure how much my wife told you, but we knew pretty early on. But in order to get where we wanted to be, we had to do the trekking business thing first. We could have joined the Red Cross or a UN organization, but we didn't want all that red tape in front of us. We'd been living and working in Nepal for so long that we knew what we could do and where we could do it. And once all the contacts were made, it was just a matter of time before we were financially stable. The donations we do get pay for just about everything. I mean, we get discounts at all of the markets because of who we are and what we do, we have one doctor that we go to who doesn't charge us, the bigger organizations drop parcels off every so often. Hien and I know them all and everyone who works for them. It all runs pretty smoothly for the most part."

On my way back to the guesthouse that night, I thought of the children I had met. I had only spent one day in Nepal, but they'd already had an effect on me. My move to Takam, although the scariest thing I had ever ventured to undertake, now also seemed the most appropriate.

The next morning, I finally met with David. He couldn't give me much more information on Takam than what was already included in the package, but he did say that exercising a certain degree of creativity in finding something to do would be useful.

"You'll have a lot of time on your hands there, so it's best to get involved with everything. Start your own projects and get the villagers involved. It could be a lot of fun, for the right person."

Like Elam, David was easy to talk to. And, like Elam, he had also led a very interesting life. At first he seemed blunt even to the point of being rude, but I put this down to the nature of his work. Frankness would have to be a prerequisite in his line of work. He was of average height and balding but looked no older then thirty-five. Listening to him, though, you could tell he was much older. In between sentences he would pause for a fraction of a second longer than most people do, which is something I have noticed people do as they get older. It was as if he was looking for the perfect word to use next in his story. He wore glasses that rested on the tip of his nose, looking over them when he spoke to me, then through them again when looking away. He had spent most of his life on the road until he had reached Nepal. Various jobs in the hospitality sector had sustained his lifestyle of short periods of work followed by travelling. In between these many trips, he would volunteer his time for months on end.

"Sometimes just to avoid the responsibility of real work," he explained. "You know, every time I had a job, it always felt like it didn't matter. It was as though if I didn't show up I wouldn't be missed at all." I recognized the same feeling from just about every job I'd ever had. "But when I was volunteering, I really felt as if I was making a difference. And there isn't exactly a list of people kicking down the door to get into this line of work. This isn't for everyone," he said, looking around the room. "Plus, as I got older, I realized I couldn't just volunteer my whole life. I had to do something to earn a living."

After our talk David showed me around the place and told me all about the photographs that hung on the walls in the hallway. He pointed out three from Takam. In one photo, many of the villagers surrounded one tall woman with blonde hair. She was hard to miss, as she towered over most of the others. Her short hair was pulled to each side in pigtails, a smile on her face stretching from ear to ear.

"Who's this, David?" I asked, pointing to the picture.

"That's Giada. She was excellent out there. An Italian girl who spoke very little English, but she enjoyed helping out as much as she could. Come to think of it, I'm quite certain she's volunteered the longest out that way."

"Certainly seems happy."

"Yeah, she was always like that, too. Great energy."

I stared at the photograph. It wasn't just her smile; every person in the picture had a similarly infectious grin pasted on their face, whether old or young, toothless or with gleaming white teeth. But then I noticed a young girl in front who distanced herself slightly from the others, her eyes downcast. Standing a few feet off to the side, it was clearly a struggle to keep her head raised.

Before I left, David mentioned the Maoists and their slow eastward advance.

"I'm not telling you what to do, but if for any reason you feel you're in danger, just get out of there and make your way back here. It's your call. If for some reason we hear of something that you haven't, then we will get in contact with you."

He walked me to the door, wishing me luck and pointing me in the direction of the bus stop where I could catch a ride to Pokhara.

And with that, I was off. I was free. I had a real job to do, just as David had said. It felt good. I was needed, and I wanted to be needed.

Chapter 4

I stepped off the bus in Pokhara at half past two. Stepping into the fading light, I had nothing to show for the journey but a sore ass and contorted stomach muscles. I took a taxi to the center of town, justifying the expense by thinking of the eight-hour walk to Takam I would set out on the next day.

Turning the corner onto the main street, I walked right into a sheer wall of camouflage - the back of a uniformed soldier. I could smell sweat and aggression through his damp fatigues. He spun around, his AK-47 just missing my face. I stood there frozen. He shouted something fierce-sounding directly into my face and kept up this vocal assault for what felt like minutes, but was probably mere seconds. When he had finished his tirade, he motioned with his gun for me to fuck off. I humbly obliged and slipped past him, head down, eyes averted.

Figuring it would be in my best interests to get out of the streets sooner rather than later, I ducked into a little restaurant just off the main road.

"Namaste," a young woman greeted me as I stepped through the door.

"Namaste," I returned.

I took a seat near the front so I could watch what was happening outside. The waitress who had greeted me brought over a menu and poured me a glass of water.

"Would you like something to drink?" she asked, a charming accent flowing from her lips.

"Yes, please. Could I get a chai and some orange juice if you have any?"

"Yes, no problem," she walked away with a smile.

My stomach began to growl as I looked over the menu, reminding me I needed something solid. When the waitress returned, I ordered a small pizza with onions and chicken and a pasta dish as well. I sipped my chai as I watched the goings-on outside. The soldiers didn't seem to be budging although it didn't appear as though they were there for any particular reason. One young soldier positioned near the bus stop was visibly drunk.

"Excuse me," I asked the waitress when she returned with my food. "Do you know why the military are here today? You know, all the soldiers?" I gestured at the one across the street and the one on the corner.

"Big rally today," she said, and was about to walk away again before I stopped her with another question.

"Rally? By who?"

"Maoists, sir. Big rally in Rapti area. Many, many peoples, all rallying." She flung her hands in the air and made a circular motion, signaling, of course, the international sign for 'rallying'.

"Rapti?"

"Yes, sir," she said, pointing out across the lake.

Chapter 5

I woke up exhausted in Takam, having spent almost ten hours on foot the previous day to reach my temporary new home. I had set off very early that morning after a quick stop at the pharmacist to pick up a few last-minute supplies. Eventually reaching a fork in the road, I stood puzzled for a few minutes before guessing. Twenty minutes later an elderly woman carrying a basket full of flowers, herbs, and an old plastic bottle filled with a mysterious brown liquid crossed my path. I stopped and took out my map, marked in both Nepali and English. She shuffled up to me and I showed her the paper, throwing in an inquisitive look for good measure. Not saying anything at first, she broke out into a crooked grin and looked me up and down. I smiled back and did the same. We both laughed.

"Takam?" I said questioningly.

She pointed back in the direction from whence I had just come. I walked beside her for a few paces, thinking we would walk together, but quickly realized I was moving a lot faster than her ancient legs could carry her.

I decided to wait at the second junction to ask someone for assistance. I sat next to a little sign I couldn't read and waited. After about an hour with no one passing my way, it occurred to me that even though I couldn't read the sign, the symbols on it would be similar to those on my map. I started off again, cursing my stupidity. But much later, when finally arriving at the outskirts of the village, my frustration and exhaustion were replaced with a great feeling of joy, like a drug sliding through my bloodstream and making everything feel alright. I knew I was there when I rounded a bend and saw houses on either side of the path. 'The burbs,' I told myself. These first few homes, though not very big, were made entirely of wood and seemed cozy enough. Further along the path I passed a few mud-brick homes, and these too appeared comfortable and sturdy. Five minutes into the village, a little girl came running round the corner of one of the houses.

"Hello!" she yelled at the top of her lungs, obviously no stranger to foreigners.

"Hello!" I yelled back, just as enthusiastically.

She laughed and ran right up to me. "Hello!" she yelled again at the same decibel level, clinging to my legs, face tilted up at a ninety-degree angle.

"Hello!" I yelled back, just the same as before. I took out the paper that David had given me. "Do you know Debu Rawal?"

"Debu?" she asked, ripping the paper from my hands. One tooth was missing from the middle of her smile.

"Yes, Debu Rawal," I repeated eagerly.

She stared at me for a few seconds, then took my hand and tugged me forcefully down the path.

"Debu Rawal?" I asked her again, pointing ahead. She was all smiles, but this time I knew she understood me. "What's your name?" I asked her.

"Alpa," she answered, beginning to swing our conjoined arms back and forth.

"Hello, Alpa. I'm Joseph." She looked at me with a childlike smile but said nothing.

A few minutes later, we stood in front of the door of one of the wooden homes near the start of the village. Alpa turned to me with a meaningful look, then pointed to the door.

"Debu lives here?" I asked. She smiled again, impatiently pulling at my arm. "What harm can come from knocking on a door?" I wondered aloud before suddenly hesitating. Meeting Debu would formally begin my stay in this tiny village, and I felt a rush of self-doubt. Could I really handle life here in the middle of nowhere? Alpa impatiently brushed past me and gave the door three hard raps, looking up at me smugly as she waited for it to open. No turning back now.

"Namaste," I said, bowing slightly as an old man opened the door.

"Hello," he replied. "I think you're Joseph, then, yes?"

"Uh," I stammered, surprised at how good his English was, "Yes sir, that's me."

"Good, good. So good to see you, Joseph." He stepped over the threshold and extended his hand.

"Good to see you, too."

He said something to Alpa in Nepali. She smiled and ran off.

"Please, come in."

Debu moved aside and gestured for me to enter. The doorway was low, but the ceiling was at least ten feet above the floor. A large iron pot hung from thick black chains in the middle of the house. Behind it, a long bench held various kitchen items. A few sheets hanging from the ceiling separated the home into two rooms of sorts.

"Humble little place, isn't it?" he said, walking to the bench and taking a pot from it. "Please, Joseph, have a seat." He pointed to the center of the room at some cushions on the floor.

"So, you're Debu?" I asked, realizing I still wasn't sure of the man's identity.

"Yes, that's me. I received a message from David a few weeks ago saying that you would be turning up shortly."

He put on a pot of chai and, when it was finished brewing, we stepped outside into his backyard. A rice field started not far from the rear of the house, extending for five more before terracing down into the valley. I hoped my own place would have a similar view. Debu, I soon learned, was a man of fifty-five, although he looked older. His skin was dark and weathered, wrinkles shooting out from just about everywhere when he smiled, which he did often as he told me about the village and his own life. He had lived in Australia for three years, going undetected as he worked various jobs to get by, saving up money for the day he would have to make a decision, remain illegally, or head back home. Luckily, for him, in his time there he had saved enough money to buy a house in Kathmandu and start his own business there. Originally coming from the vast valley of the capital, he had decided to move out to rural Nepal after his wife had passed away thirteen years previously.

"Some people said I was crazy, but after she died I just wanted peace. And you can't really find that in Kathmandu anymore." From my brief foray into the capital, I could understand what he meant.

My chai was starting to grow cold as Debu began asking me about my own life as enthusiastically as he'd talked about his own. "If I'm asking too many questions, I apologize, but don't be alarmed. It's just that not everyone here will be able to communicate with you, so they'll be asking me thousands of questions, and I don't want to lie to anyone," he smiled.

As we walked up the hill to my new home we passed a few locals who stopped and looked at me with curious eyes. They each fired a volley of questions at Debu, before smiling at me and continuing on their way.

"Don't worry, you'll meet everyone eventually," he said. "Tomorrow we'll have a welcome ceremony on the school grounds and whoever wants to come and meet you may do so."

He extracted a key from his pajama shirt pocket and unlocked the door to my new home. I was under the impression that there would be no need for locks in a village like Takam. Following the cue of Debu's welcoming gesture, I stepped inside. The building was circular, much like a Mongolian ger, except that it was made of clay and stone with two doors across from me.

Debu walked over to the area that served as the kitchen and took an old kerosene lamp off the stove, which he lit as the sun was inching its way down outside the window. The room glowed a dark yellow. He then walked a few steps and opened the closer of the two doors.

"The toilet and shower," he said, nodding for me to look inside. The floor was wooden, not clay like the rest of the house.

"I can't believe someone lugged a toilet all the way here." I couldn't believe my eyes. I was actually staring at a western toilet. There was no running water, of course; a large pipe that ran somewhere outside drained it and waste was pushed away manually using water from a bucket that sat next to the toilet. But, at least in appearance, it was a western toilet.

"Yes, Joseph, and it is not the only one here in Takam, either. You will see some houses tomorrow that have the same. And don't worry, it is not us who carry them here, it's the animals."

The shower was made of clay and stone with a tap overhead. I was told the water was partially heated by a single solar panel. The room beside the next door was my bedroom, which was approximately the same size as the bathroom, just big enough to house a single cot with some shelves along the walls overhead.

"Everything is cleaned for you and somebody will do your washing every two days. Don't worry, we will take care of you," Debu assured me enthusiastically.

The rest of the house consisted of a small picnic table in the main room, next to which was a shelving unit that curved along the wall all the way to the beginning corner of the bedroom. Towards the middle was a stove, its piping leading right to the roof, and behind it were two small but new-looking armchairs. Several small pillows stacked next to the chairs rounded everything off.

"Well, I'll leave you to get settled, Joseph. Over there we left you various foods; cereals, rice, a few vegetables, eggs, and some spice. Tomorrow I'll introduce you to the person who will be providing most of your food. There's firewood out back. Just watch your step over the toilet pipe. I don't think you would want to fall near there," he smiled as if he had a funny story to tell.

"Everything looks perfect, Debu. It's more than I expected, that's for sure."

"Well, good night, Joseph. I'll come again late tomorrow morning. You can sleep long time, as it's your first day. Subha ratri," he said, stepping out the door.

"Subha ratri," I repeated as best I could approximate, not knowing what the words meant but presuming something along the lines of 'goodnight.'

***

Taking some time to stretch, I let out a long, leisurely yawn before grabbing my alarm clock and holding it to my sleep-blurred eyes. It read half past seven in dim red. I knew I wasn't getting back to sleep, so I sat up and took in my surroundings. My bag was on the floor and some of my clothes were on the shelf above me. I hardly remembered stashing them there the night before, nor did I recall falling asleep in yesterday's clothes. I stood up and looked out the small window at the foot of the bed. The sun was up but hidden behind some very dark clouds, early morning mist still wandering about the basin below. An endless roll of green valley descended from my back window. Beyond the rear of my new home the grassy lawn extended for a few yards before vanishing from view.

Shuffling into the tiny kitchen, I rummaged through the foodstuffs that had been left for me. After locating a packet of tea and a box of sugar, I noticed a large container on the corner shelf that resembled a cooking pot, but with a spout at the bottom. I flicked it inquisitively with my index finger and was rewarded with a sharp pain. The pot was full. I took the lid off and saw a wealth of cooking water inside. 'Like going camping,' I told myself, whistling and doing a little impromptu jig next to the stove. Taking some tinder from a box next to the firewood, I built a small tepee inside the stove and struck a match. "Better than camping," I said out loud. I actually managed to make a fire on the first try.

With my mug of tea in one hand, I grabbed my jacket with the other and headed outside. The first thing to strike me was how vast the village seemed, as the homes trailed off in both directions for quite a distance. A well-worn dirt path ran the gullet of Takam. Nothing that looked like a school appeared in either direction. I circled around back, making sure to step over the toilet pipe, which ran on a slant before disappearing into the ground. Several feet separated my new Nepali home from the edge of the hill. Where the pipe ended up was anyone's guess. I found the firewood stacked neatly next to the pipe underneath my bedroom window. Next to that was an old rusty lawn chair, like the ones my family used to take to the beach when I was a child, except that this one had an ashtray attached to the arm. An empty teacup lay abandoned on the ground next to the chair. 'How long has that been there?' I wondered.

Taking a seat in the rusted old chair, I surveyed my new backyard. The view was the same as the one I had taken in from my window, of course, but more real somehow. This was fresh; I could smell the wet grass, could hear birds conversing with one another in the distance, mingling with the sound of someone whistling, my stovepipe puffing away. I was completely surrounded by green. Sap green, sea green, spring green, olive green, emerald green, moss green, everywhere green. It even smelled green. I took a sip of tea. It tasted green. I seemed to be breathing green. I sat in my greenness and wondered what was going to be expected of me in Takam, realizing I had no idea, really, what I was doing here. I had no vital skills to offer anyone. If anything, I was there to learn from them. How to be a good person. How to find a purpose, a way, an ambition. No more uncertainty, no more wasted moments. What did a young western man have on these villagers, anyway? These people had lived. I'd been around, sure, and had my share of troubles along the way, but it was nothing compared with the hardships that any one of these residents of Takam would have undergone. Would they accept me? They'd had other volunteers, the photographic evidence of which I'd seen at David and Elam's office. But what about me? Joseph Conrad Blaze Dixon, the young man with nothing to teach, no plans, a wanderer of earth, a nomad for life. 'Maybe they'll see right through me,' I thought.

Standing up from the rickety chair, I picked up the empty cup and three pieces of wood from the neatly stacked pile, feeling a little disappointment when I looked around and didn't see an axe. I'd had this image in my head that I would be chopping my own firewood. A regular Paul fucking Bunyan, a real man's man. Feeling the moisture of the firewood through my shirtsleeve, I grabbed two more pieces, knowing they would take a while to dry out, and walked around my house, my own Nepali house, a good full day's walk from any city proper. And there I was, living for free, taking up space, time, food, and water from people who needed it the most.

Debu was waiting for me at the front door. "Subha prabhat, Joseph."

"Uh...subo pra-bait," I responded in my own garbled interpretation.

"You will learn soon enough," he grinned, patting me on the back as I moved past him, juggling the firewood as I pushed the door open.

"Would you like some tea?" I asked.

"No, no, I just came by to see how you're settling in. I'm not here to take you away just yet. I am much surprise you're awake." It was almost comical how perfect his English could be, until such minor mistakes crept in. "I am going down to the village and will organize the day. I will return in a few hours. See you soon." He turned and left.

Retrieving the cheese and bread I had purchased the day before, I grabbed a knife from the kitchen and went out back again to eat my simple breakfast in the lawn chair. I took a weathered fashion magazine from the shelf in the living room on my way out, probably left behind by some other volunteer, possibly Giada. I leafed through the Italian mag, amazed at the amount of skin on show compared with this place, or even Canada.

Debu returned almost exactly two hours later, with two elderly village women in tow who he introduced as Ambu and Chapala.

"They can only speak a few words in English, but they are always willing to help," he said. "They will be doing your laundry and things. If you want to help them, then you may go ahead and do as you please, but they do many peoples' laundry. Nobody helps because it's what they do."

I looked at them both in turn and they each smiled. "Namaste," I greeted them. Chapala was shorter than Ambu, and probably shorter than most people. When she smiled not a single tooth showed, and it seemed they had long since fallen out. She kept her long and still luxurious thick black hair tied in a single braid that fell to the middle of her back. I couldn't begin to guess how old she was. No teeth, beautiful silky black hair, brown skin with wrinkles creasing her face and neck, but hands as soft and baby-like as if she had never worked a day in her life, the kind of walking contradiction I would grow accustomed to in rural Nepal.

Ambu's age, on the other hand, was far easier to determine. She was much taller than Chapala but about half the size in terms of body mass. Her face showed the wear and tear of someone who had seen more than enough for one lifetime. We both laughed when I pointed to her sweater, an old Nike sweatshirt from the eighties. She wore a blue bandana, which didn't keep a lot of hair in, as there wasn't much left to speak of on her wizened head.

The four of us strolled down the main path until we reached the end of the ridge. From there, the hill and corresponding path fell steeply down to the village proper. It seemed a great distance, but in reality it took only minutes to hike down. Here my laundry ladies left me, bidding me a cheerful "Namaskaar." They shuffled off together arm in arm, their ancient laughter ringing off the hillside.

"Namaskaar?" I asked Debu, who was busy silently disciplining two young boys who he had seen throwing stones at each other on the side of the path. He was the respected elder here, there was no doubt about that. A pointed wagging of the finger in the boys' direction was enough.

"Goodbye," he explained. "A, how you say, politeness goodbye."

"Namaskaar," I repeated. "Should I use politeness speech?"

"No, namaste is fine," he assured me.

Takam had various small, dusty streets that ran off the main artery of a path. The homes down here were built in the same fashion as those higher up the hill, but they carried a lighter economic weight. As the path descended, I noticed that each building was slightly dustier than those higher up on the ridge.

I strolled through the village with Debu, who pointed out each major building as we went. I must have met sixty people within the first hour, each with some question to ask me. One spoke English quite clearly, a few could string a sentence together, but most could not utter a single syllable. The children were the most surprising, as many had a basic grasp of the language, and I felt extremely inadequate only being able to muster a simple hello in their native tongue.

"All of these children you will be educating," said Debu. As if on cue, Alpa came running towards me from a dusty laneway filled with dirtied pots and pans.

"Hello!" she screamed with at least as much excitement as the day before, slamming breathlessly into my legs and wrapping her little arms around them.

She looked up at me with a smile, so I reached down and hoisted her up. "Hello, Alpa," I said, grasping her in my right arm.

"Ah, she likes you, Joseph," Debu beamed, "She doesn't usually let people hold her."

"Really?" I looked at the squirming little bundle of happiness in my arms. "How are you, Alpa?"

"I fine, thank you."

"Alpa, do you have any brothers or sisters?"

She stared at me for a second before what I said seemed to finally register before replying with perfect confidence, "I fine, tank you." Laughing, I set her down. She took my hand and followed along as Debu showed me the rest of the village.

At each end of the village was a small store where I could purchase a variety of necessities. There were no western treats as I had seen in most shops in Kathmandu. Chocolate bars, chips, and the like were non-existent here. I could, however, find cigarettes, laundry detergent, soap, rice, bread, pickled vegetables, alcohol, aspirin, rope, used clothing and shoes, needles, thread, tools, and other things one needs to live a comfortable life.

We covered the entire village in under an hour, ending up in front of the schoolhouse with approximately four hundred pairs of dark brown eyes staring intently at me as if I were there to perform a magic trick. Debu spoke to the children in Nepali for fifteen minutes or so as I stood next to him, feeling distinctly as though I was being auctioned off, which, I supposed, was sort of the case. Occasionally Debu turned and smiled as if he had just fibbed to the gathered crowd and I was in on his little joke. When he stopped talking and took a step back, I stood there motionless.

"Say something, Joseph," Debu intoned quietly. "They're waiting to hear from you."

I didn't know what to say. I couldn't very well tell them the thoughts I'd had that morning. It probably wouldn't go down too well to launch into a speech something along the lines of, 'Hello, uh, I really have no practical skills at all to offer you people, so I was just kinda wondering if I could hang out with you guys for a while and then, when I've had my share of this existence, leave you just as abruptly as I came, to return to my world of excessive waste, excessive eating, excessive medicine, cars, heaters, air conditioners, toasters, hair dryers, microwaves, and T.V. reality shows.'

Another few seconds ticked by as sweat began collecting on my brow. Finally summoning the courage from some unknown inner reservoir, I took a step forward and said (basically shouted, in my nervous enthusiasm) the only Nepali word I knew: "Namaste!"

To my great surprise, about two hundred voices returned my greeting with equal gusto. Feeling instantly more at ease, I took a deep breath and continued. "Hello! My name is Joseph." I waved awkwardly at the crowd, and the younger ones waved back. "I am here to help some of you that want to learn English. I am also here to help with anything else you would like me to do. Primarily I will be in the school, but please do not hesitate to come to me for anything that you may need. Thank you very much." For good measure, I yelled another "Namaste!" which brought the same hearty return as the first time. Then, all at once, as if a class bell had rung to end the school day, the assembled children began speaking to each other in excited voices. I could only guess what they were saying, but I gathered it was something along the lines of, 'What the hell did that white man just say?'

Debu took a step forward and began to speak in Nepali again. I stood staring out into the sea of eyes that were all still trained on me. I could see Ambu and Chapala in the front row knitting away, not paying much attention. Next to them was little Alpa, and in the back at a staggering six foot seven or so was Bindu, quite possibly the tallest man in Nepal, whom I had been introduced to that morning on my walk through town. He was the main carpenter-slash-builder of the village, and the surrounding villages, too. Other faces I recognized but couldn't put a name to, as I had met too many of them that morning. When Debu finished, he turned to me and told me that in a few hours we would all meet in the open space behind the school.

The school, just recently built, housed both the primary and secondary students. The previous primary school had become so dilapidated that the villagers had decided to tear it down and build a larger one. Made from both clay bricks and wood, it contained a grand total of four rooms. A library of sorts was in the room adjacent to a small empty room. It contained many randomly stacked volumes in various states of age and wear. The other two rooms were the classrooms, each with its own blackboard and a dozen desks. Wooden benches ran the entire length of the walls in each room, except for the wall that held the blackboards. Out the side walls yellowed newspaper partially covered two small windows.

"You can go wash up before we meet up behind the school if you like, Joseph. There may be some warm water in your room by now."

"OK, Debu. See you in a few hours?"

"Yes. We will have a welcome party for you tonight. Some people were very anxious for your arrival and they have been making foods all day. We will eat and drink tonight, and tomorrow you can start with your teaching. We will have much rejoicing tonight, you will see," he beamed.

Chapter 6

The pounding and ringing in my ears acted as my alarm clock. Reaching for the bottle of aspirin on the shelf above, I popped four tablets into my mouth. I managed to massage them down my throat without water by some Houdiniesque miracle. My clock beamed a disappointed six forty-three. I vaguely remembered Gunjan, the head teacher (that is to say, the only teacher), telling me that classes would begin at eight thirty. Gunjan and I had got on like wildfire the night before, our communication eased by the fact that he had spent a few years in Kathmandu studying English.

"I was working in big hotel, so I must speak good English," he told me.

I lowered my head as gently as I could to the pillow, landing with a grimace. The previous night's festivities slowly rippled into my mind's eye as I stared up at the ceiling. I remembered feeling a wee bit nervous before I'd left for the party, having followed Debu's suggestion and gone back home to freshen up, taking advantage of the lukewarm water that drizzled from the showerhead. After shaving and dressing in the least crumpled outfit I could piece together, I enjoyed another cup of tea in the greenness of my backyard until it was time to head back down to my welcome party.

As I walked down to the village in the dark, young children had run past yelling, "Hello Joseph!" That much I clearly remembered. I had felt like a B-list celebrity and not at all as awkward as I had that morning. Nearing the place where the path began to slope sharply downwards, I heard music lazily floating from the schoolhouse down below. As I approached the village, people appeared from all directions carrying dishes, smiling, whistling, and greeting me with their calls of "Namaste."

"Namaste," I replied sheepishly, wondering whether I was expected to bring something to the party as well, besides my unprepared uneducated self.

Rounding the last corner before the school, I was amazed to see practically everyone from the village in attendance. A small marquee had been set up and mini Christmas lights, though not turned on as there was no power, dangled blankly from the eaves. The desks had been brought outside from the classrooms and there were enough pillows strewn on the ground to seat a king and an army of his men. Just about every child from the village ran around behind the tent, full of palpable excitement.

Some played tag, others an impromptu game of soccer, while the littlest ones sat in the dirt looking slightly confused and misplaced.

Debu walked over and clapped me on the shoulder. "Welcome!" he bellowed, quickly ushering me inside the tent. Many of the villagers came up to shake hands and give me other hearty greetings. Celebrity status: achieved.

As I perched on one of the larger cushions taking everything in, I was introduced to Gunjan. He apologized for not being there that morning for my first visit to the school, as he had been off visiting his brother in another village.

"You will meet him too, Joseph. Very good man he is." Gunjan was the first to hand me a glass of alcohol, and from what I remembered he was the last, too. It was a real Nepali feast; thalis, curries, momos, papads, chapattis, rum, moonshine, all gleefully stuffed into me in an endless stream of indulgence.

"Everywhere is not like this, Joseph," Gunjan confided after his fourth glass of the local spirit, which tasted similar to rum but was about three times as strong by my approximation. "Many places don't have what we have. Very lucky peoples we are here. We care for each other and help each other."

I liked Gunjan from the start. He was a happy fellow who knew that he had it good and appreciated his relative good fortune. His thick eyebrows almost met in the middle of his face and seemed perpetually inverted as if he were deep in thought, a complete mismatch with the sprinkle of wispy black hairs that tickled his upper lip turned up in a near-constant smile. Over the course of the night, he would suddenly stand up and call out to someone on the other side of the tent, beckoning them over to be introduced to me. Debu joined us after awhile and the three of us sat and talked for what seemed like ages. They got up a few times and danced with the other villagers, but I was happy just to sit and take it all in, too shy to get up and join them. That is, until the alcohol kicked in.

Alpa came over to me, pulling at my hand, urging me to get up and join the dance. I eventually gave in when I realized that there was no way out of it. Downing the rest of my glass in a single gulp, I stood and followed her (or rather, was dragged) to the dance floor. Hindi music played from a radio that someone had propped up on a stack of firewood. About forty of us swayed drunkenly to the chaotic rhythm while the children, who had been ignoring the adults up to that point, came running over when they saw me enter the ring of dancers. I scooped Alpa up and did my best to keep something of a measured cadence with my feet. People clapped and cheered as I moved along with Alpa towards the center of the circle. Warm smiles greeted my eyes as my head followed my body in vague circular motions. I spun like a lazy top, a smile wider than I had known in years creasing my boozy mug. The claps and shouts of encouragement rang out from all around and the slaps on my back moved me along my clumsy tour of the dance floor with the precious little gift in my arms.

I could have continued dancing like that for hours had it not been for Gunjan pulling me away and shuffling me over to where the bucket of spirits rested.

"Tomorrow our school is at eight thirty," Gunjan yelled over the music, talking, clapping, dancing, and general revelry. He handed me another cup full to the brim with the blessed, crystal clear spirits.

Although some parts of the night after that point remained hazy, I recalled stumbling back up the hill for home at an indeterminate hour. I had evidently fallen a few times, judging by the muddied shirt I was still wearing the next morning. Willing the other events of the night to surface in my memory, I recalled how, just before leaving, the music had stopped and only Gunjan and I remained under the tent. A few other men had fallen asleep under the marquee, and some of the women had returned with blankets to cover them before retiring themselves. I remembered Gunjan, unfathomably drunk, telling about his brother and weeping. Years before, when his brother was living in far-western Nepal, he'd had his left arm chopped off by some Maoists. At the time, they had been targeting just about any government employee and anyone who they suspected of being anti-Maoist. My body began to tremble as I sat there listening to his story, overpowering the numbing effect of the spirits. Afterwards, perhaps noticing my visible shaking, Gunjan had tried to reassure me that this was in the past and that teachers were no longer being targeted by the Maoists.

"You are OK here, Joseph, don't be afraid," he had said through his tears. "Maybe when you are on one of your trips to other villages, you will meet my brother," he said. "You will be teaching elsewhere, yes?"

"I honestly don't know, Gunjan. I'm not really sure what I will be doing."

"Don't worry, it's OK."

Gunjan's brother had had his fucking arm chopped off. A sense of worry (or perhaps it was sheer, agonizing panic) slowly rose within me. 'Why the hell have they sent me out here?' I asked myself. 'They don't need another teacher here. There are, what, sixty kids max? And they only go to school for half the day. Arms being chopped off? What the fuck have you gotten yourself into, Joseph?' I buried my head in my pillow and tried to forget it, and with the pounding subsiding as the aspirin slowly took hold, I fell back into a deep but worried sleep.

Wondering upon waking for the second time whether it was normal for the village volunteer to get blind drunk with the only teacher in the village on his very first night meeting everyone, I dragged myself out of bed, filled a pot full of water and brought it to the shower to splash some on my face. Looking up into the cracked little mirror, I thought I didn't look half bad, considering. I changed into my best pair of pants and my best shirt, careful not to muddy anything.

I sauntered down the hill, hearing children's laughter and sounds of play coming as I approached the school. Rounding the corner of the building, I saw no sign of the marquee from the night before, nor did I see any desks, garbage, food, or any other sign that a full-blown village shindig had been thrown on the very spot just hours previously.

A weathered soccer ball darted in front of me; one of the younger boys shouted at me to 'pash.' My less than graceful kick was met with a wave of uproarious laughter. I knew I wasn't Pele, but I'd always thought I could hold my own on a pitch. Eager to prove myself despite the residual pounding in my head, I strolled onto the field to join them. It was a small play area, about one third the size of a normal field, but it somehow accommodated everyone. The older boys played on one half, using shoes for goalposts. When the ball came my way, I dribbled down the right flank before crossing it to the middle. It was a nice cross and would have been headed in, except that the boy trying to do so slipped and fell. The ball bounced over him and skittered to the trees bordering the field. I jogged over to the small crowd waiting in front of the goal, figuring I'd take the opportunity to break the ice since they'd let me join in their game.

"Hello," I offered. A few smiles, but no verbal response. "Namaste," I tried again.

One of the boys took a step forward and said, "Namaste." He shook my extended hand after a moment's hesitation.

"Namaste," I said in return. "My name's Joseph. What's your name?" I kept my attention on this boy who'd had the balls to speak.

"Daya."

"Hello, Daya." I couldn't quite make out his age, but he looked to be about fifteen or sixteen.

One of the younger boys then stepped forward and said with a slight accent, "My name is Indivar."

"Hello, Indivar. It's nice to meet you."

Daya looked me dead in the eyes and proclaimed, with great seriousness, "I like soccah."

"I like soccer too, Daya," I smiled back.

The other boys kept their distance, amused at the whole proceedings. The ball was thrown back into play and we all dispersed from our little circle. We played five on three and I made a few bad passes before realizing just who exactly was on my team, much to the disgust of one young man who clearly did not approve of my joining in. I heard his 'tsk'-ing noises from across the field every time I passed to the wrong team.

Gunjan showed up at eight forty-five and promptly shouted something in Nepalese to the kids, who all went running towards him. As the disapproving little shit passed me, I smiled and said, "Namaste." He returned the greeting but faced stoically forward on his holier-than-thou jog towards the school.

By nine o'clock, everyone was seated inside and ready to start. I stood near the door to the second-grade classroom as Gunjan tidied up his desk. There were thirteen students in all, nine boys and four girls. I could smell the booze wafting off Gunjan from the night before as I approached his desk and had to swallow down a sudden mouthful of bile.

"Is this the whole class?" I asked.

"Today it will be, Joseph. We divide the day up so half of the village children come in the morning and the other half in the afternoon. Same with the younger ones," he smiled, miraculously cheerful for someone who reeked that thoroughly of booze.

"And the younger ones, who looks after them in the morning?"

"I usually do, but sometimes a villager will come and watch them, too."

"So you watch both?"

"Yes," he said, as if it was the most natural thing in the world. "It is not as difficult as you think. I let the young ones play while I teach these pupils. When I have shown them something, I will walk over and check on the others. Get them to practice writings and things. You will see the children are very good at listening and doing as they are told." He looked into my eyes with concern. "You do not look as though you are alright, Joseph. Have you been having sick this morning?"

'Damn straight,' I thought, 'Thanks to you, buddy.' "Uh, yeah. A little too much of the local drop last night," I replied.

"Too much boozing, my friend, is not a good thing."

No kidding. "You don't look bad, Gunjan. What's your secret?"

"No secret my friend. No secret. I am used to this, what you say, local drop?" he chuckled. "Can you be with the young ones this morning? We will be studying maths and Nepalese here this morning, so you will not be needed."

"Um, sure." Had I not been quite so hung over, I might have taken offence to such bluntness, but seeing as I was just volunteering, I couldn't really protest anyway. Peering inside the other classroom, I saw a few small desks pushed against a wall covered with posters in English, all of them educational save for one depicting a leather-clad, motorcycle-straddling David Hasselhoff in the far corner of the room. The eleven small children sat in the middle of the room, two of them playing marbles.

"Hello," I said, sitting down cross-legged next to them. Giggles all around. "My name's Joseph." Nothing. "What's your name?" I asked the young girl sitting beside me. She smiled. "I'm Joseph," I repeated, pointing to myself. "Joseph."

"Hema," she said, smiling at me.

"Hello, Hema." I turned to the little boy on my right. "I'm Joseph."

"Ishat."

We went around the room until I had introduced myself to all eleven of them. I could only remember five or six of their names, which I figured would be enough to get me by for at least a few days. A few minutes after we had finished our introductions, Gunjan came in.

"Namaste," he said. The children answered him in kind. He gave them some instructions and they all jumped up and walked out of the room.

"They will be cleaning the book room," Gunjan told me as I stood up.

"Can I help them?" I asked.

"Yes, yes, of course. You may do what you want to do."

"Quite the party last night, Gunjan."

"Yes, it was a mighty good party. The rice will be growing many eyes high."

"The rice?"

"Yes, the rice, Joseph. Last night was our good festival for the growing of the rice. You were very lucky to have come at this precious time."

"I thought that yesterday was a welcoming party?"

"Oh, well, it was a welcome party for you and good rice grow party, too."

I thought back to what Debu had told me. Maybe he had been talking about welcoming both the 'good rice grow' and me? I patted Gunjan on the shoulder. Fuck it, it didn't matter why we were celebrating, as long as good rice grew. "It's OK, my friend. It was a good night all in all."

Next door in the book room, the children were cleaning the shelves. I stood watching as the children removed the books, wiped down the shelves, then moved on to the next section without replacing any of them until the row was finished.

"Hema," came a small voice from my feet. I looked down to see Hema gazing up at me, clutching a dirtied rag, apparently compelled to re-introduce herself.

"Hello, Hema."

"Hello." And with that, she walked off.

I searched for an index card somewhere at the end of the shelving unit, but there was none to be found. How anyone could find anything in this chaos was a mystery. If the books had originally been in some kind of order, it was clearly gone now. I skimmed over the books themselves, counting how many were in each row. For the most part, they were in English, but there were also Italian, French and Spanish. Very few in Nepalese. There averaged about sixty books to a shelf. There were four shelves in each case and four cases to each row. I estimated that there were probably close to two thousand tomes in total, all randomly stuck onto the shelves. The kids ran between the shelves as if their sole purpose was divided between hide and seek and cleaning. I ran my hand along the shelves; they were spotless. By the time lunch rolled around, I had already made a decision as to what I would spend most of my nights in Takam doing; organizing the chaos that passed for the school's library. I told Gunjan my plan and he agreed to help for as many hours as he could spare.

"Some of the older kids can helping too. Devish and Darshan definitely can. They can almost read English at my level. Maybe Geeti and Hita too, but it will be major difficult to get Hita. She doesn't talk much."

"Hita?"

"Yes, you will see her this afternoon. She will be coming today."

Gunjan and I ate lunch together behind the school. I nibbled like a sparrow for fear of hurling in the face of some poor Nepali child. Students slowly trickled in as I fought each and every mouthful down. Most ignored me and kicked the soccer ball around, waiting for classes to start.

"Only four young ones in the afternoon?"

"Today, yes. Tomorrow, maybe more."

In the quiet afternoon, I spent my time reading to the young ones. Most of them fell asleep by the end of Goldilocks and the Three Bears, Alpa among them, slumbering peacefully in my lap. Sitting on the dirty floor with four Nepalese children all silently and peacefully snoozing, I felt surprisingly at home. A voice inside me said that this was exactly what I wanted, what I needed. Something about that moment, over six thousand feet up in the Himalayas, told me I was doing something useful. I felt oddly parental to a certain degree, and I liked it. I sat motionless for about twenty minutes so as not to wake the little ones.

Gunjan crept into the classroom at around two thirty and gave me a smile. "They are liking you, no?" he whispered.

"I think so, Gunjan. What time does school finish, anyway? I've been sitting like this for almost an hour."

"Well, it can finish whenever they wanting to finish. If you like, I could get them up."

"Yes, please," I whispered back.

He walked over and gave Dayita, Kanta, and Ishar a gentle shake. I patted Alpa on the head until she stirred, eventually opening her eyes. Gunjan said something in their dialect and they all sat up, glancing at each other with sleepy eyes.

I bid Gunjan goodbye after sharing cigarettes outside the school. Smoking in front of the children was something everybody seemed to do regardless of whether or not one worked with them. Nevertheless, I felt a bit guilty.

***

After a cup of tea enjoying the greenness of my backyard, I went for a walk to the closer of the two village stores. I bought a pack of cigarettes, some yak cheese, butter, and potatoes. Walking back to my ger, I was surprised by how quiet it was, until I reached the base of the hill and heard my name being called.

"Jospet! Jospet!"

I turned and saw an ancient running towards me.

"Namaste, Chapala."

"Namaste, Jospet." She continued speaking in animated and indecipherable Nepali. I thought she was asking about food, so I pointed to my bag and shook my head. "I'm OK," I told her. She shook her head, pulling at my shirt. Apparently she was inquiring about my laundry.

"Oh, no, I'm OK. Tomorrow," I said idiotically, as if she would understand me. I used my hands to gesture a rolling ball and repeated the word 'tomorrow'. As she obviously still didn't get it, I pointed to the ground and said, "Now," then shut my eyes and pretended to sleep using my hands as a pillow, then opened my eyes and said, "Tomorrow," repeating the rolling-ball motion with my hands. Yet more incomprehensible Nepali, which hopefully included the word for 'tomorrow'. With a pinch of my cheek and a smile, she turned and walked away.

Once I had secured all of my purchases at my house, I made my way over to Debu's place. I found him outback in his pajamas, reading in one of his chairs.

"Namaste, Debu."

"Ah, Joseph. How was your first day?"

"Good. Really good, actually, considering."

"Considering?"

"Well, last night's party went pretty late, and I was a wee bit hung over this morning."

"Oh, yes, don't worry, everybody was." One big collective Himalayan hangover and I was partly responsible. Mom would be so proud.

"On that subject, what's this 'rice good grow' festival I keep hearing about?"

"The rice good grow festival, yes. Yesterday was a part of that, too." He smiled at me but offered nothing further on the subject. "Would you like a chai?"

"Yes, please, I'd love one."

The sun was falling rapidly behind the hills. I took in the view of the rice fields and tried to remember the names of everyone I had met that day, managing to recall eight names by the time Debu returned with my chai. I told him about my plans for the school's library and he nodded his approval.

"Ah, the library," he sighed. "Every time I help the children clean it, it makes me frustrated to watch them throw the books around. Most can't read them anyway, but...." he trailed off with a casual shrug of his shoulders.

"Did you get that book from the school?" I asked, pointing to the novel on the arm of his chair.

"No, I bought this last time I was in Pokhara."

"How often do you go?" I asked, taking a sip of my chai.

"One or two times a month. Mainly just to get supplies and see friends."

"You ever head back to Kathmandu?"

"I have not been there since I left thirteen years ago."

We sat in silence for a few minutes. "Debu, why am I really here in Takam, anyway? I mean, what am I supposed to be doing?"

"Exactly what you're doing, Joseph. Organizing the library, playing with the children, talking to the people. Doing what you can."

"It doesn't seem like much," I replied, not wanting to offend but wanting to share my minor crisis of purpose all the same.

Debu leaned back in his chair and fiddled absently with one of the buttons on his pajama top. "Joseph, let me tell you something. You are here volunteering your time. You are here of your own free will, just as others before you were, as will others who come after you. Many villagers here would never have even seen a foreign face if it weren't for you."

"But what's the big deal with seeing a foreigner and interacting with them?" I asked, genuinely curious.

"You take your own country for granted, Joseph. Canada has many different nationalities all in one place, and you live together there peacefully."

"Well, somewhat," I interrupted.

"In your country you can see many different types of people, and you can interact with them. You enjoy this, no?"

"Well, sure. I love living in a society with many different types of people. It's very interesting."

"So why would the people of a small village in Nepal not be the same? They are just like you, no? We are all the same deep down, we are all human. In Canada you eat many different types of food and you try new things because they are there for you to try. Most of these people here would do the same if they had the chance. You are that chance, Joseph. You are thinking like a Westerner. Here," he waved a grandfatherly finger in the air as if scolding me, "you will judge your time here with what you have accomplished in the physical sense. If you help build houses or dig ditches or even organize the library, which are all wonderful things. But what you have to do is think like an Easterner; it's your connection with the world, this world," he made a sweeping gesture at our surroundings, "and everyone around you, that you will be judged by, not how many houses you build." He took a sip of his tea then went silent.

I thought of his words and how they related to the day I'd just had. He was right. The moment I had felt the best was when I was reading to the children until they fell asleep. That moment was the most meaningful, somehow, when I felt like I was actually doing something, the moment my heart and head were one. Usually the pair were on opposite ends of the earth.

Debu smiled and continued, "It is not a matter of right and wrong, Joseph. You are still free to do as you please. Bindu is building every day and you can choose to help him every day. You can choose to organize the library, you can choose to sit in your house and do nothing. It's up to you to decide. It is your time, not ours. Just make yourself at home and do what you feel is right. You have come all this way because of the goodness in your heart." He paused for a second before adding, "Keep following that goodness."

The goodness in my heart. Was there really such a thing? Maybe, just maybe, I was finally, slowly, pulling myself out of the primordial shit I had mired myself in for all these years. We sat a while longer and he mentioned that the following week, if I wanted to, I could visit another village.

"You can stay with my friend."

"How far away is it?"

"Oh, eleven hours that way." He motioned over the hills to the left as he lit a cigarette, his tone as nonchalant as if he had just given directions to a 7-Eleven around the corner.

Chapter 7

Since my talk with Debu that second night, everything had gone perfectly. On my third night in the village, I joined Bindu and his family for dinner. He had, without a doubt, the best house in the whole village, which seemed fitting seeing as he was the one responsible for building most of them. Bindu struggled through some English, to which I listened attentively, but for the most part it was an entire night of charades as we struggled to make ourselves understood. It helped that we went through a bottle of the local spirits, too, which I found out that night was called 'Jepu' in the local dialect.

School was going great. I was actually able to teach some of the older kids. We played a few games as we went through the alphabet. I sang with my back turned against them and they called out the letters. I threw in some amazing air guitar to spice it up and almost brought the house down. We then moved on to greetings, acting them out as a group. As the self-designated director, I threw a scarf around my neck and put on a pair of plastic sunglasses that Gunjan had fished out of the toy box. I used Raju as my cameraman, giving him a shoebox, which he hoisted onto his shoulder and pretended to film. We shot pretend movies for the rest of the afternoon as the children tried to remember the introductions they had just learned. By the end of the day, just about everyone could greet each other in coherent English.

Every night I spent a few hours in the library writing down book titles and, with Gunjan's help, decided which class they were to be put in. Just as Gunjan had said, Darshan and Geeti gave us a hand when they could. The students were proud of themselves, feeling that they were a part of something extra special, which they were.

I also had my first go at rice-planting with Debu. His backyard and the hill that dropped away from it lead to four terraced fields, which he sowed himself each year. I joined him on two occasions, giving an excuse after the third invite because by that point I could barely stand upright. I told him that I was needed back at school, which wasn't really true, but I knew some of the children were having a 'game o' soccah,' as Daya called it, and my electrifying crosses were in great demand.

***

The following week I readied myself for a visit to the village of Rinrut. Debu had informed me that it would take about eleven hours on foot, so I started out at five o'clock that morning after an 'I'll be fucking damned if this doesn't wake me up' cold shower. I met Maina, a young student of fourteen, who was going to see her relatives in one of the villages along the way. She smiled, as if to challenge me to keep up with her.

The hills slowly continued their advance towards the heavens, the vegetation dwindling with every gasp for fresh air my pathetic lungs took in. Maina sustained a good lead even in her little threadbare sandals. About four hours outside of Takam, we said goodbye at an unmarked junction in the path. Apparently she knew where she was going. She looked at me and pointed straight ahead, a mischievous grin creeping its way up her dirtied little cheeks. She was enjoying feeling superior to her teacher.

The next village came into sight half an hour after I had parted ways with Maina. Talpit was a small village of no more than thirty rice farmers whose dozen or so yaks grazed away behind the ancient homes. Some of the villagers came out to say hello and even offered me some water and cheese, which I accepted gratefully. Canadians have the reputation for being friendly, but it seems underserved compared to the kindness of these people.

Three and a half hours after leaving Talpit I came across Khasil, the second and last village before Rinrut. It was similar to Talpit in size, but higher in altitude. I could feel my breathing getting heavier as I neared the village. An ancient Nepali smiled at my pronunciation when I struggled to ask if I was going the right way, then simply nodded his head.

Night had fallen by the time I reached Rinrut. Several times during the walk I'd had second thoughts as to whether or not I was going the right way. I honestly wasn't sure whether the river I'd crossed four times was the same river or four entirely different ones. My anxiety finally let up when I caught sight of a light on the plateau up ahead.

Looking for the village police station, I made my way down the middle of the village until I spotted a sign overhead that resembled the one Debu had written on my map. Rinrut was about half the size of Takam, the stone homes lining the one main street far outnumbering the wooden ones. A fenced-off area in the distance demarcated the borders of the village.

"Namaste," a man shouted from inside a run-down shack that served as the police station. I pushed open the wooden door to find a man sitting crouched over a radio, listening intently. He gestured for me to sit down with an impatient wave of his hand, and seeing as I was in a police station I did as I was told. He was a short man of about forty with a thick black moustache that drooped over his upper lip. He wore a small cap at an angle, under which sprouted six or seven long black hairs worthy more of a mole than a scalp. Thick wrinkles creased the corners of his eyes. Nicotine-yellowed fingers eventually turned the knob on the radio down to a level that could be talked over comfortably.

"Namaste," I said, bowing my head slightly.

"Josep?" he asked, clearly not accustomed to speaking English.

"Josep," I confirmed after a moment's hesitation. He stared at me for a few seconds, then smiled.

"Ma sanchai chhu," he said quickly, then proceeded to rattle off a short speech in Nepali, not a word of which I understood.

"Maile bujhina," I offered when he had finished, letting him know that I don't speak Nepali, as if that wasn't obvious already. For emphasis, I shrugged my shoulders and shook my head, which garnered a laugh from the policeman.

"Harshil," he said, pointing a yellowed finger at his broad, uniformed chest.

"Josep," I repeated, figuring it would be best to go with the Nepali version of my name. Harshil let out a hearty laugh.

Stepping around the desk, he took my hand unceremoniously in his and led me back outside. Now, I had seen men in Nepal holding hands and had thought nothing of it. But for all my perceived open-mindedness, I came to the conclusion that strutting down the only road in a tiny Nepali village hand in hand with a police officer in the middle of the night is less than comforting.

Just as I was getting ready to follow the sudden overwhelming compulsion to tear my hand away and run full-speed in the opposite direction all the way back to Canada, we came to a halt in front of an old wooden house with a dilapidated door. Harshil took a small step forward and knocked with his free hand. Seconds later, a little girl appeared in front of us. Her sad, oversized deep brown eyes were the first things I noticed. Dirt streaked her left cheek like it had found a permanent home there. She wore bright red jogging pants that were two sizes too big, folded down at the waist and clipped in place with a clothespin. A sweater with holes in both shoulders fell loosely atop her torso. I had the feeling I had seen her before. Harshil broke the brief silence by saying something to the little girl in Nepali while tickling her belly. She didn't laugh, but disappeared quickly into the house.

We followed and stepped inside one of only a few structures in the village with a second floor. A staircase to our left led to a long hallway that ran the length of the second floor. I counted six doors leading off of it.

"Hello," said a voice from down the hall.

Harshil smiled, leaned towards me and said something in Nepali. I shrugged my shoulders, lifted our still-intertwined fingers and smiled back. A young Nepali man came down the hall dressed in pajamas.

"Hello", he repeated.

Harshil began speaking in Nepali, gesticulating widely with his hands as he did so, allowing my left limb to go flailing about with his right one. He finally let go when the young man in front of us extended his hand to shake mine.

"Nice to meet you, my friend. My name is Yash."

"Nice to meet you, Yash. Do you know Debu?" I asked, just to make sure I had been brought to the right place. I really had no clue what was going on.

"Yes, we are very good friends, he and I. He had sent me a message weeks back saying that someone would be coming soon. It is so nice to finally see you." He broke out into a wide grin, his thin cheeks shooting strangely outwards but not upwards, his thick, bushy eyebrows nearly meeting at the bridge of his nose. His brown eyes were soft and clear behind a pair of old spectacles.

The two Nepalese men exchanged a few more words before Harshil turned to me and said, "Subha ratri."

"That's good night," said Yash.

"Subha ratri," I repeated.

"You must be hungry," Yash said as he closed the door behind Harshil.

He led me down the hall to a large room at the back of the house where eight young children sat around a large picnic table. As we entered the room, all eight sets of little brown eyes turned to gape at the stranger, allowing one young boy the opportunity to steal a chapatti off the plate of another. One look from Yash and the boy lowered his head and returned the bread sullenly to his neighbor's plate. The little girl who had opened the door for Harshil was sitting as far away as possible from the other children towards the end of one of the benches. I had an eerie feeling that I had time warped back to Hien and Blair's orphanage in Kathmandu.

Yash addressed the children in Nepali, and I made out the words 'Canada', 'Debu', 'Joseph', and 'Takam'. When he had finished speaking, the children stood up at once and lowered their heads. A unified "Namaste" filled the kitchen.

"Namaste," I replied, trying to make eye contact with the little girl on the end of the bench, but she kept her head lowered.

"Please take a seating, Joseph," Yash said. I sat down next to the little girl in the red jogging pants.

Two of the children brought over a plate of rice and lentils. It was cold, but it didn't matter. It had been an exceptionally long walk, and the little bit of food I had brought to eat hadn't been nearly sufficient for a body that was unaccustomed to this high altitude.

"This is our school and home, Joseph," Yash told me over the table. "Most of these children do have family left, but these children need to be here. It is better for them. They see family on weekends if they go to them."

"Who supports all this?" I asked, looking around the room.

"This house is government," he replied, which I assumed meant the Nepalese government funded it. "And some of the other peoples in Rinrut help. For the clotheses, the cookings, and the teachings, too, sometimes."

One of the little boys asked Yash a question, which was immediately followed by fits of laughter from all around the table.

"He wants to know if you have ever been to Kathmandu," Yash explained.

"Uh, yes, I have," I said, nodding. Some of the children understood me and let out a chorus of oohs and aahs.

"I have never been to Kathmandu, Joseph," Yash told me.

"Really?" I was shocked.

"I have been to Pokhara many times, but Kathmandu, I have not yet." One of the children asked another question. "He wants to know if you speak Nepalese."

When all eyes were once again trained on me, I did my best to try out as many of the phrases that Debu and Gunjan had taught me. With each attempt the laughter at the table grew more deafening. I even managed to get a slight smile out of the little girl next to me.

"What's your name?" I asked her once the laughter had subsided. She turned her head back to her food.

"She may not speak to you, Joseph. She does not speak very much. She does speak some English, though. Her parents were many times educated."

"Why is that? I mean, why doesn't she speak much?"

"Her parents are killed during this war. They were officials of very high standings, but a few years ago they were in a police station that was attacked by the Maoists. Her grandmother is in Khasil. She sometimes goes to see her."

"I've been to Khasil," I said, turning to the little girl again. "What's her name, Yash?"

"Kunjana is her name." This was met by yet more laughter around the table from the other children. Yash said something in sharp Nepali and the laughter stopped just as fast as it had started.

"Kunjana, I have been to Khasil. It is a very pretty place. And that is a very pretty name, too. Kunjana." She sat staring at her food, not moving an inch. "That's OK. You'll speak when you want to speak, right? There's no hurry."

I introduced myself to the rest of the table and the children in turn did the same. I met Yogi, a young boy from Marang who had many relatives but who was a mischievous little boy, sent to the school on occasion to study for a week or two before undertaking the nine-hour walk back home. Matsendra sat right next to me with a smile that never left his face during the entire dinner. Only six years old, he had lost his family in a landslide when he was just a baby. He had been at the school ever since. Meha sat next to Matsendra, the two seeming to form an inseparable pair, and she shared his unshakeable smile. Her father worked for seven months out of the year as a guide and couldn't watch over her during the tourist season. She had lost her mother to polio when she was four. Considering what had happened to most of them, and what they were still going through, their bright and cheerful dispositions were a shock to me.

After dinner, I helped Kunjana wash the metal plates, giving each one a quick scrub before handing it to her to rinse. I tried several times to get another smile out of her, but to no avail.

Once the dishes were clean, I helped tuck a few of the younger ones into bed upstairs. The house being of a considerable size, four of the older children had their own room, while the younger ones shared another. Kunjana shared with Nalika, a girl of seven who had been at the school for three years after her parents had abandoned her one night in Rinrut.

Back downstairs, Yash and I talked over a cup of tea at the picnic table in the kitchen, the room chillier, now that the dinner fire was dying.

"How long will you stay here, Joseph?"

"In Nepal?"

"No, here, in Rinrut."

The light from one of the two lanterns flickered, then went out. "I don't know. I haven't been given a schedule or anything like that. As long as I think I should, really." I paused, stirring my tea with my fingertip. "What exactly do you need from me the most?"

"Teach English to children and me. Help with what we do here every day."

Yash stood and walked to the wood burning stove. After opening the metal door he poked at the remaining logs, embers cracking as the fire was brought back to life.

"Well," I answered, still unsure as to my actual role, "I'll stay for a few days this time, and when I get back to Takam maybe I'll write up a schedule for myself."

"This is very good plan, Joseph, very good plan."

Over a second cup of tea, Yash told me about his upbringing in the Seti region of eastern Nepal. He had gone to college in the small city of Silgadhi, the only proper city in the area. After graduating with a diploma in Children's Services, he had spent time in India volunteering in Puttaparthi, a small town in Andhra Pradesh.

"That is where I stayed for a few years. After my times there, I decided on returning to my own country to continue my helping here."

The steam from my chai wafted up to my nose as I looked up through the window at the glittering night sky and the whitecaps of the Annapurna range that seemed close enough to reach out and touch. The stars shone with a surreal intensity, mindlessly muttered something to that effect. Yash gave me a quizzical look.

"Surreal, I like this word," he said, so much so that he repeated it three times.

After Yash showed me to my room, I laid awake in bed, unable to drift off. It was much colder than it had been in Takam. I pulled back the curtain of the window directly over my bed. It never seemed to be cloudy at night in Nepal. Taking in the thousands of glittering points of light, I reflected on whether being in Nepal was helping me become a better person. Maybe I had found something that would lift me out of the proverbial gutter I had been dragging myself through. At twenty-five years old, I still hadn't figured out what to do with my life. At least I had started to feel less sorry for myself, after seeing what these kids had been through. I pulled the quilt up to my neck and rolled over under the distant light of infinite stars.

Chapter 8

Children's footfalls in the hallway woke me the next morning, accompanied by the rise and fall of laughter and intermittent whispers. Sliding out from under the covers, I crept across the wooden floors as silently as I could. I could still hear them whispering as I placed my hand over the doorknob. In one swift motion, I turned the knob and pulled the door open, springing forward like a wild animal, eyes wide and teeth bared. The children erupted in hysterical screams and laughter, scattering in all directions. Yogi, the chapatti thief, was so frightened that he turned and ran headlong into the opposite wall, falling to the floor in a riot of limbs and tears. I rushed over and propped him up, not so sure the gesture would be taken as consoling considering I could barely contain my laughter.

We ate breakfast at the picnic table in the kitchen, everyone sitting exactly where they had the night before. Kunjana was once again sitting by herself until I came down to the kitchen after splashing some ice-cold water on my face and joined her at the end of the bench.

Yash wanted me to teach the kids English in that day's class. I decided on teaching them to introduce themselves and say where they were from. "It worked in Takam," was the only assurance I could offer.

The school in Rinrut was a one-room, clay-brick building, the kind you see in National Geographic magazines without ever thinking that you would actually come across one in real life, let alone end up teaching in it. The lone blackboard at the front of the room hung from a single nail and the children sat on simple wooden benches. I reused the movie-making idea in my lesson and the kids loved it, although one young girl, Uma, didn't quite grasp the concept. After a few minutes I figured out that she might not know what a movie was, possibly having never seen one. I noticed Kunjana kept her distance from the rest of the children, never really committing herself to the lesson. I tried to get her to join in, but she shook her head 'No' as soon as I moved towards her.

That afternoon, I asked Yash if I could take the kids for a walk.

"Yes, my friend, as you like," he replied.

We left the village at just past two o'clock. I was curious to see how far the mountain path went, so we set off in the direction of the Annapurna range. When Meha grabbed hold of my hand, Matsendra copied her and took the other one. Kunjana stayed quietly close behind me. We walked for an hour or so, the vegetation growing sparser with each step, turning the landscape into something more lunar than terrestrial. To keep the little ones entertained, I sang the few children's songs that I could remember. 'Frere Jacques' was followed by 'This Little Light Of Mine', which I remembered from my very brief stint spent sweating it out in a church basement. I even belted out 'Oh Canada', rounding off my repertoire with 'Itsy Bitsy Spider.' By the end of it I had the children all singing along with me with varying degrees of enthusiasm, pronouncing everything endearingly wrong. Even Yogi seemed to be enjoying himself, making a concerted effort to have his voice heard above all the others.

As we crested yet another steep hill, I stopped abruptly to take in the surroundings. The place looked eerily familiar. We had arrived at a vast plateau that extended for a half a mile or so. The path continued down the right hand side of it, and mountain walls shot up on either side. A few feet down on the left hand side, I could make out three small openings in the mountain wall.

The nine of us traversed the plateau towards the caves. Yogi and Umesh, the only student who Yogi seemed to get along with, went running ahead. Matsendra and Meha took off together as we approached the mountain wall. Kunjana came up beside me, taking my hand. I watched as the children climbed, wondering whether I should stop them, but soon realizing from the fluidity of their movements that they had done this before.

"You want to go up, too?" I asked Kunjana, who looked up at me, shielding her dark amber eyes from the sun. She did not reply. I smiled and pointed my thumb over my shoulder towards the caves, "How about we go up together? All of us," I said, glancing around at the remaining students, who nodded eagerly. They then took off hurriedly as Kunjana stood still. I reached down for her hand and her small fingers folded around my middle finger. Together we made our way up the stony slope, and it wasn't long before we reached the top and entered one of the caves. I could make out the back wall in the permeating sunlight. Yogi and Umesh had already moved on to another cave some distance away to the left of us. Three of us sat down on the dusty floor with our legs swinging from the mouth of the cave. I joined the kids in yelling out into the plateau just to hear my voice bounce off the mountain walls.

I left the children shouting gleefully into the void below to examine the adjacent cave, which penetrated much deeper into the rock face. I made my way slowly to the back, my hand pressed to the cool stone wall as my guide. The smell of incense soon filled my nostrils, growing more robust with each step. The wall grew warm to the touch. The cave narrowed suddenly and, as I moved my hand downwards, the warm wall crumbled between my fingertips. Running my fingers down to the floor, my hand plunged into soft, warm sand and thin, brittle sticks of wood jabbed into my palm. Countless years of incense ash sifted between my fingers. The noise of gigging children rising up behind me broke my reverie and I made my way back towards the light.

The children's songs once again took precedence on the walk back to the village, and I even attempted to join in their Nepali songs. Everyone seemed in good spirits, and even Yogi was well behaved. We marched into the village just before dark and the kids ran to the house to wash up and prepare for dinner. I walked into the kitchen and found Yash at the picnic table with Harshil.

"Ah, Joseph, you are back. That is good."

"Yeah, we walked for about an hour into the mountains and found these three caves on a plateau. Really neat stuff."

"Yes, Kalikot. You found it, that is good."

I joined them at the table and offered Harshil a tired smile. "Namaste, Harshil," I said.

"Namaste," he returned.

"Joseph, Harshil has just told me that he has heard on the radio that there are Maoists very short distance away."

I stared at him, not quite sure what to do or say.

"They may be here in the next few days, Joseph. Maybe tomorrow you go back to Takam. There is a military post not far off the path to Takam. You will be OK."

A military post? What was he talking about? I had just walked the path yesterday and I hadn't seen any military post.

"Which post, Yash? I don't remember seeing anything."

"It is not on the path, Joseph. It is beside the path. You would have walked past it. Harshil may be going, too."

"Is there going to be trouble?"

"Probably not. The peoples here have shown no sign of commitment to the government, so we will be OK. But Harshil is a police. He is a government official and it would not be wise for him to be here if they arrive. The rest will be OK. Some even want them to come. Some people here say that they will bring good things. They may build a road for tradings and things."

"Why would I have to go, then?" I couldn't believe I had voluntarily put myself into this situation.

"Just to be sure, that is all."

Harshil nodded, his face beaming as if nothing in the world could disturb his inner peace. I wondered what he was so happy about.

"When should I head back, then?"

"It is too late tonight, unless you bring torch. But there are setters too, and you don't want to run into any setters."

"Setters?"

"Yes, Joseph, the peoples who kill the animals."

"Hunters?"

"I think that is the word too," he said, puzzled. "Setters set traps for animals, then kill them or sell them. They are not good men and many in area. That is why there is a military post. It was put here for them, not Maoists."

"Oh, poachers. Gotcha. No one has told me about them until now. Thanks for the information, though," I said, unable to hide my sarcasm.

That night over a few cups of chai, Yash tried to assure me that there wasn't going to be a problem with the Maoists.

"No one in this area has bothered to walk the twelve hours to vote in many years." He looked around the tiny village now only illuminated by the bright moon. "There is no reason Joseph," he said somewhat discouraged. "The Maoists are not stupid, and they may bring good things to these peoples."

Asking him whether he felt safe as an educated man living in the hills, Yash was silent at first, then answered, "I am not afraid, Joseph. They may do what they will, but I am not afraid. I am here to help, and if they show me they are caring peoples too, then I shall help them as well."

"You're a good man, Yash. I can see it in your eyes." He laughed. "And this whole business about the Maoists coming here and being so close and everything? Surreal, eh?"

"Ah, yes, my friend, surreal it is." He smiled with just a hint of sadness in his kind eyes as he took a sip of his tea.

Chapter 9

Word came to Takam, both on the radio and through Harshil, who had passed through during his escape to Pokhara, that the Maoists had indeed taken over Rinrut and Khasil. Neither had resisted and both villages had actually welcomed the change. Better that than death, I could only presume. The military post that, it turned out, was closer to Talpit than either of the occupied villages, had remained dormant. The Royal Nepalese Army had let the Maoists take the villages without so much as a squeak of protest.

"You may return to Rinrut if you choose," Debu informed me one night over tea in his backyard.

"I've been thinking about it," I offered vaguely, trying not to let my underlying fear make itself heard in my voice. The thought of entering the communist-controlled villages both excited me and scared the shit out of me. "Debu, did you know that there was a little girl in Rinrut whose parents have both been killed by Maoists?" For over a month, poor Kunjana had been on my mind, every thought of her an itch I just couldn't reach to scratch.

"No, I didn't know that," he said slowly, drawing out each syllable. He took a pack of cigarettes from his pajama pocket and passed one to me.

"Yeah, she has a grandmother in Khasil but she stays with Yash at the orphanage." The early evening fog was beginning to form, the smell of wet grass and trees floating amongst the mist as Debu lit the cigarette for me. "Do you think they, the Maoists I mean, would hold any spite towards her?"

"Spite?"

"Do you think she could be harmed in any way?" I clarified.

"Oh, I don't know, Joseph. It's possible some will have bad feelings toward an entire family. But I do not know them and their practices." He took a long drag from his cigarette. "You are free to go and see," he added, smoke drifting lazily upwards from his pursed lips.

A helpless feeling, like watching a loved one suffer from afar, had taken over me in the past week. I was a foreigner in the mountains of Nepal who had absolutely no idea just how dangerous the situation in which I found myself could be. What would stop the Maoists from moving further eastward to Takam? The military post outside the village didn't seem likely to be much of an obstacle. Violent scenarios, like getting caught in the crossfires or taken hostage, played out in my head a dozen times with a dozen different endings.

I could still return to Rinrut and continue to help out at the orphanage if I wanted to. No one was stopping me. Killing a volunteer wouldn't seem to be a positive step for the Maoists' agenda, but then again, what the fuck did I know about their agenda?

We were more than a third of the way into cataloguing the books in the school library. Gunjan, Geeti, and Hita remained devoted to the project. Darshan and Devish's enthusiasm, however, had waned after the first couple of weeks, and then totally disappeared after the third.

My time in the community had grown to be more than I had bargained for. Once a week I had dinner with Bindu and his family, and we would finish off a bottle or two of the local spirit. I supplemented my weekly intake of the booze by way of an unlikely pot connection: Chapala.

One evening, I got a great surprise when I walked to Chapala's house on the other side of the village to pick up some vegetables I had been told were waiting for me. After a few knocks on the door went unanswered, I decided to see if she was around back. A very distinct odor drifted towards me as I walked to the backyard, where I found Chapala hunched over a tub of soapy water squeezing the suds out of a perfectly bleached sheet. She clasped a long clay pipe between her lips with a towering pile of marijuana poking out of the tip. Despite my best efforts to speak to her in Nepali, I ended up pointing at the pipe, then pointing to myself, and giving her a big smile. She laughed and handed me the pipe, along with a box of matches that rested beside the pile of laundry. The two of us worked on her laundry well into the evening and smoked ourselves silly. When I left a few hours later I had a box full of vegetables, a set of clean sheets, a sizable pouch of marijuana, a stomach sore from laughter, and a head full of good fuzzies.

A few nights later, after leaving Debu half-asleep in his lawn chair, I made my way home, rolled some of Chapala's pot, and, as I smoked it under the stars in my backyard, came to the conclusion that I was going back to Rinrut. I would finish the week off in Takam and make my way to Rinrut on Sunday morning. I couldn't shake the feeling that somehow I needed to go and help Kunjana, Maoists or no Maoists. Of course, I had no idea how I could possibly help, and I had a fleeting thought that maybe I was just trying to be a hero. But by the time I had inhaled the last of my joint, I was at ease with my decision and had a gut feeling that everything was going to be OK. It didn't occur to me that I was probably just really stoned.

Debu and I left Takam at half past four in the morning that Sunday. He was on his way to see a friend in another village, and to get there he would need to follow a path that ran off the one to Rinrut.

Debu eyed me carefully. "You're still scared."

"Shit, yes, I'm still scared."

He let out a laugh. "Then why go?" he asked, bemused.

I lied. "I don't know," I answered slowly.

"You'll be fine."

"I know. I hope so, anyway. By the way, why did Harshil go all the way to Phokara?" And why did Gunjan's brother get his arm chopped off? And why am I doing this again?

"Harshil was scared, Joseph."

We walked in silence for a while, leaving me alone with my thoughts, which were less than reassuring. As the first streaks of sunlight spread across the sky, I asked if he was going to the military base.

"No, why?"

"I don't know, maybe they have information for you."

"With Maoists all around and closer than ever, I do not want to be seen talking to the military. I want to live."

'I want to live, too' I thought to myself with increasing anxiety.

Debu wished me well as we parted an hour later, and I thanked him for accompanying me. I knew he didn't really have to go see his friend, and I wasn't entirely sure he even had one in the next village. He had suddenly announced he was coming along after one too many talks about the Maoists.

I reached Talpit less than an hour later, my urbanized feet having grown accustomed to the dips, bends, and ravines of the country road. As had happened on my first time through, two of the villagers, a young man and woman, stopped tending to their yaks to speak to me. I politely declined their offer of a drink of water from their canteen, then we had a very short conversation in two machete-hacked languages with a bumbling of sign language tossed in for good measure. They were puzzled as to why I was going back to Rinrut. The young man was especially concerned, shaking his head back and forth in a gesture of warning. This frightened me even more than I already was, but I gave him a hesitant thumbs-up and handed him the letter Debu had written for me should anyone ask for an explanation of my presence along the way to Rinrut. When he had finished reading the letter, he looked up and nodded his head as if we were in agreement. I nodded back, not knowing what I was supposed to say or do. Eventually the pair lost interest in me and waved good-bye, returning to their yaks.

An hour shy of Khasil, I sat down next to the river and took out the small packet of cheese and bread I had brought from Takam. I dug into this small meal with a mountaineer's gusto, after which I rolled a small joint and puffed away. All rested, I dusted myself off, packed up my belongings, and continued my long day's trek. I knew I was getting closer to Khasil when I reached the spot in the path that veered away from the river. My reddened eyes scoped out my surroundings, looking for a sign that I might be being watched or followed. The pot had hit me harder than usual. Every three minutes I turned abruptly, expecting to see a bunch of toothless, gun-toting Maoists snickering behind me, making grunting noises whilst placing bets as to who would fire the shot that finally brought down the imperialist pig. Nothing of the sort happened, but it didn't stop my paranoia.

I walked into Khasil entirely unnoticed. A new building had been erected near the entrance to the tiny community. A sign overhead written in both Nepali and English read, 'Khasil Community Maoist Office'. The door to the office was wide open but empty of Maoists. The villagers of Khasil were nowhere to be seen, either. I sat down on the steps outside the office and lit a cigarette, hoping someone would return soon. I thought maybe someone could contact Rinrut through the radio and announce my arrival so that it wouldn't startle anyone, thus making it less likely for my head to be blown off by an AK-47-toting, trigger-happy communist.

After twenty minutes of waiting there was still no sign of anyone, Maoist or otherwise, so I decided to move on. I really didn't want to arrive in Rinrut after nightfall. Walking out of the village, it occurred to me that Kunjana's grandmother lived there. I turned to look at the small mud-brick homes and wondered which one was hers.

Another two hours and I was nearing Rinrut. It was getting on in the afternoon, but I knew I would make it before dusk. "This is good," I said aloud, repeating it for reassurance, after which I heard a noise coming from up ahead. I stopped and listened, unable to make out exactly what it was. For a moment I thought about jumping off the path and hiding in the bushes. Instead, I stood there frozen as the sound approached. .

Throughout the entire day I had not seen one other person besides Debu and myself on the path proper, only as I passed through Talpit. The last time, I had passed many a villager along the way, some transporting goods with their yaks, some out picking herbs and flowers, and others on their way to visit friends and family. Then, just as the noise seemed to be getting even closer, it suddenly began to recede. I stood very still and faintly made out what sounded like someone crying. Making my way up the hill, a lone figure came into view. I could see that it was a child.

Feeling simultaneously relieved and saddened, I jogged towards the figure. It took only a few seconds for recognition to hit.

"Kunjana!" I yelled, "Kunjana!"

She looked up, then put her head back down and continued her slow walk towards from me. "What's wrong?" I asked, when I had caught up to her. "What happened?"

She stopped, her face buried in her hands. She was wearing the same red jogging pants I had seen her in last, the same sweater with the two shoulder holes draped across her skinny frame. I knelt down beside her and pulled her into my arms. She let go of her face and wrapped her arms around my neck.

"It's OK," I said. Her tears soaked into my shoulder while I tried to console her. "What's wrong, Kunjana? Why are you crying?"

She let go of me and said something in Nepali. Only catching the word for 'grandmother,' I couldn't be sure what she meant.

"Is that where you're going now?" I asked. She nodded. "You're going to see her?" She nodded again. "It's getting dark now, Kunjana. How about you go tomorrow? OK?"

She shook her head and said "No" in English. Damn it. The kids in the hills wandered off by themselves all the time, day and night, and it wasn't considered a big deal by any of their parents. But I wasn't one of those parents. Every day it scared me to death to think how far some of the children walked alone at night, let alone a grown man. "Fuck," I muttered. "Do you want me to come with you?" I asked Kunjana.

"No, Joseph."

"So you can speak English, Kunjana?" She nodded and wiped her tears. "Why were you crying then, hmm?" She didn't answer. "Did something happen to you? Are you hurt?" I turned her in a circle to inspect her tiny frame. She shook her head, then repeated the word for 'grandmother' in Nepali.

I looked down at her. Her eyes and cheeks were red from crying, her hands a pale brown color as her tears had washed away some of the encrusted dirt. Why did she have to suffer like this? I thought about taking her back to Takam with me.

"I can't exactly walk into town holding a screaming, crying child though, can I? Shit," I muttered to myself. "This is not good, Kunjana. You know where you're going, yes?"

"Yes, Joseph."

"You had better hurry. It'll be dark soon."

I fished a sweater out of my bag and handed it to her. "You might need this." I grabbed my flashlight and gave that to her as well. "Look," I said, showing her the button to turn it on and off. "Go now, hurry."

She gave me a quick hug before running off down the path. I watched as her little retreating form disappeared around the bend in the path. I had doubts about whether I had made the right decision.

Chapter 10

Yash, who had just left Rinrut to take a stroll before dinner, greeted me on the path.

"Did you know Kunjana just left to go see her grandmother?" I asked, forgoing an actual greeting.

"I know, Joseph." He took off his glasses and wiped them on his shirt. "This is OK. She knows where she is going. All these children know where they are going. Most know many more secret places and paths than us older peoples."

"She was crying when I saw her. Do you know why?"

"Oh, yes, I noticed her crying too, and I heard her and Nalika had arguing. I do not know what this is about. Kunjana never speaks me."

"Nalika?"

"Yes, Nalika. They used to share a room together."

"Ah, yes, I remember now. Used to, you say?"

"Yes, a few days ago Nalika asked to sleep in her own room. I do not know why, but we have extra bed so I said yes. I asked Kunjana if this is OK, and she nodded to say yes, so I moved them."

As we walked back to the village, Yash filled me in on what had been happening in Rinrut since the Maoist takeover. Except for Harshil, who had fled before the Maoists had arrived, the village had essentially stayed the same.

"In fact, Joseph, he was still going to stay on as our policeman, using the Maoists' law, of course. This is what I have been told."

We climbed the steep hill into the village. At the top, we met a young man who introduced himself by way of pointing to his chest, fingers inches away from his gun, intoning "Prakul," in a brusque voice. He then pointed at me with his middle digit. "Jospet?"

"Namaste, Prakul," I nodded, carefully eyeing the weapon strapped to the young lad's body.

"Why does he know my name?" I leaned in to ask Yash as Prakul walked on ahead of us.

"I have told them of you, and of the other volunteer peoples that come to Rinrut."

Just before reaching the police station, Yash stopped and said that he had to get home to help prepare dinner. He looked at me then to Prakul. I understood I was to follow the Maoist.

"Please come join us when you are finished, Joseph."

I didn't like that I was being left alone with a man who had a gun strapped to his back.

"Jospet," Prakul said, motioning for me to follow, seeming indifferent to my unease.

The old police building that Harshil used to man was now, according to the sign overhead, the 'Rinrut Community Maoist Office.' Underneath this it read, 'Myagdi Regional Headquartars'. I figured it was best not to mention the spelling error to Prakul, who was still fondling his gun as we stepped inside. The office seemed cluttered, not with objects, but with energy, a dense feeling that made it hard to breathe. Physically, the small space hadn't changed at all. The radio Harshil had been listening to that first night was still perched on the rickety desk. Just like that first night, there was someone crouched intently over the little device. A portly man with a thick black moustache turned to look at us as we entered the doorway.

"Namaste," I said, bowing slightly.

"Namaste," he answered.

Prakul began speaking in rapid-fire Nepali to the man bent over the radio, who interrupted him in harsh tones. I wished I hadn't come. I wished I was back in Canada drinking beer and watching hockey. I wished the war would end. I wished I hadn't let Kunjana go. I wished they would just leave me alone. When they finally finished speaking, the man with the thick black moustache stared up at me, saying nothing.

Finally, Prakul broke the awkward silence. "No English, Jospet. He not know what to say."

"My Nepali isn't very good either," I stammered, "Please tell him that I hope I can be of some help here in Rinrut." Maybe expressing my willingness to help would aid me on my quest to keep all of my limbs intact. Prakul spoke a few words in Nepali to the mustached man, who eventually let a grin cross his lips. I smiled back, fighting my instinct to run.

The formalities at the police office seemingly over, Prakul escorted me to the orphanage.

"I can manage, Prakul. It's just right over there." 'Please get away from me.' I thought.

As we approached the building, Prakul halted abruptly and informed me, "I am watching, always watching I am. Soldiers anywhere to strike against us. Always watching, I am." I kept my mouth shut and walked as quickly as possible to cover the remaining few steps to the front door, keeping as much distance between the two of us as possible.

A smiling Nalika opened the door. She took a few steps towards me, then jumped up and wrapped her tiny arms around my neck. "How are you, Nalika?" I asked as I set her down. She offered a wide grin in response.

Down the stairs came Yogi. Surprisingly, he greeted me with a smile, too. "Hello, Yogi. How are you?"

"I'm fine," he answered in Nepali. OK, maybe he wasn't so bad.

From the kitchen, I could hear the sound of laughter and the voice of more than one adult drifting from it. I pointed towards the back of the hallway, "Who's here, Nalika?" I asked the little girl who had latched onto my legs with seemingly no intention to let go anytime soon.

She grabbed my hand, pulling me towards the kitchen. I walked in to find the kids sitting around the picnic table watching two adults I hadn't seen before preparing dinner, and entertaining the kids as they did. None of the children even noticed my entrance. Yash, who had been standing at the back of the room overseeing the cooking, came over and clasped my hand warmly.

"How was it, this first meeting with Vikram?" he asked.

"Fine, I guess. He doesn't really speak any English, so it was brief. I think I prefer it that way," I answered, lowering my voice self-consciously.

"He is strong man, this Vikram. I don't like very much. He is not nice to children." At my quizzical look, he continued, "He is rude to them, this man. He shouts many times to them. They are not his soldiers, but still he shouts."

"Will he stay in Rinrut?"

"Yes, he is here since first day. He is area leader. There are others too, but he stays here."

"So, how many people, you know, Maoists, have moved into Rinrut?"

"There are…" He paused for a few seconds to count, "maybe ten."

"Soldiers?"

"Yes, mostly. Four are just common peoples like me. Nice peoples they are," he said with an emphatic nod of his head, as if to reassure me, or perhaps himself.

Sensing this was the end of the conversation, I turned my attention to the young couple entertaining the children. I couldn't make out what they were saying but everyone, including Yash, would burst into laughter every few minutes at their antics. The man did most of the talking while the woman chopped the vegetables, occasionally interrupting him to correct something that he had said. It was a bit strange to see an impromptu comedy routine being performed in the kitchen of an orphanage in a Maoist-controlled village of the Nepali Himalayas.

"Who are these two, Yash?" I asked quietly.

"They are a helping peoples. They come here once a month, sometimes more. They do most of the cooking and they help with the children. Very funny they are."

Later that night once the children had been put to bed, the four of us, Yash, the couple, and myself, enjoyed some local spirit outside on a bench that Yash had brought from the kitchen. Yash played the interpreter. I learned that the two newcomers were originally from the city of Mihang in Mahakali, located in the far western area of Nepal. Sahana and Ranjiv had been married for twenty-two years. Long enough for them to start to resemble each other; the pair practically looked like siblings. They both had wide, almond-shaped eyes, the chestnut color of their irises matching their weathered skin. Ranjiv had been orphaned himself at the age of three after his parents had died of tuberculosis, hence why they volunteered their time in Rinrut.

When I asked Yash what the pair did when they were not volunteering at the orphanage, he informed me, "They own a farm about two days that way." He pointed in the direction of Takam. "They stay here with us when they come to Rinrut. It is very good for the children."

"What do they think about the whole Maoist situation?"

Silence followed after Yash translated my question. The pair looked at each other as if to check whether it was OK to speak. They both glanced around worriedly before offering a short, hushed reply.

"They say that they afraid of them," Yash translated, "In their village, people have been forced into the Maoist ways. The army do nothing to protect these peoples, they were never around. They will say 'Yes' when asked whether they believe in the Maoist cause, but they are not really sure what to believe."

We stayed outside long enough to have two drinks each before heading back inside for the night. Ranjiv and Sahana were leaving early the next morning, so I said goodbye to them before retiring to my room. As I passed Kunjana's room, I thought I heard a noise coming from inside. I knocked gently, but there was no answer. I opened it a smidge and peeked around the corner, but there was nobody there. 'Strange,' I thought, slowly easing the door shut.

The night was cool, and yet I was sweating. I lay awake for most of the night, eyes wide open, eventually drifting off to a fitful sleep.

I awoke in sheer panic, my heart racing in an erratic rhythm. Extricating myself from underneath damp sheets with shaking fingers, I rushed to the window to see if something was going on outside. Nothing. Just the orange-yellow glow emanating from the small window of the Maoist office.

"Something's wrong," I said aloud. "Shit. I never should have let her go. You stupid fucker, Joseph." I began pacing the room. Starting the trek back to Takam or Khasil was out of the question. It was too dark and I would never be able to find my way once I hit the tree line. Talking to Yash was no good, as he had to stay here with the kids. Ranjiv and Sahana could possibly help, but I couldn't communicate with them. "They wouldn't believe you, anyway," I told myself aloud. But they were leaving early in the morning. I could get Yash up when they were leaving and explain the situation. All they would have to do would be to check up on her in Khasil.

I began formulating my plan as I quietly made my way downstairs. In the kitchen, I drank some water, then wrapped my blanket around my shoulders and went outside for some more fresh air. Why hadn't I stopped her?

I spent the next three hours downstairs in the main room of the house, next to the fireplace. An empty fireplace is one of the coldest and loneliest of sights, but it was the only room in the house with a proper chair. I pulled it over to the window and gazed absently out at the stars.

After some time alternating my gaze between the empty fireplace and the stars, I managed to fall asleep. The sound of the door closing startled me awake, and I leapt to my feet. Looking around frantically, it took a few seconds for me to register where I was. Stumbling towards the door, I flung it open and bounded outside into the pale daylight. I spotted Ranjiv and Sahana up ahead. Throwing the blanket that was still clutched around my shoulders to the ground, I dashed towards them, nearly running into Ranjiv when I caught up to them. I asked them to wait in a garbled mix of broken Nepali and frantic hand gestures, then dashed back inside, straight up to Yash's room. I tore the door open, slamming it against the wall and waking him in the process. He bolted upright, rubbing the sleep from his eyes.

"Joseph, what has happened?" he asked groggily, staring at me wide-eyed and confused.

"Yes, yes, something has happened. I'm not really sure what, and maybe it's nothing, but you have to come."

"OK, OK" he said wearily with a wave of his hand, dragging himself out of bed.

I practically pulled him down the stairs to where Ranjiv and Sahana were waiting on the porch step.

"Yash, you have to explain to them that they must check on Kunjana."

"What? Why, Joseph?"

"I just have this feeling that something has happened. I can't really explain why, I just do. I need them to check to make sure she is OK."

Yash gave me a bemused look, but then turned to Sahana and Ranjiv and began his explanation. When he had finished speaking, Ranjiv replied in slow, measured Nepali that they would check in on her, and that if something had happened they would send someone back to Rinrut with the news. Watching their retreating figures descend the mountain path, I noticed a swath of grey-black clouds hanging low in the early morning sky.

Yash went back to bed, but I knew I would not be able to sleep. I took a glacial shower to take my mind off the wait. By seven thirty, Yash and I were in the kitchen making breakfast for the children. As he put a pot of water to boil on the stove, he spoke of Kunjana. "She makes that walk many times, Joseph," he assured me, "She knows where is going."

"I understand that, Yash," I said, rinsing some rice in a plastic bucket. "It's just that I had a gut feeling last night. When I saw Kunjana on my way to Rinrut yesterday, I didn't want to let her go to Khasil. I thought of forcing her to come back here with me. Maybe I should have."

I sat next to Nalika at breakfast, giving her most of my rice in an attempt to get her to open up to me and find out what had happened to make Kunjana so upset. The day passed with not so much as a word from Khasil. Another day passed, and still nothing.

Chapter 11

Sahana appeared the next day while I was outside with Yash and the kids washing the yak-skin cloths that the village used for transporting goods. She went straight for Yash, grabbing his arm and pulling him inside. Checking to make sure the kids were all busy at their task, I crept over to the door, which stood ajar enough for me to make out Yash and Sahana standing in the dim light of the hallway. Sahana spoke in a hushed voice through quiet sobs. I tried to understand but all I could make out was Kunjana's name spoken intermittently.

Giving the door a quick knock so as not to startle them, I stepped towards Yash. "Yash, tell me what's up. What's happened?" I tried to keep the anger and fear out of my voice, without much luck.

"This is not good, Joseph. Bad peoples here, very bad peoples."

"Tell me what has happened," I repeated, my voice cracking slightly on the last word.

"Kunjana," he uttered, his eyes fixed on the floor. Grabbing him by the shoulders with more force than I'd intended, I asked again, this time in Nepali, what had happened.

"Very bad peoples, Joseph," he repeated. "Joseph, the setters have done terrible things. Very bad peoples they are."

I remembered my talk with Yash about the illegal poachers. I wanted to scream, but instead I muttered through clenched teeth, "Where is she?"

Yash said a few things to Sahana in Nepali, who responded through wet fingers. "She is still in Khasil," he said, finally meeting my eyes. "She is with her grandmother now."

I released my iron grip on Yash's shoulders. I don't know how long I stood there before Yash gingerly touched my shoulder.

"Joseph," he intoned softly. "You can go to Khasil tomorrow. You can see her."

How could I ever look into those almond eyes again? This was my entire fault. I stood motionless.

Once Yash had settled Sahana in the kitchen with a cup of chai, he led me into the front room to tell me the entire story. Two setters had attacked Kunjana. They had come up behind her and pulled her into the forest. Although she was obviously no match for two grown men, she did manage to make enough noise to finally persuade them to let her go. The severity of the attack was unknown as Kunjana refused to speak to anyone except for her grandmother. Sahana had stayed with her the previous two days before returning to inform us. Ranjiv and two other villagers had gone off the next day in search of the perpetrators.

"Kunjana's grandmother is not well, Joseph." Yash and I were sitting outside the next evening. "Sahana said she is not very good at all. Very sick people, she is." Earlier that day, we had bid Sahana farewell as she was going back to Khasil before moving on to her own home the following day. Ranjiv, she said, would keep looking for the setters as long as they remained at large.

"Why hasn't Vikram done anything?" I asked, pointing towards the office emanating its sickly yellow glow. "What the fuck has to happen before they do something? They're the goddamn police, aren't they?"

"Yes, Joseph, they are our police peoples now, but we cannot tell them what to do. Maybe tomorrow they send some peoples out. I told you I do not like Vikram, but I will speak to him. What you want him to do?"

"He has a radio, why doesn't he use the bloody thing? Call some more people and get them over here to search for the bastards." I wiped my lips of the spittle that had escaped along with my outburst. "They spend all their time worrying about the military while real criminals are out there. They sit around playing cards and telling the children what to do. It's because her parents were killed by them, isn't it? That's the reason they don't give a shit. What the fuck is wrong with these people? It's not her fault!" I was angry at the Maoists, I was angry at the setters, I was angry at everyone. But most of all, I was pissed off with myself.

"They can't really do much, Joseph. The villagers are searching for these two very bad peoples."

"I know, I know." I finished my tea, then slammed my cup on the ground, almost shattering it. "What will happen, Yash, if they get caught? I mean, who judges them now? These dickheads are the police, but who judges and who convicts these people?"

"That, Joseph, I cannot answer." He looked upwards as he said it. We then sat in silence, with nothing else to add.

I spent another sleepless night in Rinrut, tossing and turning for hours, unable to get the idea of little Kunjana struggling for her life out of my mind. Why had I let her go?

Before breakfast the next day, I set off for Khasil. Dragging my feet, the walk took five hours instead of the usual three. Other travelers passed occasionally and I eyed them all suspiciously.

When I finally glimpsed Khasil through the trees at the final bend in the road, it dawned on me that I had no idea exactly which home belonged to Kunjana's grandmother. The thought of heading to the Khasil Community Maoist Office made me shudder with revulsion.

As I made my way down the solitary path that ran through the village, a tiny figure darted out of a doorway. I recognized the bright red jogging pants immediately as they went fluttering before my eyes like a tattered red kite. I kept an eye on the doorway from which she had just fled. As I started up the dirt road, Sahana materialized in the doorway, a large cloth bag slung over her shoulder.

"Namaste, Sahana."

"Namaste," she returned.

In broken Nepali, I asked if this was Kunjana's grandmother's house, which she confirmed with a quick nod.

"She sick," Sahana said in halting English, glancing back worriedly at the small hut. Switching back to Nepali, she told me that she had to go, but that Ranjiv was still out searching for the setters with some of the other men from Khasil. She told me Kunjana had gone to fetch water. I bid Sahana goodbye for the last time in front of the tiny, mud-brick dwelling.

Watching her leave, my heart sank. I turned again to face the house and, after taking a few moments to collect myself, wiped the sheen of sweat from my forehead and stepped over the threshold.

Kunjana's grandmother lay on a thin mattress atop a flimsy wooden bedframe. She lay motionless except for a gentle fluttering of breath moving the heavy blanket covering her from toes to chin. A simple white cloth was draped over her forehead and tiny puddles of sweat filled the creases above her upper lip. I stood with my head bowed, not knowing what else to do. I settled for asking whatever higher power might be listening for her to recover, to be full of life again. Some omnipotent being, celestial entity, or divine presence, the concept of which I had always took for granted as non-existent, was now needed.

Placing my bag on the ground, I looked around the tiny dwelling. The room was small, with another room opposite of approximately the same size. A threadbare sheet acting as a curtain hung over a thin rope tied between two wooden spikes in the walls. Partly pulled aside, it revealed a kitchen where few plates and some cutlery soaked in a large bucket half full of dirty water. A grey bucket with a scant amount of clear water sat on the floor next to it.

Grabbing the bucket of clean water, I gingerly lifted the cloth from the ancient's forehead, rinsed it thoroughly, then gently replaced it on her brow. I sat next to the cot and watched her. Deep wrinkles of time were etched into her face, but they were soft, not nearly as defined as the ones I had seen adorning the faces of other elderly Nepalis.

I sat there holding her hand, almost nodding off myself. Just as I was about to refresh the damp cloth on her forehead, the door opened. Expecting to see Kunjana, my eyes were met not with her small frame, but that of a young man of about thirty, wearing the same checkered shirt that I had seen both Prakul and Vikram wearing. Definitely a Maoist. He sported a moustache like Vikram's and his hair was pushed back from his face and adhered to his skull with wax. His eyes were small and beady, his nose narrow. He barked out a few words in incomprehensible Nepali. Trying my best to communicate, I told him in both English and a sacrilegious form of his own tongue that I knew the woman lying in the cot and that she was very sick

"My name's Joseph," I offered in English, placing my hand on my chest. The young man walked over to the kitchen and pulled the curtain wide. I wondered what exactly he was looking for. Turning back to me, he pointed to my pack which was resting on the ground and asked whose it was, first in his own language and then with grunts.

"It's mine," I said, pointing to myself again. He took a step towards the bag and poked at it with his baton. A feeling of relief flooded over me when I realized he wasn't carrying a gun.

Bending down and without so much as a look in my direction, he unzipped the bag and proceeded to dump its entire contents onto the floor. The first item to hit the ground was the little bag of marijuana from Chapala that I'd stuffed in my pack as an afterthought before leaving Rinrut. I kept my eyes glued to the little baggy as it miraculously disappeared under some wrinkled clothes.

After muttering something about Kunjana's grandmother in a dialect I had not heard before, he finally turned to leave. Just as he set his heavy booted foot on the threshold, Kunjana appeared just outside the doorway. One look at the Maoist and I saw instant fear materialize in her eyes. She stood motionless, gripping a plastic bucket of water in tiny clenched hands. The soldier barked something at her, but she didn't move; she was frozen solid. He yelled at her again, this time gesturing at me with his baton as I hastily gathered up my belongings and stuffed them back into my bag.

Kunjana's eyes flew wildly back and forth between her grandmother and me. "It's OK," I assured her, doing my best to maintain eye contact.

The soldier resumed shouting at her, all the while staring at me, shaking his wooden baton inches from my face. This time, she responded and I understood some of what she said; she told him that I was a worker in Rinrut at the orphanage and that I spent most of my time in Takam. At the mention of Takam, he bent over and stared menacingly into my eyes.

"I am a volunteer," I said in English, my voice quivering. "I am just here to help." Kunjana began translating for me. "What's his name, Kunjana?" I asked her when she had finished interpreting.

"Prabal," she whispered.

"Prabal," I began tentatively, "I am sorry. I mean no harm. I am going back to Takam today." I looked back towards Kunjana and said slowly. "Kunjana, just tell him that I am leaving. In a few minutes I will go. You understand, yes?"

She nodded and began translating what I had said. As she spoke, I kept my eyes glued to her face. She didn't look at the man, but kept her eyes fixed on something in the dingy kitchen. When she finished, Prabal took a few steps toward the door and, as Kunjana tried to move out of his way, he gave her a push, swatting at her like a stray dog with his baton. She fell against the wall of the house and dropped the bucket, spilling it onto the dirt floor.

Waves of guilt came crashing down upon my shoulders as tears rolled down Kunjana's cheeks. I crawled over to her, putting my arms around her as she fell into my chest sobbing. Her tears soaked into my shirt as I held her, rocking gently back and forth.

Through the open door, I watched as dark clouds gathered in the sky above. A distant bird sang, the bells of a herd of yaks clanked in an uncontrolled rhythm, the cacophony of my mind a dire emotional cocktail of anguish, regret, and sorrow, seizing power over my thoughts like the Maoists had Rinrut. I wanted to tell Kunjana it was alright. I wanted to tell her that things would get better, but instead I said nothing. I knew that she was stuck, that there was no light at the end of her tunnel. No prince in shining fucking armor would be coming to rescue her and sweep her off her feet. No glass slipper was ever going to fit her tired, bruised, and callused country-worked foot.

I went to retrieve more water to replace the bucket that Kunjana had spilled. When I re-entered the doorway to the small, mud-brick home, a tiny ancient sat at the bedside with Kunjana.

"Namaste," she greeted me.

"Namaste," I returned.

"Nisha," Kunjana said, pointing at the old woman.

"Joseph," I said, pointing at myself.

Kunjana told me the old woman was her grandmother's friend and that she lived in another village near the main path. At least, I think that's what she said. As Kunjana explained, the ancient looked up at me with sad, glossy eyes. She held her friend's hand lovingly, the way only a grandmother can. I spoke through Kunjana, trying to find out what was going to happen. Nisha would stay for as long as it would take for Kunjana's grandmother to get better. I looked at Nisha and inclined my head. She returned the gesture knowingly.

After a cup of tea prepared by Nisha, I finished gathering up my belongings.

"You go?" Kunjana asked in English, coming over to stand next to me.

"Yes, Kunjana, I have to go. I'm sorry, but I'll be back, OK?" She looked up at me, then turned and went back to her grandmother.

Hoisting my bag over my shoulder, I stood and bid Kunjana and Nisha goodbye. "Kunjana, I'll be back, OK? I promise."

"Bye bye," she said, coming back to me and clasping her tiny arms around my legs. I fought back the tears.

"Thank you," I said to Nisha in Nepali. We caught each other's eyes for a few seconds before I turned to leave. Walking past the Khasil Community Maoist Office, a feeling of rage and helplessness overtook me. I wanted to rip the building apart, I wanted to burn it, destroy it. But most of all, I wanted the young man inside it to pay.

I walked through Talpit at around nine o'clock, but there was no one to greet me this time. Everyone was asleep, not a single hearth fire to be seen glowing from the wood-framed windows I passed. I had shaved almost two hours off my normal trip time, arriving in Takam at just past midnight. Making my way up the hill to my house in the moonlight, I then sat in my chair and lit a cigarette, tears already forming in my eyes.

Chapter 12

A chill consumed my body from head to toe, sweat dripping from my temples. Looking down, I noticed the cigarette I had been smoking a few hours previously lay abandoned at my feet. I went inside, grabbed the quilt off the bed, then went back outside to my greenness. Wrapping the old, tired blanket around me, I lit another cigarette and sat staring out at the rolling hills.

"You're getting sick again, Joseph," I said aloud, punctuating the thought by coughing up some phlegm.

"Then maybe you shouldn't be smoking," said a voice to the right of me. It was Debu.

"Shubha prabhat."

"Good morning to you too, Joseph. How was Rinrut?"

Rinrut was the last thing I wanted to talk about that morning, but I had to tell him. Of all the people in this corner of the world, Debu was the one man I could really talk to. He was the de facto father figure of the village and, by extension, my own father figure as well.

"Not very good," I answered him.

"Why is that, Joseph?" he asked, taking a cigarette from his pajama pocket and lighting it. A mystic smoke enveloped his head at the first strong puff. I sat without speaking for a few minutes as he stared out at the hills with me, not pressing me to answer.

"You know Debu, sometimes everything is just wrong, and the wrong people end up with the wrong type of power."

He stood in methodical silence before answering. "This is true, Joseph, but is it not also true that good people sometimes end up in power as well?"

"Yes," I answered slowly, thinking that was fairly obvious. "Just not from what I've seen."

"You are young, Joseph. You will experience many more happenings in your life." He took a drag of his cigarette. "Both good and bad, I'm afraid."

After a short pause I cleared the remaining phlegm from my throat, and began to recount what had happened over the past few days. Like a breached dam releasing a torrent of water, I let go of everything I had. When I had finished I was completely exhausted, breathing in lungfuls of the fresh mountain air. The whole time I was speaking, Debu gazed out silently at the hills around us, his face inscrutable, responding only with a vague nodded affirmation.

Eventually he turned to me. "You really should stop smoking if you are not feeling well, Joseph. A sound body helps achieve a sound mind."

"I know. I don't even know why I bought these." I threw my half-lit cigarette into the can of rainwater at my feet.

"When will you be returning to Rinrut?" he asked, stroking his chin.

"I don't know," I replied, already aware of the conviction to return to the Maoist-infested village. "I don't know what the point is, really."

"Come now, Joseph. You know exactly why you will be returning."

I spent the rest of the day lying in bed, as well as the next day, and the one following that. I wasn't violently ill, but it felt as though the slightest movement was the only catalyst needed to provoke it. Chapala came by every night, dinner in hand. She left it on the chair in the living room, said something in indecipherable Nepali from the bedroom doorway, then departed on her long walk home. Each morning she returned to a half-eaten chapatti and a dish of cold dhal. I tried to get most of it down, but cold tea was all my body wanted. On the third day, Debu came by in the morning just as I was reheating the dhal from the night before.

"Feeling better?"

"Good morning, Debu. Yes, I am, thank you. Much better."

"The children were getting worried about you."

"So I've heard," I said, taking a towel from the shelf and wrapping it around the pot handle. I sat down in one of the living room chairs with my breakfast. "Well, at least I thought that's what I heard. Chapala mentioned something about children, and I thought I heard the word 'worry', so I figured she was saying as much."

"Alpa has been asking about you every day. I had to warn her not to come here. I knew you needed rest."

"Any word on the situation in Khasil?" I asked as I blew on a spoonful of dhal.

"Not that I have heard, Joseph, no."

"I suppose no news is good news for Kunjana's grandmother, then."

Debu offered a half smile before excusing himself with the promise to return later once I was back from teaching.

I found myself surrounded by a throng of jumping, beaming children as soon as I walked through the door to the school. I had arrived an hour late and the older students were well into their math lesson, but I wanted to stop in and say hello nonetheless. Even Naresh welcomed me with a smile, probably happy that I had missed a soccer match during my illness. Gunjan excused himself from the class and the two of us went outside for a talk.

"Everything is going well, Joseph. The girls are still doing a good job in the library and the little ones are really enjoying the songs you have taught them."

After our talk I visited the younger kids and, not being in the mood to actually teach, played games with them until lunchtime. After lunch, the girls and I worked on the library. Geeti and Hita were visibly thrilled to show me all the work they had accomplished in my absence. I knew Gunjan had been doing most of the classifying, but the girls were responsible for the documentation and I had to admit that their handwriting was a hell of a lot neater than my own.

That afternoon I left school early and went over to Bindu's house. He was away working on some project, which was all I could garner from his wife's explanation in Nepali. I told her I would return later, but I don't think she understood me either.

Passing Chapala's house, I decided to stop by and thank her, and also tell her that she need not worry about bringing over my meals anymore now that I was better. As I reached her home, I caught the distinct odor of our favorite plant wafting from the backyard. Heading in that direction, I saw that she was once again bent over at the waist with a pipe in her mouth. We spoke briefly and she accepted my thanks for tending to me while I was sick like water off a duck's back. She would have none of it, repeatedly waving her hand in front of her face to tell me that it was nothing. She offered me a smoke, but still not feeling one hundred percent, I had to pass. I thanked her again and made my way home.

**

A week passed with no new information from Khasil. I was hoping Nisha would somehow manage to get word out to me about the situation. I was finally back to full health by the time I received a letter from Dave and Elam. I kept my reply short:

Dear Dave and Elam,
All things considered, I'm doing fine. I worry about the others, though. Still here, and planning to stay for now. Don't know for how long, though. Will keep my passport and take my chances later.
Regards,
Joseph

Debu appeared in the doorway as I was delivering a lesson on prepositions to the older students. Gunjan stepped outside and I could hear the rumble of their voices as I distractedly continued my lesson. At the first opportunity, I left the kids with some exercises to do on their own and joined the two men outside.

"Debu, Namaste."

"Hello, Joseph."

Gunjan glanced at me, then quickly lowered his gaze.

"She's gone, isn't she?" I asked, knowing the answer already.

"Yes, Joseph. Three days ago she passed away."

I looked at them both, not knowing what to do nor say. I had known it was coming, yet I was suddenly speechless.

"I'm sorry, Joseph," Debu intoned softly.

"And Kunjana? What will happen to her?" I finally managed to blurt out.

"Still unsure," he said, taking a few cigarettes from his pajama pocket. Lighting mine first, then Gunjan's, and finally his own, we stood together in smoke-infused silence. "But there is also good news, Joseph. I have been told that the setters have been caught."

How was that possible? I had seen the fear Kunjana had for the young Maoist in Khasil, that fuck Prabal. I had come to doubt there had ever been any setters.

"Really? Who are they?"

"Well, I'm not too sure. I have just been told that two setters were caught and that they will face a court in Rinrut. It's the Myagdi area center, you know. I think they are from China."

"Just how are they going to do this?" I asked, stubbing out my cigarette.

"They are waiting for the court to come. They will use one of the highest officials in their party. I do not know who or when, but it will be soon."

Voices floated from the classroom. The students had stopped speaking English and were now, I presumed, busy talking about the same subject we were.

I looked to Gunjan, who stared back at me. "You can go as you like, Joseph," he said. He tossed his cigarette away and went back inside the classroom.

"He's angry with me?" I asked Debu.

"I don't think so, Joseph. He understands," he said patting my shoulder.

Chapter 13

Packing as many clothes as my bag would carry, I grabbed my passport as an afterthought. Having it with me might just help as I crossed and re-crossed the line between Maoist-controlled Nepal and the rest of the country. The next morning at five a.m. Bindu was waiting at the bottom of the path into the village. A faint orange glow of sunlight emanated through the early morning mist, illuminating the white peaks in the distance.

"Good...morming," Bindu said in broken English. He had heard through Debu that I was walking back to Rinrut and had volunteered to accompany me. Having firsthand knowledge of the setters, he wanted to be there in case anything happened, but Talpit was his limit; he had no intention of entering the Maoist-controlled area. Trying to get a reason for this out of him was, as I soon found out, futile, as neither of us had a good enough grasp of our newly acquired second languages.

Luckily for me, Bindu had the foresight to bring along two bottles of the local brew, the sweet jepu of which I had become so fond. He managed to convey to me that the second bottle was reserved for his walk back alone. By six o'clock that morning, under the steady drizzle that had started just after we left the village, I had a solid buzz on and a ten-hour walk ahead of me.

An hour before we reached Talpit we stopped and tied a small blue tarpaulin between two trees, sat underneath and ate some bread and sweets that Bindu's wife had made. We finished off the first bottle of booze in the process, which miraculously increased our ability to understand each other. From what I made out, he had been in a fight with some Maoists and was now deathly afraid of being caught out by them. That, or he was looking for a fight and would very much like to beat some Maoists to death. It definitely had something to do with fighting.

We were a few hundred yards away from Talpit when Bindu bid me good-bye and started off on his return journey. To my surprise, he pulled out the second bottle of jepu and handed it to me. I politely refused, figuring he could use it more than I could.

It was half past ten. If I kept up a good pace, I knew that even in the now pouring rain and biting wind, I would make it to Rinrut by nightfall. Thinking about walking through Khasil again brought a sick feeling to my stomach. Prabal's sneer was burned into my memory, as was the look on

Kunjana's face when she had seen him standing inside her grandmother's home. I knew he was to blame for what had happened to Kunjana. I could feel it. There had been no setters; Kunjana had made up that story out of fear, or perhaps she had been instructed to tell that version of events.

"Think man, think," I muttered. Suddenly wishing I had taken Bindu up on his offer of that bottle of spirits, I quickened my pace. I arrived outside of Khasil just after two o'clock. I decided to walk through the forest that flanked the far edge of the village so that I could check if anyone was at home at Kunjana's without being seen myself. I crept slowly through the dense foliage, ducking behind trees every few feet and keeping as low to the ground as I could. The steady rain would make me harder to spot, but also hampered my view of the houses. About twenty yards in I spotted Kunjana's grandmother's home. Making a run for the biggest tree I could find, I crouched down next to it, took an extra jacket out of my pack and threw it over my shaking shoulders.

Saying a silent prayer that Kunjana had left the village for Rinrut already, I settled into my soggy post and decided to wait an hour before continuing on my trek. An hour is a long time to wait when you're crouching in the mud in an official war zone. Thanks to Bindu's booze, my eyes began to drift shut, and I let myself get distracted by the swirl of stars at play behind my eyelids instead of watching the house. When I awoke two hours later, the rain had stopped and an oppressive humidity had taken its place, soaking me through with sweat.

"Fucking dumbass, Jo-" I started, before I caught a glimpse of someone on the other side of the trees. I recognized Prabal by the AK clutched under his arm like he was carrying a baguette. I held my breath as he turned to face the exact spot where I was sitting, then slowly exhaled as he stretched lazily and ambled away down the path. He returned a few minutes later with a bucket of water and entered the house next to Kunjana's.

I waited another twenty minutes but saw no one else enter or leave the house. Content that at least in all probability Kunjana was safe in Rinrut, I quietly organized my things while picking tiny insects off of me, then set off to join her. Pushing aside the branches in a low, darting walk, I finally met up with the path that veered left out of Khasil. I was sure I could still make it before nightfall as long as I hurried.

I entered the village just as the sun sunk behind the distant wall of mountains to the west. Walking straight past the Maoist office with my head held as high as I could manage and forcing my face not to betray the fear in the pit of my stomach, I made a beeline for the orphanage.

"Joseph! Come in, come in," Yash greeted me breathlessly. "I never thought I was going to have seen your face again."

"I heard about the setters being caught," I said, skipping a proper greeting in favor of getting straight to the point of my visit.

"Ah, yes, it is wonderful thing them peoples being caught. Very bad peoples, very bad."

"Debu told me they were Chinese?"

Yash put his hand on my back and led me down the hall towards the kitchen. "Chinese, yes. Very bad. From Tibet these setters. They are here in Rinrut, at the office they are. Tomorrow the court will start. Would you like some tea?"

"That would be great, Yash." More information on these Tibetan setters and their impending trial was what I really wanted, but I'd settle for a cup of tea first. I sat down at the table across from Yash, two cups of steaming chai before us. My foremost thought was that I had to find out whether Kunjana had returned safely to Rinrut, preferably without conveying what a nervous wreck I was. "Where are the kids?" I asked in the closest approximation to nonchalance I could manage.

"Playing," Yash replied with a vague wave of his hand in the direction of the backyard.

"And Kunjana? She's here, isn't she?"

"Oh, yes, she is here. Terrible thing that is, her grandmother." He took a sip of tea before continuing. "She has been here for a few days now. Just after her grandmother dead."

"How is she?"

"I think OK, but I do not really know. She does not speak to me, if you remember."

"How does she look, Yash?" I asked, angered by the lack of care he was displaying.

"She looks OK. She is upstairs now. She doesn't really play with anyone, either."

"Not surprised," I said in a low and bitter voice.

"Yes, but she will get better."

I finished off my chai then excused myself. My heart raced as I made my way up the stairs. I tapped on the door to Kunjana's room and, hearing no response from inside, gave it a gentle push. Kunjana sat on the floor, two well-worn dolls held in her tiny hands, a dejected look on her face. A soft, sad smile crossed her lips as she glanced up at me. In that moment, I knew what I had to do.

"Namaste," I said, entering her room and taking a seat at the edge of her bed. "How are you?" I asked in Nepali.

"I am fine, Josep," she replied in English.

"I'm sorry about your grandmother," I offered in a mix of our two languages, hoping my concern would be clear if my words were not.

Her gaze shot back down to the two dolls, which now lay in her lap. "Kunjana?" I said softly, in slow, careful English. "Do you want to get out of here?" Her eyes darted up to meet mine instantly. "Do you want to come with me? I can take you somewhere safe. I know some place far away where no one can hurt you and you'll have good people and friends to take care of you." Surely Hien and Blair had room for one more at their home in Kathmandu.

"I want to leave," she said in Nepali, her eyes glossed over with unshed tears.

"It's our secret, OK?" I put my finger to my lips, and she nodded. "We will go soon," I said in Nepali in what I hoped was a reassuring tone.

"Do you have any other clothes?" I asked. Not knowing the word for clothes, I tugged gently on her sweater. She pulled a little box out from the under the bed. Inside was another pair of jogging pants that looked to be about three sizes too big, two sweatshirts, and a worn brown t-shirt. "A bag?" I asked in Nepali. She nodded, pointing under the bed. I understood that all her worldly possessions were kept in the small compartment. I smiled reassuringly, "I have to go now, OK? But be ready soon."

***

"So, what happens now?" Yash and I were sitting outside after having just put the children to bed.

Taking a sip of his drink, he answered, "I do not really know, Joseph. I have been told that a leader is coming. He will make the decisions with the others. Vikram, the man here now, do you remember? He and the leader...and Prabal will be judging."

I practically choked on my drink. "Prabal? From Khasil?"

"Yes, I think this person is in Khasil."

"Fan-fucking-tastic," I sighed, throwing my gaze up at the stars.

"What does this mean, Joseph?"

"Nothing, my friend."

***

The next morning I woke early, stretched, washed my face and brushed my teeth, then made my way to the kitchen for a breakfast of cold rice and potatoes. At just past eleven Yash made his way back to the care home. The children and I had been playing movie star again, as it was one of the few ways they actually enjoyed speaking in English. The initial novelty of having a Westerner around had faded drastically and I was now seen as just another authority figure, or some variant thereof. Yash entered the school and said something to the children in Nepali. They all darted for the doorway in a mad scramble to see who would be the first out the door.

"Joseph, the leaders are here. The head peoples have just arrived and are now at the office."

"When does the trial start?"

"Prakul said they would begin this afternoon."

"They don't waste any time, I guess."

He looked at me in confusion. "No, Joseph, no time wasting," he repeated.

After lunch, which the children and I prepared as Yash was busy finding out what was to happen with the trial, I went upstairs and packed a few things. I figured the whole thing was a farce anyway and I had no intention of allowing Kunjana to stay there any longer. She had spent most of the morning upstairs, only coming down for lunch.

"Kunjana, you know they are having the trial today?" I didn't think she understood me, but I had a feeling the sound of someone else's voice would comfort her. "I think they will ask you to go and identify the men, Kunjana. I'm sorry."

She would be made to stand in front of a room full of strangers and practically be forced to say that it was the Tibetan setters who had assaulted her. All the while, the real perpetrator would be staring right at her, through her, putting the fear of God into her if she were to say anything but the pre-rehearsed version of events. I saw the whole thing play out in my mind's eye and it made me feel sick.

I weighed the pros and cons of Kunjana staying in Rinrut versus leaving the mountain village. In Rinrut she would never be a normal little girl. She had already been ostracized by virtue of what had happened to her parents. In all likelihood, she would be assaulted again. In Kathmandu, she could start afresh; she could make friends with others who had undergone the same misfortunes, she could attend school fulltime.

'You could have prevented one tragedy and you fucked up,' I told myself. 'Don't fuck it up this time.'

Yash came to find me later that afternoon to inform me that the trial was about to start. It would be held at the school, as the Maoist office was too small.

We pushed our way past some of the villagers gathered inside the schoolroom, not a difficult task seeing as the average height of the locals was around five foot three. It was very crowded; steam lifted off the sea of heads, sweat droplets formed on brows. I could barely raise my arms over my head. Squeezing our way to the front of the crowd shoulders first, I spotted the leader. Dressed in fatigues like all the rebels I had seen in Nepal, with a red sash draped over his body, this elder sported a perfectly trimmed, greying moustache in the Indian fashion. His dark, sincere eyes scanned the crowd through a pair of spectacles much too large for his small head. Sitting next to Vikram, the two could have passed for father and son.

Sitting next to Vikram was Prakul. On the other side of the leader sat that son of a bitch Prabal, looking smugly pleased to be sitting next to the man in charge. I eyed him for as long as I could, but he never glanced in my direction. He sat with both hands resting on his lap like royalty, a slight smirk on his face and a cup of tea resting on the desk in front of him. Hatred burned inside me.

"Where are the two Tibetans? And who's the guy with the red sash?" I asked Yash, pointing at the man seated next to Vikram.

"The Tibetans have not arrived yet. Before they begin that trial, there are few things that other peoples from the village want done. The leader, his name is Chandra Prakesh."

"Chandra Prakesh," I repeated softly, staring at the man, appraising. "So when will it begin?"

"I do not know, Joseph." Before Yash could finish his sentence, Prakul began to address the crowd. The look that crossed Vikram's face when Prakul spoke told me he clearly wasn't happy; there was evidently some kind of power struggle going on inside the party.

Yash leaned into me, translating as best he could. Prakul told the crowd that they were honored to have such a valiant and determined comrade in the village of Rinrut, and indeed in all of the Myagdi area. Comrade Chandra Prakesh had been fighting for their cause since the very start, back in February of 1996 when the party had first declared their People's War. Many years before that, he had been the group's leader in armed conflicts with the Royal Nepalese Army.

"Many fellow comrades have fallen," Yash translated, "And we all to take a moment of quiet to reflect on their lost live as we continue struggle for a People's Republic of Nepal."

The smell of compressed bodies and dirty clothes penetrated my nostrils. The people pressed into the small space were farmers and yak herders left alone for the most part by the capital; they were country people of the hills who had no use for an armed struggle against anyone, especially against a government that had all but abandoned them already. But there they were, heads bowed en masse, in memory of people they had never met and probably wouldn't have liked anyway.

After Prakul's address, Comrade Chandra began to speak, and Yash continued his hushed translation.

"They will have more disruptions, Joseph," he said, his voice penetrating the trance I had fallen into listening to the leader's somber, mesmerizing speech.

"Disruptions?" I asked hazily.

"Yes, some peoples have things they want the court to do judging."

"Ah, disputes, gotcha."

"Yes, this is what I said, disputes."

The court deliberated over the cases brought forth by four people from various nearby villages. One of the disputes dealt with a stolen yak; another had to do with property lines, which I found ironic seeing as we found ourselves in a communist court, and two others had to do with dowries that had not been paid in full. It was less like a courtroom scene and more like teachers breaking up a quarrel in a schoolyard and having the misbehaving children shake hands. Each judgment would not be valid in the eyes of the country's capital, but would nevertheless be implemented in this remote corner under its de facto rulers.

At just past five, when the sun had almost completely disappeared beneath the cloudy horizon, Comrade Prakesh ordered the two accused to be brought into the courtroom. Hushed voices echoed throughout the schoolroom. The guards returned with two diminutive men who showed clear signs of having suffered a recent beating. Dragged in shoeless, the bottoms of their feet bled leaving four faint trails of crimson behind them.

The crowd parted as best it could as they entered. The sudden movement of bodies sent the dust, stench, and steam into the air, the low ceiling trapping it just above my head. Everyone shuffled to make room for the newcomers, the scrape of sandals on the dirt floor amplified in the tiny chamber.

The two accused were released roughly into a corner at the front of the room, where they tumbled to the floor, cowering. I felt a stab of pity; sure, it was true that they had been poaching animals and that they were probably not 'the nice sort of peoples,' as Yash put it, but still, they had nothing to do with Kunjana.

I stole a glance at Prabal as they lifted the two men onto a bench. He turned and met my eyes for a fraction of a second, as though he could feel me watching him. We exchanged knowing stares.

As the charges were read out, the anger of the villagers grew more palpable, their whispers growing into shouts. A sandal whizzed through the air from the back of the room, just missing the smaller of the two Tibetans. Comrade Chandra stood abruptly and ordered the assailant to be removed from the schoolhouse, but the man was already leaving of his own accord, reeking of jepu and muttering something incoherent. The situation devolved quickly as two more men were ordered to the back of the room after spitting on the accused.

Prabal told the court, of which he was a presiding judge, that he and some other soldiers had come across the two accused in a camp that they had set up not far from Khasil. They had apparently been there for quite some time, as they found many skins ready for selling. Prabal pointed to the two in disgust and repeated the accusations against them no less than four times, each time with growing vehemence. The crowd once again worked itself into a frenzy, shaking fists added to the shouts and spitting in the general direction of the accused.

With a firm raise of his arm, Comrade Chandra brought the villagers' rants and cries for justice under relative control before calling for Kunjana to be brought into the courtroom. Head down, tears streaming down her cheeks, she was guided by two rebels to stand in front of Chandra. I shoved myself through the compact mass of bodies until I was standing right behind her. Suppressing the overwhelming urge to slam together the skulls of the two rebels flanking the little girl, I became acutely aware of Prabal's eyes on me and planted myself more firmly on the dusty ground, fists clenched.

Comrade Chandra began speaking to Kunjana in a gentle tone, and she met his eyes for a fleeting instant before turning her gaze back to her feet. He pointed to the accused, but the little girl refused to look, head held down resolutely, taut with fear. Prabal, apparently fed up with her frightened obstinacy, barked something at Kunjana; at the sound of his voice, she suddenly burst out into uncontrollable sobs. This only served to encourage Prabal to launch into an even more vicious invective, but Chandra quickly silenced him with a slight raise of his hand. The bastard slammed his lips shut. The leader leaned forward and murmured something to Kunjana, so softly that I could barely hear him from my spot a few feet behind her. Her whispered reply was just as hard to distinguish, but I did make out a barely perceptible shake of her downcast head.

Slowly sitting upright in his chair, Chandra addressed the crowd with quiet authority. All the while, Prabal stared at Kunjana with a look to kill. I took a step forward, only inches behind her now. Chandra Prakesh locked eyes with me and gave the slightest of nods. Taking that as my cue, I scooped Kunjana up in my arms and made for the door, the crowd looking at the two of us with confused stares.

We made it back to her room before she fell into a fresh bout of tears. I placed her on the bed and knelt down beside her.

"It's alright, Kunjana. We're going tonight, OK?" The tears continued streaking down the sides of her face, filling the hollows of her ears. "I'll be here at twelve o'clock." I made sure to say 'twelve' in Nepali so that she would understand me. As I bent down to give her a hug and kiss her forehead, she flung her arms around my neck. Tucking her into bed, I brushed away the remaining moisture from her cheeks, kissed her forehead again and said goodnight.

Once I had assured myself she would be safe for the time being, I made my way back to Yash in the schoolhouse. He began speaking in a rushed, quiet voice before I even reached his side. "Kunjana said she did not know, Joseph. She said it was too dark so they can't do anything to these bad peoples."

"That's it? They're free to go, then?"

"No, no. All peoples get really angry when Comrade Chandra tell us this, but then he said that they have done other crimes and that they will be judged for those. We cannot keep them here, so they are being taken with Comrade Chandra when he leaves tomorrow. They will take them to jail and decide on them later."

Prabal led the two convicts away. As he passed my way I felt my fists clenching involuntarily. He leaned into me, bumping against my shoulder with much more force than strictly necessary to make his way through the still-packed room. I stumbled forward, my head colliding with Yash's shoulder. As I turned to face the brute, everyone else in the room began to fall away and I felt my fists lift, then in one excruciatingly slow motion my arm raised, cocked back, then made contact with the side of Prabal's cheek. His head spun away from me, dark eyes wide. A scream came from somewhere in the crowd. As if he had expected the blow, Prabal responded with an elbow to my stomach. I instinctively bent over, falling right into him. I put my arms up, expecting a furious deluge of punches that never came. I felt a rush of damp air as the space immediately behind me emptied out, its former occupants making for the door. My right arm was still on his Prabal's shoulder; I could feel the cotton of his red sash between my sweaty fingers. I pulled myself upright with one arm, throwing a punch with the other that missed him entirely. Then Prakul landed on top of me. I was kicked, once, twice. I felt my head being pulled back, someone's fingers anchored in my hair. More screams. The kicking stopped.

As my head lolled to the side on the dusty ground, I looked through the open door and noticed absently that the sun had gone down completely; the chilly air hit my sweaty body.

"You must leave, Joseph," Yash said, hovering over me with a look of pained desperation. A few villagers watched as I allowed Yash and Prakul to help me up.

"You don't know, Yash," I mumbled, shaking my head. Through the door, I saw a blur of commotion outside the Maoist office. People gathered outside looked pointedly in my direction.

"It no safe for you," Yash continued. They led me to the care home and quickly escorted me to the sitting room, depositing me gently in the armchair next to the fireplace. I heard the pattering of feet upstairs accompanied by a chorus of young, high-pitched voices.

"You do know, don't you," I said, more a statement than a question. Yash and Prakul stood by the door, engaged in hushed conversation, occasionally shooting worried glances in my direction.

"No Joseph, I do not, I know not what you say," Yash said, not meeting my eyes.

I felt a trickle of blood run down my cheek, my eye beginning to swell shut. I coughed and felt the kicks once more. Prakul left the room. Yash stared at me wordlessly as the clamor of voices outside intensified.

Comrade Chandra gave permission for me to stay till sun up, at which point I would be sent on my way, escorted almost all the way to the frontlines of the war. I was told to wait where I was until the children had fallen asleep. Yash left without so much as a word, and I couldn't really blame him.

Chapter 14

At twenty minutes to twelve, I crept out of my room into the moonlit hallway. Slowly, and ever so quietly, I pushed open the door to Kunjana's room and peered inside. She stood next to the bed, wearing the same red jogging pants and ripped sweater she'd been wearing the first night I'd met her, a clothespin once again holding the pants in place. All of her earthly possessions had been packed into a little green backpack missing one of its straps. Easing the door shut behind us, I ushered her down the stairs. We stepped outside into the cloudless night and I grabbed hold of Kunjana's hand, moving as noiselessly as we could to the rear of the house. I knew it would be safer to take the path behind the houses rather than risk taking the main road. The Maoists would be on guard; I could make out a light shining like a sinister star from their office.

I pointed to the bushes at the edge of the path and nodded my head in that direction. Kunjana nodded in understanding. Within seconds we were hidden amongst the thin cover of the trees. Not wanting to lose her for a second, I kept hold of Kunjana's hand until we had distanced ourselves sufficiently from the village.

"OK, Kunjana. You have to do everything I say now, alright?" I said softly when we had stopped to catch our breath. "We don't have to run anymore. We can make our way back to the path now, OK?"

She gave a terse nod and let go of my hand, as if to assert her bravery. I started off with Kunjana close behind. A few seconds passed, and I heard a strange rustling sound coming from over my shoulder. Panic hitting like a nauseating wave, I turned sharply and was flooded with relief when I saw Kunjana standing there, pointing in the opposite direction, directing me toward the path which, in my adrenaline-heightened state, I had somehow managed to miss.

I could just make out the bend in the path that marked the way to Khasil through the eye that wasn't swollen completely shut. Kunjana marched on ahead of me without hesitation, blazing our trail through the undergrowth. We were passing the exact spot in the path where I had fallen asleep in the rain no more than two days previously. To our left was Kunjana's grandmother's former home, a house that up until the previous week had been the little girl's home, too. She didn't even give the building a passing glance, her gaze held resolutely forward on the path that lay ahead of us.

The sun began to rise at around five o'clock, making the path a dangerous place to be since we still hadn't left the Maoist-controlled area. Kunjana stopped and waited for me to catch up. We were nearing Talpit, the front line of the war and we were walking right through it.

I was so absorbed in these thoughts that I nearly missed the noise of someone much larger than Kunjana approaching behind me. As I turned to look over my shoulder, my head suddenly spun like a top and I found myself face down on the ground. A sharp blow landed on my side. Through my one good eye I saw Kunjana turning to face the attacker, seemingly in slow motion. She screamed as my vision faded to darkness. Just before all the light was gone, I made out her small form as she turned and fled among the trees.

Rain pelted my forehead as I came to, I don't know how much later. A millipede ran along my cheek. I felt its tiny pairs of feet gripping my skin. I dragged an arm out from underneath my stomach and threw it out to the side. A buzzing noise filled my ears, blocking out all outside noise. My immediate view was of close-packed earth, the smell of moss and foliage filling my nose. I blinked twice, then winced. As the memory of the fall, the kick to my ribs, the fleeting glimpse of Kunjana making for the forest came rushing back, I pushed myself painfully into a sitting position, then even more painfully to a stooped crouch. Smudged black tread marks dotted my shoe from toe to ankle. Someone had tried to break my foot.

I hobbled my way through the brush, keeping out of sight as much as possible. At the bridge crossing I had to abandon my cover, the river much too fast to attempt a swim across. Bells jingled faintly behind me, and the corresponding herd of yaks was practically on top of me before I could even register how close they were. A frail old man transporting a bulky collection of goods along with his seven yaks strode past. He stared me up then down before pointing to the yak at the front of the line, a wordless offer of assistance. The beast, which looked just as old and stooped as its owner, waited patiently as the old man helped me onto its back.

Takam loomed up ahead as night drew in. Raising his hand, the yak herder let out a whistle and the animals came to a shuffling halt. The old man spotted me from below as I dismounted, shuddering as my bruised ribs brushed the animal's side. The old man smiled as he continued on his way, a dark crevice where his teeth should have been.

The village was eerily and almost expectantly quiet. I knocked on Debu's door and heard him stirring inside.

"Joseph!" he half shouted. He stepped out and placed an arm around my shoulders, ushering me inside.

"Debu, it's wrong," I slurred, my words distorted by the throbbing in my head and the numb panic enveloping my heart.

"This way, this way." He guided me over to his bed where I took a seat, Debu hovering over me worriedly. "What has happened, Joseph?" He walked hastily across the room and bent over to light a fire in the hearth.

I explained the recent events as best I could, pausing every few seconds to take a shaky breath and gather my thoughts inside my pounding head. "You must go soon," Debu said when I had finished. "It is not safe for you here." He handed me a cup of tea, which I could tell had some herbal medicine added when I detected the bitterness on my swollen tongue.

Everything from that point onward moved in slow motion; the flares of light from the small fire across the room, Debu working on my injured ankle with slow, methodical motions, the bitter herbs slowly making their way into my bloodstream. Somewhere between the motion of taking the last sip and setting the cup down unsteadily on the floor next to the bed, I was asleep.

***

The sun shone in patches through silver clouds. I flew above a field, darting in between the beams of light. Below, Kunjana raced up a hill, zigzagging east then west, a smile on her face. Her wind swept hair bounced along, trailing her crosses. Beyond the hill, a battle field, soldiers in the midst of war. Guns popped, millions of cartridges littered the ground, reflecting the sun. Corpses lay everywhere, soldiers fought on. Booming sounds of metal on metal echoed like thunder. Wails of pain and anguish whipped about like wind. On Kunjana ran, smiling. An unknown force pulled me towards the middle, framed by the war around it, an untouched plot of green in amongst the sea of silver casings. Faster now I dropped towards it, unable to stop, a man in the middle with a sinister grin stared upwards, a gun pointed. There's nothing you can do now Joseph I heard someone say. You must go home.

Part II

Chapter 1

Twice during the night I awoke from a dream and watched the moon shining in through the barred window, forming a shadowy pattern of stripes on the seat next to me.

"Hey, you all right? You were mumbling again."

Wiping the sleep spit from my chin, I leaned towards the voice. "Oh, it's you." It came out irritated. "I was sleeping again," I added in a friendlier tone.

Outside, an inland sea of rice pools glistening in the twilight almost had me convinced I was travelling by boat. I shifted my position and closed my eyes. The slow, methodical motion of the bus lulled me to sleep in minutes. Hours later the bus sputtered to a halt, and with the turn of a key exhaled what sounded like its final breath. Wafting up through the floorboards, a stench of motor oil, brake fluid, sweat, and curry penetrated my nostrils.

"Well, you coming?"

The dim light streaming through the dusty windows accorded me the pleasure of watching the owner of the voice walk away from me, a light cotton dress hugging her perfect inverted heart of an ass. I waited for the mayhem to subside before walking to the front of the bus and out into the night. I stood shivering for a moment, the night air hot and sticky in contrast to my feeble body. With a thud, my bag landed at my feet, engulfed in a dust cloud. A cacophony of shouting voices drifted through the still, thick air as people barked orders at each other. I sought out one particular voice as I slung the dusty rucksack over my shoulders.

"You can do this," I murmured to myself.

"I know you can," came a voice from behind me.

"Oh, there you are. I was looking for you."

"I've been standing behind you the whole time," she smiled.

Caught up in the press of bodies, we were violently shoved into the flow migrating towards the border. I had just spent over three months travelling through India, a short time compared to its perpetually reincarnating inhabitants. With a population of over a billion, India seemed to me like the universe itself; ever expanding, its natural destiny forever pushing it outward, forward, and beyond man's ability to comprehend such enormity. One massive land of absolute chaos and unfathomable beauty and all I wanted was to get the hell out.

My weary, broken body and hundreds of others continued our close-packed, slow march towards the six customs officers at the open-air immigration queue. Seated outside on the low porch of a one-room building constructed from pieces of plywood with obvious past lives as pallets (and, by the looks of it, thrown together sometime before the birth of Ganesh) were the customs agents. I had no idea what the penalty for overstaying a visa was. India is a country where things are not always done by the books. This was also a country where violence was an everyday part of life, like shitting.

Standing between the immigration officers were a few young soldiers armed with AK-47s. None of them looked too happy. None, that is, except one, who happened to be a terrifyingly big man. I took one long look while he faced the other way and immediately tried to position myself so as not to end up at the immigration desk next to which he was standing. The customs process, from what I could observe, consisted of fifty seconds or so of questioning and suspicious glances, then a stamp in your passport and you were through. If I timed it right I would be standing in front of the old man at the end of the queue, and thus safely out of harm's way, away from the huge man I had been eyeing before who I had already dubbed "Chief" in my mind. I stopped to reorganize myself, allowing the people behind me to move ahead.

I walked up to the old man, keeping my bag slung over my shoulder. He eyed my passport suspiciously as I trembled under the weight of my belongings. Eventually he reached for the stamp, wetting it on the inkpad...and then he stopped, as did my heart. He removed his coke-bottle glasses to look me squarely in the face. He didn't say a word, but leaned back in his chair and instantly, as though he had been summoned, the big fucker in the middle sensed his services were needed. He stood leaning against the rail post, staring out into the chaos that was his daily life. He took a deep breath and made a hissing sound as he sucked the night air into his lungs. Chief then ambled over with one hand on the gun strapped across his chest and the other used to take a deep drag of the beedi he held pursed between his lips.

The old man handed him my passport and muttered something under his breath. With one swift motion the brute jerked his head to the left, telling me wordlessly to join him in the back room of the plywood shack. I stared at his massive back as he walked towards the door, then took a deep breath and followed.

There was no chair to sit on. Behind a desk the brute sat in a plastic patio chair and tossed my passport onto the table. I watched it fall in slow motion, lips pressed together tightly. Leaning back, and speaking without a trace of an accent, he said, "You know, you should have been out of my country four days ago." As if to punctuate his point, a fly that had been circling the lone, naked bulb overhead fell to the table, quivered, then flew off again. "Do you understand that this is now a matter for the courts? Legally, I am obliged to take you in and wait for a court's decision." He took a drag of his beedi and the resulting smoke swathed his dark features in a bluish haze. "The nearest cell is thirty miles south, and its Friday night." He grinned, his teeth betel-red. "I don't think you'll be seeing a judge 'til at least..." Here he drew out the end of the word for a few seconds "...Tuesday," he finished with a glint in his eye.

After a coarse swallow of the unhealthy amount of saliva that had formed in my mouth, I mustered the courage to look him in the eyes. "How much will it take to get me to the other side?" My voice was shockingly steady, my words slow and measured.

His lips parted slightly and his cheekbones gradually disappeared into a well-practiced smile. "Twenty American should do it," he replied through his grin.

"OK," I answered, trying in vain to keep my immense relief out of my voice. "Just need to get something out of here, alright?" He nodded slowly, his hand far too close to the AK. My shaking fingers fumbled for my travel wallet. I retrieved a crumpled twenty and put it in my right hand (always the right hand in India, as you wipe your ass with your left), then handed it over. Chief leaned forward and took the money like a true professional; no awkward stumbling, strictly Hollywood. Then he leaned back and just sat there, utterly silent and eerily still. I grabbed my bag and passport, turned on my heel, and fled, fighting the impulse to break into a run. Walking under an arched gateway, I crossed the border. It felt damn good to be in Nepal.

Chapter 2

A thin little man with friendly eyes and a uniform in need of a wash stood behind a desk watching me enter. "How are you good sir?"

"Fine, thank you." The door slammed shut behind me and I started, dropping my bag to the floor. "Still a little sick, though," I muttered as I bent over to pick it up.

"Sick?" he asked. "Did you take a fever?" His accent was noticeably different than the Indian one I had grown accustomed to hearing. After India, standing in the newly constructed Nepal immigration office was like being transported into the future.

"Yes, sir. Down in Agra I had a bout of food poising." I figured honesty was the best policy. He quite literally held my future in his hands.

"Ah...do not worry, my friend. That will not happen to you in Nepal." He opened my passport and began flipping through the tattered pages. "Welcome back," he said with a broad smile before stamping me through.

Shaking the blank look off my face, I offered a tepid smile before leaving the office and stepping back out into the night.

Guesthouses lined either side of the main street. Aware of the fact that I was about to stay near an international border I had just bribed one of the officers to cross, I put my head down and kept moving down the road. The left-hand side was chock-full of street vendors peddling their wares, the usual stuff they sell all throughout Asia; soap, buckets, pots and pans, cheaply made t-shirts, plastic sandals.

After ten minutes of searching, I singled out a hotel that was far enough from the border for comfort. As I approached the front counter, an exceedingly small man looked up from his paperwork and smiled at me in greeting.

"Yes, my friend?"

"Do you have any rooms free? I'd like to stay at least two nights if I can."

"Yes, yes, no problem. We room for you." Clambering up on a wooden stool, he stretched to grasp a set of keys. "All rooms are share toilet and shower. Is this OK to you, sir?"

"Yes, that's fine, as long as the bed is soft."

He started towards the back of the restaurant. "Do you want an air conditioning?"

"No, just a working fan will do." Taking in my surroundings, I was surprised; the building didn't look like it could sustain the weight of an air conditioner.

"Two hundred rupees. Many sorry, but they are all double beds," he said over his shoulder as we climbed the rickety steps.

"Bargain," I replied.

"No, we don't have those, shower and toilet are shared."

I stared at the top of his head. "And you do take Indian rupees, don't you?" I said, trying to make it sound like I knew exactly what I was talking about.

"Yes sir, no problem. Same rate as a bank, sir, no problem."

God, I loved Nepal.

Sitting alone in my room, I found it to be much nicer than I had expected. A bit dusty, granted, but the entire town seemed to be covered in a thin layer of dust from the dirt road running down the gullet of it. Turning on the shadeless lamp on the bedside table, I lay back, closed my eyes and rolled over, expecting to be asleep in seconds. The lopsided melody of the ceiling fan, coupled with the low, insistent growling of my decidedly empty stomach, however, brought my eyes open.

I went down to the restaurant on the ground floor, where the little man from the front desk handed me a menu and asked if I wanted something to drink.

"I'll take a chai. Can I grab one of those bottles of water, too?"

"Sure, sure," he said with an acquiescent gesture of his hand and a quick nod.

I took a bottle of water from the fridge and went back to reading the menu; dahl bhat and achar, thali, fried rice, fried noodles, sandwiches, all your usual fare. I ordered a dhal bhat, figuring it would be best to have something not too heavy that I would be able to get (and keep) down without much chewing.

From my table at the front of the restaurant, I looked out into the night, letting my thoughts drift back to the voice, wondering if she had made it over the border alright.

A steaming chai was set in front of me and I wafted the vapor towards me, inhaling deeply. The smell of the spices kick-started my appetite and my stomach began to ache in anticipation of a solid meal.

Once I had finished my dhal, which filled me up to perfection and made no immediate threat of making a return appearance later, I sat staring out into the chaotic roadway. Lit only by the headlights of passing vehicles and the lights emanating from the small shops on the roadside, it was like a sort of Times Square of days long past.

"Is it always like this?" I asked the old man, who sat watching television behind the front counter.

"Yes, sir, always this," he replied, glancing out into the night, not seeming to take in the teeming bustle and eagerly turning his attention back to the television.

I realized that I had stopped sweating, which was a good sign.

"I think you might have cured me."

"Very well, then?" he asked.

"Yeah, much better, thank you."

I was just about to head back towards the stairs when, out of the corner of my eye, I caught sight of a woman with light hair standing on the roadside. It was her. Leaning forward for a better view, I watched her pick through a cart full of socks and lungis, then, as if sensing my eyes on her, she turned and looked directly up into my staring eyes.

"There you are," she said, smiling brilliantly, as if it were perfectly normal for a quasi-stranger she'd just met on a bus to be staring openly at her from several feet away. "I was wondering what happened to you after I lost you at the border." Her clear, almost crystalline eyes reflected the traffic passing between us. "I turned to look for you after I got to the front, but you were gone."

"Yeah, funny story, really," I said, but upon realizing that it really wasn't, promptly shut up completely.

"Oh yeah?" Her smile faltered ever so slightly.

"Yeah." Dammit, Joseph, get it together.

"Well," she paused, looking back towards the border. The awkward silence grew between us. "Well," she repeated, "I'm glad to see you got through OK." Glancing back in my direction, she added, as if it were an afterthought, "I'm going to check out the birthplace of Lord Buddha tomorrow, and you're welcome to come along if you want. You know, if you think you'll be up for it."

A pride of man-eating lions straight from the dusty plains of Africa couldn't have stopped me. "Oh definitely, yeah. What time were you thinking of going?" Please don't say early, please don't say early.

"About eleven or so."

Yes! "Eleven sounds good. You staying near here?" I asked, trying to keep my tone casual.

"Just a little further up the road. So, I'll come by in the morning then and get you?"

"Yeah, that'd be great. I'm in room...uh..." I turned and yelled over to my friend at the counter, still engrossed in his television program, "What room am I in?"

"Sixteen, sir," he said, leaning over the counter, his attention suddenly diverted when he realized who I was talking to.

"Well, then I'll see you in the morning, Joseph."

"Yeah, I'll see you in the morning, uh…"

"Skye," she said, her smile twisting into a smirk.

"Sorry, right, Skye." You dick, Joseph.

***

Trekking with nothing but my pack slung over my back, surrounded by enormous mountains, the peaks of which seemed to loom directly on top of me. I had to crane my neck just to take in their cloudy white peaks. I was alone, and I had no map.

That's the funny thing about dreams; you can never really trace them back to where they start. There you are, playing the leading role in your own little mental movie, but someone always forgets to tell you the start time and, in most cases, neglect to give you the script as well. You show up halfway through, wing the rest, and hope for the best.

I rounded a turn and found myself facing a terraced village that reminded me of a giant Greek amphitheater. My breath shot out in one long, wispy line as it cut through the mountain air. Following the plume through the air, it led to a vision of a partially stuffed yak's head, staring straight back with its empty, blood-encrusted sockets. Empty pits filled the spaces where its ears used to be. Around the whole grotesque tableau, the coagulated blood attracted swarms of droning insects.

Holding my breath, I made a run for it to the top of the hill, where I stood looking out onto a large plateau surrounded by two walls of mountains, one smooth and sheer, the other pocked with indentations which I soon realized were caves with tiny figures moving about inside them.

Before I could investigate further, I was interrupted by the pounding at my door.

Chapter 3

"Just a second, shit!" I struggled to disentangle myself from the mosquito net. It was too early for it to be Skye, but it occurred to me I had told her what room I was staying in the day before. A smile crept over my face as it dawned on me what the very insistent knocking on the door might entail. A single faint beam of light emanated from the peephole, illuminating millions of dust motes. Stumbling forward in a half-asleep stupor, I placed my eye to the light source. Standing just outside my door was a young Nepalese man of about my age, no older than twenty-five. I opened the door, wiping the disappointment off my face and the sleep from my eyes.

"Excuse me, sir," the young man said with a betel-stained grin composed of shockingly few teeth, which were tinted a shade of red bordering on deep purple. "My grandfather told me you arrived last night and that you will be staying for a few days."

"Yeah, that's right. Do you know what time it is?" I asked absently.

"It is seven o'clock, sir."

"Is this about check in?" I asked, wiping the remaining sleep from my eyes and trying to keep the annoyance out of my voice. "Can't I take care of that a little later?"

"Oh, yes, sir. No problem. But this is not about check in. No, no. Do you smoke, sir?"

What the hell? "You mean cigarettes?" I guessed his true meaning, but it couldn't hurt to clarify.

"No, sir. I have hashish." And with that, he pulled out a chunk about the size of a fruitcake from a green plastic bag that had been clutched at his side.

I stared at the molasses-brown mass. Not once since my arrival in this strange place had someone displayed the testicular fortitude to knock on my door and produce an amount of drugs that could keep an entire high school stoned for a week straight.

"Suppose I could use some," I said, trying not to let the shock register in my voice. "How much do you want for it?"

The hash strung out like taffy under his deft fingers as he tore off a piece about the size of a child's fist.

"Eight hundred rupees."

"Eight hundred?" I repeated, faking astonishment. I knew it was much more than the going rate in those parts, but the fact still remained that it would've cost a week's wages back home in order to purchase such an amount. "Hold on a moment."

I rummaged through my bag and scrounged up six hundred rupees from my wallet. Holding them out to the young man, he shook his head slowly, not breaking eye contact, but I knew he was just doing his job.

"Those are Indian rupees," I pressed. In most parts of the world, a bag of dope will cost you a fixed amount of money, and that's it. If you have the money, great, and if you don't, well then, you can just fuck off. But Asia is different. It's amazing, quite frankly. Since there's so much hash circulating that you couldn't put a fixed price on it anyway, you can always haggle. Sensing that I wasn't going to budge, the young man accepted the rupees with a slight nod and wordlessly slipped away down the corridor. It was clearly far more then I would need for the next six weeks, but at Asian prices you always end up buying more than you need.

Setting the charas down on the bedside table, I decided a few more hours' rest was in order. I stared up at the ceiling fan. It was already intensely hot, although the sun had only just risen.

I awoke just before eleven, feeling even groggier than at my first wake-up call that morning. Making my way to the third floor, I stepped into the welcoming cool of the shower, surrounded by damp cement colored various shades of green and gray from infrequent cleaning and indeterminable age.

"Sorry for the wait," I called out as my feet touched the ground floor of the hotel. Skye was waiting at a table near the front. "Have you been here long?"

"Only ten minutes. Have you had anything to eat yet?" she asked, her lilting Australian accent really coming through. I caught myself breaking into a goofy grin in response.

"Not yet. Breaky, then?" I asked, taking a stab at imitating her twang, which either went completely unnoticed or was so offensively awful that she didn't deem it worthy of commenting.

"Sounds good to me."

I slid in across from her, taking in the long auburn hair falling past her shoulders like rich port wine. She was one of those people who turn a perfectly toasted brown in the sun, in stark contrast to my white-pink pasty skin, which bore an uncanny resemblance to a plucked chicken. A constellation of freckles started at her chest and exploded up and out, racing each other down the sides of her lean arms. A long leather necklace, the pendent hidden within, dipped into her cleavage. You could tell she had curves, gorgeous, mid-nineteenth-century type curves. When she smiled, tiny wrinkles sprung up at the corners of her blue-green eyes. I could tell she smiled a lot. I broke into my second goofy grin of the morning just looking at her.

"So, chai, you reckon?" she said, breaking what I hadn't even realized was a full-fledged awkward silence.

As we waited for our chai, I admitted that I really had forgotten most of our conversation from the previous day on the bus, so she would have to bear with me if I repeated some of my questions to her.

"No worries," she said with a grin, the little wrinkles near her eyes distracting me. "You did seem pretty out of it. I'm just glad you made it through alright."

A waiter emerged from the kitchen and served our tea. "Anything else?" he asked, looking pointedly at me.

"Uh, yeah. I'll have some muesli with yoghurt and some toast, please."

"Excellent, sir." He continued to stare at me, so I added, "And Skye here will have..." I looked across at her, waiting for her to jump in with her order, but she just stared blankly back at me. "Muesli and yoghurt for you, too?" I asked. She gave one quick, angry nod and turned her gaze out the window.

When the waiter had retreated back to the kitchen, Skye let out a sigh that contained no shortage of annoyance. "You know," she began, "some say chivalry isn't dead, and it isn't, but the man should never order for the woman. In any country." She took a sip of her chai, looking thoughtful for a second before adding, "But he'd probably just stare at my tits if he took my order, anyway." Which pretty much summed up what I was doing at that very moment. I quickly averted my gaze and turned to look out the front window, taking a hurried sip of my chai and promptly burning my mouth.

Tense breakfast aside, it was an exquisite day in southern Nepal. Cook a curry on a rock hot, but beautiful nonetheless. We were being bumped along in the back of a pickup truck, taking in our surroundings in silent awe. The land around us was flat and dry, but in the far distance, beyond the Kathmandu plain, the Himalayas shot out of the earth in all their tectonic magnificence.

The "Information Center" the pick-up dropped us off in front of looked as if it hadn't served that function in several years. Outside the one-room building was a small, long-abandoned parking area with weeds blotting the numerous crevices in the pavement. We wandered a dirt path to the left of the Information Center until we reached a stone pillar no more than three feet in height and enclosed by a rusted iron fence, which I had read marked the exact spot where the Buddha was born.

South of the pillar was a small pool filled with shallow, stagnant water. Queen Mahamaya, the Buddha's mother, was said to have given her son his first purification bath in the very same water. Tranquility reigned supreme all around us. A gentle wind blew in from the north, bringing with it the subtle aroma of wildflowers and rippling the fetid water of the sacred pool. A pair of monks wandered the garden paths in contemplative silence under the watchful eye of the mountains in the background.

I sat down beside Skye at the edge of the pool and watched the ripples race each other to the other side. Being strangers in a foreign land, there were a million things we could have talked about to fill the silence, but we both felt no need to disturb the all-encompassing calm around us.

My eyes started drifting shut of their own accord, so I pulled myself to my feet. "I'll be right back," I told Skye, whose own eyes had drifted shut, a blissful smile pasted on her sundrenched face.

After taking a quick tour amongst the gardens, which were filled with a treasure trove of dormant, dust-collecting ruins, I returned to Skye, who was sprawled out on the ground under a large tree facing the Himalayas, her lungi folded neatly under her head. I sat down next to her and rested my back against the trunk of the tree.

"Didn't get much further than the pool," she murmured lazily, "Didn't really feel like I had to, to be honest."

"Yeah. This place is kind of hypnotic, huh?" I closed my eyes.

We dozed off for over an hour. It was so tranquil I didn't even think about making a move, not even once.

Chapter 4

Heavy mist hugged the road and the steps leading up to the hotel. An old dog who had taken shelter under the table next to mine lay motionless. I lit a cigarette, pulled up a plastic chair and sat down to wait, thinking of the adventure ahead. During the previous day's excursion to Kaplivastu, Skye and I had decided to do the Annapurna Circuit trek together. My thoughts of travel were admittedly overshadowed by the thought of spending extensive time with my attractive traveling partner. A three-wheeled tuk-tuk whizzed past, the morning's first indicator of the mayhem about to descend upon the thoroughfare. My canine friends night had finished, mine too, it was a new day.

The bus terminal was jammed with people jostling about with no real sense of organization, while six buses sat idling at varying stages of readiness, most of them loaded perilously with goods. Finally locating the vehicle that would take us the first leg of our journey, we threw our bags up to someone on the roof and climbed aboard.

About an hour later, Skye suddenly turned in her seat and said, "Hey, I don't even know your last name."

"It's Dixon."

"You have a middle name?"

"Yeah." I said, offering nothing further. I had my reasons.

"Well...what is it?"

Addressing my reply to the back of the seat in front of us, I sighed. "My full name is Joseph Conrad Blaze Dixon. And yes, I've heard quite a few giggles over it, thank you."

"No, no, I'm not laughing because it's a funny name," she said, stifling a grin. "It's a perfectly respectable name." And for a split second I believed her, until she smiled again, vainly suppressing a chuckle.

"What about you, then?" I asked.

"Skye Violet Duchesne," she said out unceremoniously and, before I could speak, "So, Joseph Conrad, your parents' writers or something?"

"Not exactly, no. My old man thought of himself as a budding journalist around the time I was born, and he considered himself a writer back then, I guess. Blaze was my mother's contribution, and then you've got...Dixon."

I rolled my head to look out the window across the aisle. A dirtied Nepal whipped past at dizzying speed. I hadn't thought of my parents in a very long time. And I could not recall the last time we had been in touch.

Was it over a year? I didn't know. I felt someone watching me and my eyes were pulled to the old woman in the aisle seat opposite me. Her head rested against a mat of oily gray hair. Creases graced her dark brown skin. She stared back at me as if reading my thoughts. Uncomfortable, I feigned a smile. A sweat bead crept down the woman's cheek. She did not respond, her eyes remained glued on mine. Her look kept my eyelids open, though I wanted to close them.

"Tell me about your family, then. You said you had a sister, right?" I spoke outward, not towards Skye at all, but to the woman who held my gaze. But I heard Skye start to answer before I managed to pull my head back towards her direction

"Yeah, I told you that, but it was on the bus coming up from India, so I wasn't sure if you remembered."

"Well, I did. It was…" I paused trying to remember her name, "uh…Brylee right?"

"Close enough. It's Brooke."

"That's right," I said, mentally repeating the name over a few times. "Tell me more about Brooke, then."

"What do you want to know?"

"I don't know, how old is she? What does she do for a living? What's she like?"

"Well, she's taller than I am, but thinner. She's twenty-seven, so not much older than me, and she works as a journalist for a small magazine back home. She really enjoys travel, much like myself, and she's a bit of a go-getter. If you ask me, slightly too intense sometimes." I nodded, but said nothing. She added, "We weren't necessarily close growing up, but we have found a certain bond with each other now that we've grown up a bit. I think her being the older one, most likely the prettier one, and the go-getter of us both gave me a lot of resentment towards her growing up. You know what I mean?" she asked, looking up into my eyes.

"Only child," I answered with a shrug of my shoulders. Skye didn't look amused. I quickly added, "Yeah, but honestly, after everything you've been up to yourself, it doesn't sound like you were the black sheep or anything. You finished school and all, and you're well-travelled."

"Yeah, but…" she paused for a second, "I wasn't exactly a perfect child growing up. I mean, I finished school, but it was just college. Brooke graduated from university, then she went off and travelled through Europe and all the way through Russia, alone, by the way, before I even stepped foot outside of Australia. In fact, I guess what I'm saying is that if it wasn't for her, I might not have cleaned up my act. Trying to compete with her has made me a better person, I think. And now that I'm older I can accept that and even thank her for it."

We were gradually entering the Inner Terai. Beyond the grasslands I could make out the Duns, small valleys that just touched the southern plains before rolling towards the foothills of the Himalayas. Skye, like most everyone else on the bus, eventually got tired and managed to fall asleep. I stayed awake, consciously keeping my head turned to the right. Not wanting to chance getting locked into the gaze of the old woman across from me.

The bus pulled off abruptly to the side of the road. Outside the window I spotted a few army-green sandbag barricades straddling both sides of the dirt road. A handful of soldiers stood leaning against them, guns perched on the bags, adjusting their sights. The driver vacated the bus for a short time and returned with two burly soldiers, who began questioning passengers at the front of the bus. Skye was asleep. I felt no need to wake her, despite the twinge of fear that ran through my stomach at the sight of the guns strapped across the soldiers' backs, or perhaps because of it. Two passengers were ordered off the bus before the soldiers had even made it halfway down the aisle.

As they made their way towards the back of the bus, one of the soldiers, who sported three elongated scars on the left side of his face, leaned in to say something to a man sitting a couple of rows away from me. The man shook his head. Without a moment's hesitation, the soldier picked the passenger up with frightening ease and dumped him on the floor, where he lay on his stomach, his right foot resting inches away from my left shoe. Delivering a swift kick to the prone man's ribs, the soldier then hoisted the man up and hauled him off the bus.

A funereal silence filled the vehicle as the doors slammed shut and the driver started the engine. Four soldiers stood at the side of the road shouting at three former passengers, all of them on their knees, heads bowed. Those who had been awoken by the commotion had already gone back to sleep. Some had slept through the whole ordeal.

I decided to let Skye keep sleeping, sure I should be more concerned than I was about what had just happened but figuring dwelling on it wouldn't make us any safer. Instead, I looked out the window as Nepal grew in color by the minute. Wildflowers flew past, blurring into the mud-brick homes and grassy hills. I watched it all fly by with my own gaunt reflection superimposed atop the landscape. When we finally began to twist and turn, most eyes opened. Orchids that clothed the stems of trees were forced to watch us as the wind from our bus dragged their necks in our direction. The young captain made some startling recoveries, taking each turn and bend at a speed not known to the western world. Large, weathered signposts announcing Bhairahawa and

Bharatpur sent chills of anticipation through my tired body. Hours later, I spotted the slightly larger signs for Kathmandu and Bhutan.

Under the oppressive heat of the midday sun, our bus came to a shuddering halt at the base of the hills. Skye and I stretched our legs before figuring out how to reach the next stop in our journey.

"We're heading to Thamel," I told an inquisitive pair of brown eyes amidst the throngs of countless others jostling for our attention, looking dazed and slightly lost as we were with our heavy packs and sunburnt skin.

"I take you. Where you stay? I take you nice place," the hawker said with a broad, toothy grin.

***

"What a good score," Skye proclaimed, sauntering into my room without knocking. Not that I minded terribly. "We've both got a view of the main street, too." She leaned over the windowsill, her shirt creeping up, revealing a few inches of her lower back. Tearing my eyes away, I sat on the bed. "Wonder if we can see the mountains from the roof."

Sure enough, the roof offered a stunning view of the Himalayas, towering over everything and stretching across the entire northern skyline. We were so much closer than we had been in Lumbini. We stood staring into the distance, speechless. The majestic, monolithic beauty of them inspired me to recount the dream I'd had two days previously to Skye, who mostly just kept her eyes dreamily and wordlessly fixed on the mountains.

Later that afternoon, we wandered the labyrinthine streets of Kathmandu. The atmosphere was so much different than what I had experienced in India. The shopkeepers didn't hound us to come inside and take a look; most simply said hello or nodded in greeting. People were far more relaxed than what I was used to seeing over the past few months, and I liked it.

Skye and I eventually found a trekking guide in a used bookstore. "Here, you hold onto it," she said, placing the book in my hands. "Try to get a feeling for something. Maybe your dream was trying to tell you something." Somehow I didn't care how trippy-hippy that sounded.

Chapter 5

Durbar Square, the center of the old city, consists of three loosely linked areas; the open Basantapur Square, which Freak Street, the backpacker and hippy Mecca of the seventies, runs off of, Durbar Square proper and the area of Makhan Tole. We wound our way through the streets of the old city, taking in the stalls, temples, stupas, and shrines, all bound together in a sort of organized anarchy. The people of the city, the ones who didn't have anything to do with the tourism of it, just plain ignored us, with the exception of two young boys who did not stop pestering me to have my shoes cleaned. It's probably worth mentioning that I happened to be wearing sandals.

We entered a restaurant off a small side street, which was more of an alley than a road.

"Namaste," the waitress greeted us. "Would you like drink?"

"What are those guys drinking there?" Skye asked, nodding towards the table opposite us.

"That's tongba," I answered before the waitress had a chance to respond. I noticed she held her gaze on me longer than was strictly necessary, a smile quirking the corners of her lips.

"How you been?" she asked.

A faint but persistent buzzing rang in my ears, I stared at the menu, convinced I must have misheard her.

"Sorry, what did you say that was?" Skye asked, watching the men at the next table pour hot water into their mugs.

"It is Tibetan beer. Tongba, like he say."

"I would like one of those, please," I said, ignoring Skye's inquisitive look.

"Make that two," said Skye.

The waitress returned with two large wooden mugs of millet and a very large container of boiling water. I poured the water over both our beverages then waited a few minutes while the millet fermented, as Skye looked on, seemingly impressed if a little bemused.

One of the men at the next table caught Skye's eye and smiled. "Hello," he said cheerfully. Eyeing the guidebook on the table, he asked if we were planning to do a trek.

"The Annapurna Circuit," Skye nodded enthusiastically.

He told us he was a trekking guide from the Mustang region, and introduced himself as Barati.

"Do you think we'll need a guide?" Skye asked.

Silly question I thought, stirring my millet. Like asking a safety inspector if you need a permit.

"Honestly, my friend, you do not need guide for that trek. It is marked for you, and if you get lost, please ask one of the many peoples you see along the way. They will help you." He smiled encouragingly as he added some more hot water to his tongba.

The men from his table had ordered a dish of dumplings called momos, so we did the same. While we waited for our order, Skye and Barati continued to chat until Barati's tongba turned transparent.

"Good luck, my friends," he said, getting up to leave when our food arrived.

"What do you think, Joseph?" Skye asked as I swirled a momo around in a puddle of hot sauce. "I think it sounds perfect," she said, before I could answer. "We can camp most of the way, as long as we get some gear and it doesn't get too cold."

"May take up to three weeks," I pointed out as she reached for the last momo.

"That's all right. It's not as if we're starved for time." I had a feeling that was partly the tongba talking.

With heads full of fresh enthusiasm and stomachs full of tongba and momo, Skye and I headed back to our respective rooms. I settled into bed and thumbed through the guidebook. The trek seemed to be exactly what I wanted out of my time in Nepal. The section on the trek explained that we would be following an ancient trade route over the Thorung La Pass, although there was a notable lack of advice on where to camp. Eventually, the sheer mass of information weighed heavy on my eyelids and I drifted off to sleep.

***

Struggling for escape, my hands and body wet with perspiration. Kicking and punching from within some kind of giant blue plastic bag, I fought as though I were drowning, relentlessly trying to gain one more lungful of air. Just when I thought I was about to lose consciousness, I was thrown forward and tumbled into a tent. It was dark, but I could sense it was already occupied. I felt along the length of the body next to me, searching for a spot that would allow me to identify it; a leg, an arm, a breast, anything that would help me determine what I was dealing with. Then there was a scream. A loud, piercing shrill that lasted only a few seconds, then cut off sharply like a smoke detector that you think will never stop, just before it suddenly does.

Chapter 6

"Joseph, I'm not sure I can do this."

Those eight words did not bode well for us. Ten miles into the trek, and we still had another two to go before we reached our destination of Bahundanda. We had been hiking along the Marsyangdi River, a crystal-clear ribbon of water that starts in the heavens and winds its way down a serpentine path carved in the rocks. My back ached almost as much as my ankle.

"It's another two miles to the next village. I, for one, put forth the idea that we stay in a guesthouse tonight and lick our wounds." Our first day and we were already abandoning the whole camping idea.

"I second that motion," Skye yelled from behind me. She had been trailing me since we'd left the first village of Besisahar. Initially I had stopped every now and then and waited for her to catch up, but this just seemed to annoy her, so I gave it up a couple of hours into the trek. We had set off at eight o'clock that morning, thinking it would take us around six hours or so to reach Bahundanda. It was already half past three.

"You've got to be kidding me," Skye panted as she came up behind me, assessing the steep climb ahead of us with an air of defeat.

"That's our paradise, right up there," I said, pointing at the top of the slope. "But first, take a look over there." I grabbed her shoulders and turned her around towards the valley. "Imagine how much better the view will be from the top. Magical."

"It had better fucking be." It was the first time I'd ever heard her swear. I must admit I liked it.

Leaving Skye to catch her breath, I continued climbing and hoisted myself up onto a precipice, not so much to wait for Skye or to make sure she got up OK, but basically because I absolutely could not take another step.

A few minutes later, Skye's head appeared below me. Pulling herself up next to me, she laid her sweaty torso across my legs.

"Please tell me there's no more," she said breathlessly.

"That's it. We can find somewhere to sleep tonight. Like right here."

We watched as the evening set in, the sun transforming the color of the snow-capped mountains from a blinding white to a light grey, and then finally to a thousand shades of pink, orange, red and purple.

Bahundanda is a fantastic place to stay, because you have to, quite simply. Seven bhattis lined the single partially cobbled road arching over the hill. Four were boarded up, but we managed to find a tiny guesthouse overlooking the valley on the other side. It was cheap and the owner was extremely cheerful.

Skye dropped her pack on the floor of our room, sprawling across two single beds that were pushed very close together, an arrangement whose benefit I was too exhausted to fully comprehend.

"I am not afraid to admit that that was the most physically grueling day I've ever had in my entire life," she proclaimed. "I'm honestly not sure I can do this."

I sat on the edge of one of the beds and began the painful task of taking my shoes off.

"What happened to your ankle?" Skye asked, her head hanging over the mattress.

A large bulb stuck out the side of my foot. "Must be from all the walking," I answered, pushing down on it, then feeling a pain shoot through my entire leg.

An hour later, we sat waiting for our dinner with our new friend Kartik, the owner of the guesthouse. He was a very cheerful upper-caste Hindu Brahmin, a fact that he had no hesitation in pointing out to us before we had even sat down, then at twenty-minute intervals in our conversation. For being part of so priestly a lineage, he was pretty full of himself.

"So, how many of these little ones are yours?" Skye asked as six or seven kids ran back and forth between the guesthouse and the shed in the backyard that acted as the kitchen.

"I only have two children to myself, lady." He pointed out two of the kids scampering off in the opposite direction. "Those others are friends of mine own children."

Turning the topic of conversation to the number of seemingly abandoned hotels we had passed on our way to the guesthouse earlier that day, Kartik confided that the village was not doing so well.

"No, good sir, it is not so good. It would be very better if not for the many problems that some peoples like to cause. I keep this radio on most times to be aware of all the happenings." He patted the radio fondly. "Sometimes the governments can say where the Maoists have been, and it give us a chance to leave most quickly."

"What do you mean, leave quickly?" A flash of panic crossed Skye's tired face.

"These Maoists, you know, they will take all my food and money if they want it. I have no real danger of being hurt; I am not official, I merely run a most small honorable business. But it is good to know when I should take my children into the mountains."

"You mean you just up and leave, hide in the bush?"

"I tell my children we are going camping, and they most really enjoy it."

On that encouraging note, Kartik left us to enjoy our meal, returning after dinner to offer me a smoke.

"How often do you have to run into the mountains?" I asked, handing the chillum back to him.

"Oh, not often my friend. Maybe three times this year."

"You've never had any real trouble, though?"

"No, my friend. Although a friend of mine is no longer here because of the trouble. He was government official, a police officer. How do you say in English, top police?"

"Chief of Police?"

"Ah, yes, this what I want to say. Many years back now, my friend."

Skye lifted her head sleepily from its resting place on the back of the bench and announced that she was off to bed.

"Goodnight, good lady. Good sleeps to you," Kartik called after her.

"I think I'll be heading to bed as well, Kartik. Not exactly an easy day today," I said, rubbing my aching calves for emphasis.

"Ah, my friend, it will get better," he replied, a big, broad smile crossing his face.

I left Kartik to his chillum and went to join Skye in our room. I found her already fast asleep, lying in the middle of the two beds with her unzipped sleeping bag tossed over her as a blanket. Fighting through the pain that encased me like a second skin, I crawled underneath her sleeping bag and threw mine over top of us. I wanted to curl up next to her. I wanted to make her dream sweet and wonderful things. More than anything else, I wanted to sleep her. But I did none of these, instead rolling over and slipping into a dull, dreamless sleep.

***

"Every muscle in my body is killing me," Skye moaned, pushing herself up onto her elbows. I remained in the fetal position, unwilling to accept the fact that I would soon have to move. The mere thought of walking made my body ache. Skye somehow found the strength to get out of bed to take a shower.

I bit my tongue to keep from cursing and sat upright. Waiting for Skye to return, I stared out the window that overlooked the entire valley. The mist still hung low over it, blanketing the treetops with dew as the sides of the mountain shot upwards through the fog. It was almost nice enough a view for me to want to stand up and get a better look. Almost.

When Skye returned, I stole a couple of glances of her toweling off and instantly began to feel a little better. Nakedness, even when not in its glorious entirety, is still one hell of a natural painkiller. While drying the last of her hair, the towel wrapped around her body fell clean off, slipping to the floor. She let out a shriek as she bent over to grab the towel, her immaculate breasts swaying in perfect unison. I didn't want to laugh, I really didn't, but I just couldn't help it.

"You finished?" she asked, her voice raising half in anger and half in amusement. "Now that you've seen me, I'm going to have to see you, too, you know."

"Well, it's pretty cold in the mornings and damn cold at night, and on top of that there's no hot water, so I'm afraid you won't be seeing much of anything." I quickly slipped out the door to go wash up before she could offer a rebuttal.

The guidebook said that the walk from Bahundanda to Chame would take just over three hours. I gave us two pathetic individuals about six. We were going to stop for lunch, and there was an accessible hot spring below one of the villages.

"So, you're still up for camping?" Skye sounded hesitant. "What Kartik said made me feel a bit iffy."

"We'll be fine. It's an easier walk today. We'll stop just outside of Chame, set up camp, and head in for dinner and maybe a shower. We've got sleeping bags, we'll be well-fed, it'll be fine." She looked thoroughly unconvinced, but shrugged her shoulders and continued walking.

Jagat had been an old customs post, or so said a barely legible sign at the side of the road. A ramshackle building a few feet past the village entrance still had painted Nepali Rupees adorning the side of it.

"It says here that the hot spring is just below this building here." We were standing in front of an abandoned home two doors down from the tax post.

"Let's do it," said Skye, her head resting on my shoulder, the feel of her breath on my neck stopping me short.

As we drew nearer to the spring, we heard voices, seemingly in English, rising up from the rocks below. A man and a woman were soaking in the natural bath water inside the tub of cement and large rocks pushed close enough together to sit on.

"How's the water?" Skye called out.

"It's bloody lovely, mate," the man called back. "You've really got to try it."

We went behind a boulder to change, using our towels as a partition, Skye resorting to the old turn-around trick when she got to her bra. Drawing the strings of my swim trunks together around my newly scrawny waist, I remembered her head resting on my shoulder and decided I would have to make some sort of move soon.

I dipped a tentative foot into the water. "Woo, that's hot."

"That's the idea," said the woman. Not in a snotty way, just in that Australian, pointing-out-the-obvious way.

"The name's Joseph." I stretched out my hand to each of them in turn.

"Trev, mate."

"Hi, I'm Jacqui."

"So, where are you guys from?"

"We live in Melbourne," said Jacqui. "Originally from the Victorian countryside, but we've been in Melbourne for a few years now. And you?"

"I'm from Canada, and Skye there is from your neck of the woods."

"What you reckon bout all this Maoist stuff?" Trev asked. "Pretty crazy. I mean, we've done this route before at roughly this time of the year." He looked to Jacqui, who nodded in confirmation. "It was chock-full, mate. Most guesthouses had no vacancies whatsoever."

"We were a bit hesitant at first, but then we decided to just go for it. Most of the people we spoke to said it was OK. Honestly, I really didn't know much about the situation before I got here. For the past few months or so, I've been travelling around India. Not that that's an excuse, but..."

Jacqui and Trev told us they had just made their way up the east side of India. This trip was their honeymoon sort of speak, as they were not married, but they had been together long enough to realize they had found what they were looking for.

"Are you guys staying in the guesthouses or camping?" I asked the pair.

"We decided to stay in all the places we skipped last time," Jacqui replied. "Everyone basically follows their guidebook, and all the little spots in the middle are left out. Tonight we're in the Everest Hotel. Just above us, I think."

When we told them we were planning to camp most of the way, they seemed surprised.

"You do a lot of camping?" Trev asked.

Wanting to say yes, I'm a regular lumberjack, I instead opted for honesty. "It's been a while," I answered.

"You smoke, Joe?" Trev asked. Not bothering to wait for a reply, he jumped out of the spring and wandered over to a guitar that was propped up against some rocks. Reaching into the body of the instrument, he pulled out a leather tobacco pouch, then returned to the spring with both pouch and guitar in hand. In a matter of minutes, he passed an adeptly rolled joint over to me and I sucked in a slow drag with an appreciative nod.

Sitting in the bath, I had a moment of smoke-wreathed clarity. The rocks I was sitting on were there before man had even arrived to this place and would be there for thousands of years afterwards. I loved them and loathed them because they were rocks, simple stones which knew their part in this great big world and I was still trying to find mine.

"You're pretty stoned, aren't you, darling?" Jacqui asked. Just as I was about to answer, I caught the telling look she aimed at Trev.

"Yeah," he smiled and left it at that.

"I think we should probably get going, Joseph," Skye said. "We still need to find a place to camp tonight."

We said goodbye our new friends and readied ourselves for the short walk ahead. The trail out of Jagat rose steadily for forty-five minutes, which would have been a hell of a lot harder had it not been for the much-needed rest at the hot spring. Just outside of Chame, we passed yet another waterfall where I stopped and stared in a pot-induced haze of awe until Skye yelled to me from some distance ahead, apparently weary of taking in the scenery and wanting to continue on.

Chame itself was smaller than I had expected. We passed a school that was oddly familiar to me, though I had no idea why. Skye stopped to take some photos.

"So how far are we going to keep walking before we find our spot?" she asked.

"Well, the river runs down and to our right, so I think we should find somewhere over there," I said, pointing to the left.

Ten minutes into our search, Skye stopped and pointed into the underbrush. "What do you think about in there?" The trees grew thickly around us, mainly oak and maple, making it difficult to see more than twenty feet in. "Should we go take a look?"

"Maybe one of us can go scope it out while the other waits here. I don't plan on going that far in."

"Oh, so you're going in, are you?" she asked.

"I didn't think you'd want to. I'll stay here if you want, that's fine with me."

"Alright, you can go this time," she said, "but I want to make the second discovery."

Thirty feet in, with my head still buzzing from the hash, the trees which had looked so welcoming and protective from the path, now took on a sinister appearance. Suddenly overwhelmed with the need to lean against something but not wanting to touch the gnarled, creepy looking trees, I bent over and rested my palms on my knees. When I raised my head, everything began to lurch sickeningly around me. I repeatedly told myself it was just the hash, which didn't seem to improve my situation much.

Finally regaining some composure, I stood up straight and scanned my surroundings. I took a few steps to my left, now unsure which way the path was and which led further into the unknown. A foul odor crept up my nostrils. I doubled my pace, turning left, then making a sharp right. I tripped over what I thought were my own feet and landed on the spongy ground, sending a pile of foliage into the air. The stench of something rotting beneath the leaves quickly overwhelmed all my senses. I put my hand to my nose and gagged, the smell so strong the air seemed thick with it.

When I finally dared to look down at the cause of the stench, I saw, no more than a yard away the decaying husk of a long-abandoned body. After squeezing my eyes shut and taking in a shaky breath, I forced myself to take a second look and confirmed that the body was indeed human. I lay there frozen, staring at it like it was going to spontaneously reanimate at any moment. The head was turned to the side, both eyelids missing, two greyish-white balls staring back at me. Most of the hair had fallen out of the scalp, and insects busied themselves scavenging for anything that could be used as food, making their way through the nostrils and out the mouth.

"You're fine. It's OK," I said aloud, darting my head in all directions as if I myself were somehow responsible for the dead body lying at my feet.

Two small bullets had penetrated the body, perforating the light green uniform. Red- and purple-stained leaves acted as a sieve for blood as it dripped its way down into the earth.

Scrambling to my feet, I noticed my shoe was covered with little clumps of the soldier's innards, dirt and tiny insects mixed in with the bits of decomposed skin. I had quite literally walked right into him. Kicking off my shoe in revulsion, I turned and leaned over to support myself on the nearest tree, dry-heaving as I did so. 'What are you going to do, Joseph? If you say anything, there could be trouble. There will be trouble.'

"Keep quiet," I said, louder this time, looking around wildly for something to clean my shoe with. Grabbing the largest leaves I could find, I held my breath and scraped the putrefied pieces of human off my footwear, the dry heaves once more taking full control. The devastatingly horrific and cruel nature of the world had just been permanently imprinted in my mind. I inched my way slowly back to the path holding my breath as much as I could manage, the trees offering me support and anchoring me to the physical world around me as I grasped for the solidity of their trunks.

"So, how was it?" Skye asked from her perch atop her pack.

"Too many fallen trees," I managed to gasp out.

"Too many trees?"

"Yeah, the space was good, but there were fallen trees everywhere. Impossible to set up a tent. We'll have to go a bit further." I picked up my bag, not yet daring to make eye contact, and started walking down the path.

"Joseph?"

"Yeah?"

"You're going the wrong way."

Half a mile or so up the path, we decided to try again. Skye, wanting to be a part of the decision-making process this time, demanded she be the one to scope out the campsite. She returned a few minutes later, emerging from the forest with a wide smile.

"There's a good spot not too far in. Could you still see me?"

"I could still make you out, yeah. But spotting a tent would be difficult unless you knew what you were looking for."

We had our evening meal at the Lhasa Guesthouse, sharing a pot of mint tea and a bowl of potato soup before tucking into a plate of vegetable fried rice each. Halfway back to camp, we ran into some military personnel. They were coming towards us with torches, but they strutted past with no more than a cursory glance in our direction, saying nothing.

Five strong fingers pushed down into my arm. "Joseph, why would there be soldiers on the actual trekking route?"

"I don't know. I expected to see them eventually, though. It's a good sign, Skye. They're here to protect and serve and all that shit. Don't think too much about it. Here, we're almost back to our spot now. No one can see us from the path at night." She didn't reply, but dropped my arm from her death grip.

We reached our marker, an old t-shirt of mine knotted around a tree branch, but just as I was about to lead the way into the forest, Skye stopped abruptly.

"Everything will be fine. You'll see," I urged. We held each other's gaze.

I took her hand again. Unzipping our sleeping bags to form two blankets, I wrapped my arms around her as she nestled in. I had to do something; time was ticking, and after the moment we had just shared together it was the perfect time to act. She grabbed my hand and pulled my arm closer to her body so it rested just a few inches below her breast. Ah, sweet heaven.

"How high up are we, anyway?" she whispered.

"Five thousand feet or so. Why do you ask?"

"Oh, no reason. I just thought it would be colder than this. I figured we were higher up. Bloody well feels like we've walked further."

I smiled and pulled her in a little closer, but the proximity did nothing to keep the decomposing soldier from my thoughts.

Chapter 7

The cheese we had brought with us was still good in the middle. Neither of us could decipher what kind of cheese it was, but it was edible. The bread had hardened, which was fine, and we still had some sweet biscuits. As we reached the path, I pulled out the guidebook.

"It seems like it'll take us about six and a half hours to reach Bagarchhap, including a stop for lunch."

"And how far are we climbing today?

"About two thousand."

"That's OK, hey? How much did we do yesterday? About the same?"

"Yesterday was about five hundred, Skye."

"Oh." Pause. "Well, shit."

The path dropped steadily before leveling off just outside the village of Tal Basi. The village seemed empty; we saw no one wandering through the streets, nor in the fields. We passed a couple of guesthouses, both empty. Through the dusty window of one bhatti we could make out a kitchen and dining area. Some cooking pots had been left on the stove, and some glasses on the table appeared to be filled with water. Apart from the two hotels, which were themselves just two big homes, there were only two other houses, shacks really, made from stone and mud brick. Both had been abandoned, too.

"I think we should keep going," said Skye, peering into the window of the other guesthouse.

It was there in that tiny, abandoned village that I finally got the impression that everything wasn't alright in Nepal. It wasn't the military presence, nor even the dead soldier, but Tal Basi, a hastily abandoned village a three-day hike from any city proper. Maybe there were entire villages that had been caught up in the trouble, and they just hadn't been reported. How long would it take for news that a little village like this one had been ransacked?

The path ascended again after a short walk through abandoned maize fields, eventually bringing us to Tal. Tal resembled an old Western movie set, every building a replica of one found in a frontier town. The flat, dusty plateau on which it rested added to its Wild West feel; the Annapurna Conservation Area Project (ACAP) building that could easily pass as an old Sheriff's office was in the center of town, with hotels surrounding it that looked hand-picked by John Wayne himself.

Stopping in at one of the hotels for a rest and expecting only the ubiquitous chai to be on offer, the owner surprised us by presenting us with a menu that, at first glance at least, appeared full of a wide variety of hot beverages. After browsing through the long list, however, we noticed there were actually only four kinds of tea on offer, listed in their various permutations; with or without milk, sugar, lemon, even including the size of the cup. Each of these menu items warranted its own line, of course, the working assumption being that if something looked like more, quantity-wise, it was intrinsically better, or so I can only assume. We shared a pot of mint tea before heading off to the village's only shop to buy some water and more biscuits.

As we entered Bagarchap, I noticed a memorial plaque for those killed in a landslide some years back marking the entrance to the village. According to the guidebook, we would be camping in roughly the same spot where the disaster had happened. The village itself was composed of a number of cobbled streets lined with small Tibetan shops selling jewelry, pottery, and, of course, tea, all carted in from distances further than my mind could fathom.

"What do you think?" I asked as we walked through the main thoroughfare. "Pretty quaint little place, no?"

"Yeah, it's very cute." Skye stopped to inspect a pair of earrings. "Are we gonna keep going and find a spot to camp for the night?" An old woman sat watching Skye with a three-toothed smile. Skye held the pair up to her ears.

"Nice," I nodded.

We hiked outside of the village for fifteen minutes, Skye's new earrings jingling with every step. The trees that surrounded us now were completely different, conifers and ferns that had begun to spring up a few miles previously now dominating the landscape.

"We should be able to find a spot in there," Skye said, pointing in amongst the leaves.

"Off you go, then," I said, smacking her on the bottom. One of those things it just feels right to do at the time, but with potentially disastrous repercussions. Luckily for me, she just smiled, albeit with a slight furrow of her brow, thrusting her pack into my hands.

"If I'm not back in..." she started to say before I held up my free hand.

"Yeah, yeah. Come on now, be serious."

She frowned before turning and delving into the forest. "Might be a bit prickly!" she yelled from a few feet in.

The sun was dropping fast but still shot through the needles of the trees to bathe the path in a fiery orange. As I was admiring the vista, trying not to worry obsessively over the fact that Skye had slipped from view, I noticed two men in the distance walking steadily towards me. They were carrying guns, but they weren't in uniform. I swore I felt my arteries lose compression for a second and then, wham! My pulse smacked out again with a rush of blood that pounded into my chest. Feeling an inevitable confrontation in the air between the two men and me, I turned to meet them when they were a few feet off.

"Good evening," the man closest to me said, his voice deep, his tone neutral. "Are you enjoying your stay in Nepal, sir?" Now that they were standing right in front of me, I could see the red sash tied around each of their left arms.

"Uh...yes, I am, sir." I replied, taken aback at his near-perfect English. Neither of them was overly big. Years of trekking up and down the mountain slopes had shaved everything but the slightest of fat off of their bodies.

"Are you alone?" asked the same man.

I felt a chill on my flushed cheeks as I stared at them both. The image of the dead soldier reappeared before me; the smell, the insects, the glazed white eyes, my shoe caked in decomposing flesh. A sudden rush of acid flared up in my stomach and my mouth watered before I forced myself to swallow the bile down. I risked a furtive glance down at the incriminating two bags at my feet.

"Are you alone, sir?" the soldier directly in front of me asked again, his voice now crisp and irritated.

"No, no. Just waiting for my friend." I pointed into the forest. "One of those moments when nature calls."

I could feel the eyes of his silent comrade on me, holding me in place; I opted to focus my attention on the inquisitor, who somehow seemed less threatening.

"Your name was?" The soldier fished a notebook from his front pocket.

"Conrad," I said, hoping that the grain of truth in my response would make me sound more confident.

"Conrad, we are taking our own park fee. You see, we are in a struggle with certain peoples of Nepal and we feel it is our right, and our duty, to ask for a small fee ourselves. You have to admit a small amount of money for experiencing such wonderful surroundings is a very small price to pay indeed. Wouldn't you say so?" Where had this guy studied English? His fluency was unnerving, somehow.

"Well, no..." I didn't like where this was going. It's one thing to bribe an official member of state for your own convenience; there's an equal share of respect and hatred being felt on each side. You're both caught up in the same thing, you can both be brought down. "I wouldn't say a small fee is too much to pay at all." I desperately didn't want Skye to emerge from the forest and see me standing there next to two armed brutes.

"Do you know much of our cause, Conrad?" the soldier asked, jotting something down in his book.

"I have to tell you, sir, that I know very little of it, but that doesn't mean I'm totally ignorant of the ideology behind it. I understand the struggle of people who have not been given a fair chance at life. And I know it is morally and fundamentally wrong for the world to continue how it is today."

"Good, Conrad, Very good," he nodded in approval, but not elaborating any further, either about their cause or the money I was to pay them.

"You see, the thing is, I, well...we hadn't really planned on the trip being this expensive. Not that we mind spending and all. Don't get me wrong. Everyone deserves their share, I know, but it's just that we only have so much money left to get us back to where we started." As I said the words, I became acutely aware what it sounded like: 'Take all my money, rob me blind, be my guest.'

"Yes, I understand, Conrad. We have a standard fee that we charge. No harm will come to you."

Uneasy at the casual mention of the word 'harm', I asked, "How much is the fee, then?"

"It's the same as what you have already paid." I reached into my pocket and carefully took out the allotted sum without showing how much money I had on me. He scribbled something in his notebook, tore off she slip of paper and handed it to me.

I took the piece of paper and moved aside to let them pass, kicking the bags away from them as I did so. The soldier who had done all the talking gave me a chillingly insincere smile as he walked away. His comrade was clearly displeased, or else he had no idea what the conversation that had just taken place had been about. The whole episode had only lasted a few minutes. I peered between the trees and saw a figure stumbling over some fallen branches.

"There's a nice little spot in there. A little further back than I thought I'd go, but it'd be a nice place to camp for the night," Skye said as she reached the edge of the forest. Then, seeing the look on my face, which I had only half managed to compose between the soldiers leaving and her arrival, "What's up with you?"

"Oh, nothing. So, it's a good spot, then?"

"Yeah, a little ways in but....Joseph?"

"Yeah?"

"Why are you smiling?" I was trying not to, but it was the closest thing to a normal expression I could muster under the circumstances. As much as I wanted to tell her, something told me it wasn't a good idea. I had paid another park fee and that was that, as far as I was lead to believe by the unreadable note in my hand.

"Nothing at all, Skye. You just took a while, that's all. I was worried that something might have happened, like you got lost or something."

"Don't worry about me, Joseph. I'm fine. Shall we have a look at my spot, then?"

***

"Let's smoke outside." We sat cross-legged in our tent. I had just packed the chillum after returning from dinner in Bagarchhap. We stepped outside and I lit the pipe for Skye, letting her have the first go. I watched her eyes close. There was something about the way the moonlight touched them, making them appear to move in slow motion, the silvery whiteness slowly disappearing as she inhaled. The mountain caps shone in perfect miniatures in the reflection of her eyes when she opened them again. I stood transfixed, completely forgetting what it was we had been talking about just a moment earlier. She let out a delicate cough that brought me back down to earth, then handed me the chillum.

"So, what you're saying, then," she went on, "is that because I am travelling with you, then that makes you an OK person."

"Essentially, yeah," I mustered, speaking through the chillum, still unsure of what I had just said to prompt such a reply.

"That must mean you think a lot of me, then?"

"Yeah, it does. I wouldn't argue that point." Think, Joseph. Don't fuck this up.

"Well now, do you think you know exactly who I am, Joseph? We haven't known each other very long. The last time I checked, it takes quite a while to truly get to know someone."

Just go with it. Say something. "I'm not saying I know who you are exactly, not at all." I took a drag from the pipe as if the answer was to be found within it. "For all I know, everything you've told me so far is a lie. But I don't think it is. And even if it is a lie, I would still be correct in thinking you're a good person, because you would be pretending to be this nice person who likes to hang around nice people. So insofar as all that..." I was feeling the first hit now, big time. "Then I would still stand to be an OK person. Do you get me?"

"Not really. Let's just say for the sake of argument that I was lying about everything that I've told you so far. That would make me a deceptive person, wouldn't it?"

"Yeah, that would make you a deceptive person...more along the lines of bitch, really."

She laughed as I took another drag from the chillum. "Well, then," she continued as I held it out for her to take, "who I chose to hang around with, and tell my lies to, would have no bearing on the character of that person. Don't you see? I still couldn't be trusted."

"No, not really. I mean, I see your point, but I disagree. It would take a certain kind of individual to believe those lies. That is, if they were lies. What I mean is, it would take a certain kind of person to believe those lies and still want to hang around the liar. You see? Someone else who may not have believed you would have done something ages ago to break away from you, or they might have simply told you to fuck off. But the fact remains that, lies or no lies, I believed you, and do believe you, and that makes me an OK person because your lies, if they were lies, were believable, and I felt something for you."

"You feel something for me, Joseph?"

"Yes, Skye, I do."

I just exhaled my remaining smoke before she grabbed me and pulled me towards her. Our lips met with such a jolt that I dropped the chillum. The smoke definitely had something to do with it, but fuck it, we were attracted to each other, and yes, she was right, we had only known each other for a short time, but we cared for each other. She pulled away and I saw the look in her eyes that mirrored my own feelings; frustration, pity, anger, longing, wanting...it was everything that was going to divide us in the all-too-near future, every emotion that would seep from that inevitable wound was holding our eyes together as if to tell us, 'There, you see that? Look deeply, behold what is out there, fall deeper into it, get as close as you possibly can, but in the end I will win. I will dominate you as I have dominated millions before you and will continue to dominate for millions of years to come. Behold! I am Separation!' Yeah, I was stoned.

Crawling under the sleeping bags and wrapping our limbs around each other, we lay with the tent flap open, allowing in the night air and the peaks of the Annapurnas. Skye drifted quickly into a chillum-induced sleep. Eventually the arm that was pinned under Skye beat me to sleep. Under the watchful eye of the towering Manaslu at over twenty-six thousand feet above us, I reached over to close the tent flap and surrendered to sleep myself.

***

The sound of gunfire is a startling thing. I awoke in darkness to the final rounds of a distant gun being unloaded. It was not a hunting weapon; it was a repetitive assault, meant to defend and kill repeatedly.

"Please, God, tell me that wasn't what I think it was." Skye lay motionless next to me.

"Shit," was all I could come up with.

"It was far off, right?" She rolled over, sitting up slowly.

"I think so. How many shots?"

"I heard at least six or seven. What do we do?" she asked. "Just pack up and go?"

"I don't think it's a good idea to be walking around at night, no matter how far off those shots were. But there are mountains everywhere, Skye, everything echoes. It was far off, I'm positive. We had dinner in town not long ago, and nobody there seemed to be worried." The abandoned villages we had passed that day forced their way to the front of my mind.

No more shots were fired that night, but neither of us slept. Our bodies would ache the next day. Before the sun had broken across the horizon, we were up, packed, and back on the trail. At seven thirty in the morning, we reached the village of Bhratang, where we bought some biscuits and yet more undistinguishable cheese from a small shop. I asked the shopkeeper, an old man sitting on a grimy plastic chair, about the situation. He smiled, blissfully ignorant of what I had just asked.

"Maybe we should walk back, Joseph." Skye stood staring absently at a water-powered prayer wheel at the far edge of the village.

"I'd thought about that." I walked up next to her, placing a hand on her lower back. "But something inside of me is telling me we should just keep going."

"Those shots though, Joseph."

"I know. But, if I had to guess, I would say they came from further behind on the trail."

"Why would you say that?" She kept her eyes fixed on the ancient wheel, shoulders squared and back rigid under my hand.

"Not sure." Kartik's words about fleeing into the mountains were burning on my tongue, so I clamped down on it, tasting blood. Below us, the roots of a bridge long ago washed away rested on opposite banks; somewhere downstream were the remains of its core. The powerful roar of the Marsyangdi below us overpowered the tranquility I could only guess the prayer wheel was meant to elicit. I consciously pulled my eyes away from the rotations of the cracked wooden wheel. "We should keep going, Skye."

An hour before we reached Pisang, where we planned to stop for the night, I spotted a line of green uniforms coming down the ridge in the distance. Skye jerked her head toward the forest; I nodded in agreement, and we headed into the cover of the trees to wait. The rhythm of military boots pounding the sacred ground joined the rattle of necklaces and clinking of bullets in a sinister melody in time with my own crazed heartbeat. We waited motionless, hidden thirty feet or so into the forest, Skye crouched behind me.

"How many?" Her fingers gripped me tighter with every unified step the battalion took.

"Twenty three," I whispered, not taking my eyes off of them.

"Guns?"

I looked back, nodded, and then winced as her nails almost drew blood through the thin fabric of my sleeve. We waited until we were absolutely sure the last of them had passed, nibbling at our dry biscuits on the forest floor. I abruptly stopped chewing and involuntarily spat half of mine out when my eyes happened to graze over the sole of my left shoe, stained with what looked suspiciously like a patch of coagulated blood.

Chapter 8

Behind Pisang proper, we followed a dirt path that brought us beyond the eleven thousand feet of elevation we had already attained. Kartik's words echoed in my mind, accompanied by the macabre vision of the dead soldier propped upright in front of a distorted microphone, repetitive gunfire playing bass while soldiers' boots beat out percussion. We approached an old wooden bhatti about the size of a small barn with a sign that read 'Hotel Shanti' above the door.

"Hello! Please, please, come in, come in," we heard a voice call from a room off to the left.

We made our way into some sort of foyer where, to my relief, a crackling fire blazed in the hearth. A woman entered carrying a huge pot, gliding past us with a broad smile despite how heavy the vessel looked, and deposited it on the hearth with swift, expert precision. I could see the wrinkles forming around Skye's eyes as she took in the tiny woman's strength.

"Hello," she said as she turned to greet us.

"Good evening," we replied simultaneously, which made her laugh as she grabbed the two chairs that were closest to her and pushed them towards the fire.

"Please sit."

The small room was constructed of wooden planked walls holding up a thatched roof. The chipped and splintered rafters crossing above our heads looked like they had only a few more years left in them.

"You here for night?" our host asked.

"Actually, we just thought we'd grab some dinner. Is that OK?" Skye asked.

"OK, no problem. We have no many peoples this year. You staying where?" she asked.

"Haven't found a place yet," I jumped in.

"Oh, OK. Just many place here doing by the rule that you stay in hotel, you eat in hotel."

I wasn't sure what to say, and it was apparent Skye didn't either. We stood watching as she lumbered back towards the hall, pausing by the door to turn to us expectantly, waiting for an answer to her unspoken question.

Skye broke the silence first. "Yeah, we have found that, it's just that today we started off earlier than usual and we figured since it was still pretty early, we would come up here and have an early dinner."

Our host smiled gently before continuing wordlessly on her way out of the room, leaving Skye and I alone by the fire.

"I reckon we can ask her about all the crazy shit that's been going on." Skye held her hands held up to the fire. "Fuck, it got cold today, no?"

"Almost twelve thousand feet, Skye," I said, my words coming out more biting than I had intended.

The woman returned with two menus and two cups of tea. "Please, good tea for you," she said as she placed them in front of us. It didn't smell like tea. It was also too hot to drink, practically scalding my hand as I gingerly gripped the cup.

"Where you come from?"

"I'm from Australia, and he's from Canada."

"No, no, I mean where you from, now, today?"

"We're coming from Bagarchhap," I told her.

"How is tea?" she asked, apparently satisfied with my answer.

I still hadn't tasted it; the smell alone was enough to put me off. Skye tried hers first and from what I could tell actually enjoyed it, or else she was a much better actor than I would have thought. Feeling the pressure, I brought the cup up to my lips and held my breath. I took a sip. I didn't vomit, so that was a good sign.

"Tibetan tea," she said, breaking into a wide, toothless grin. Her hair was a mix of various whites and greys, pulled back above her expansive brow. Dark skin peppered with tiny liver spots framed dark brown eyes, which shone almost coal black in the dimly lit room. Although her build was small, she had big, strong hands and feet. When I was looking down at my tea, I noticed just how far apart her toes were; apart from being exceptionally wide, her feet also seemed larger than life for such a short woman, and rendered almost void of arches from a shoeless lifetime. Her hands were much the same. The light from the fire hit them directly, illuminating countless wrinkles that traced a life of hardship that I didn't dare fathom.

"Are you from around here?" Skye asked, interrupting my study of our host and snapping me back to reality.

"No, no. I come from Tibet." She pointed in a direction I could only assume was north.

"And this?" Skye pointed to her exceptionally colorful dress, festooned with a riot of ribbons and mirrors that glinted in the firelight, giving her small figure a slightly larger-than-life effect.

"Tibet," she said with a single nod.

"It's amazing. Look at the work, Joseph." Skye bent over to examine her garment. I preferred to admire from afar, smiling and nodding as I took another tentative sip of my tea.

"You want eat?" she finally asked after Skye had done poring over just about every stitch.

"Yes, please," I said. "By the way, my name's Joseph." I stretched out my hand.

My whole hand was enclosed in her larger one. "Choden," she said, before rising to her feet and shuffling off to the kitchen.

"Wow. A Tibetan refugee, Joseph." Skye shook her head gently from side to side before turning to hold her hands to the fire once more.

Choden reappeared a few minutes later to ask if we were ready to order. "We'll have one thali, and one vegetable fried rice please," Skye told her. "Maybe we should stay here tonight, Joseph," she said after Choden had left.

"Really? You want to stay here?" I swallowed the last of my tea. It was oddly crunchy.

"Well, maybe. I mean, Choden seems lovely and you heard her, she hasn't had many people this year. Look, did you see anybody else up here as we came in?"

"Not a soul."

"Well, let's give her a break. It's getting cold and we still have plenty days left to camp."

"And the whole military situation?" I asked.

"I think we'll be OK. We'll ask Choden about it later."

We'll be OK? Our host for the night was a Tibetan refugee, and the rebels trying to overthrow the government were Maoists. 'Pretty sour cocktail,' I thought as I stared into the fire.

I didn't dwell on thoughts of rebels and warfare long, as the smell of dinner stewing wafted in from the kitchen and the warmth of the fire soothed my tired feet and legs. Clean, crisp air from the open windows cleansed my lungs. Choden returned with three plates of rice, one with a few chopped vegetables mixed into it.

"I eat here, OK?" she asked, sitting down opposite us.

Choden ladled the dhal from the pot and we tucked into the food with gusto. The room filled with the sounds of lips smacking and metal spoons scraping the bottom of metal plates.

"The Chinese took our land," Choden said abruptly about half way through the meal. I paused with a mouthful of food, afraid to take another bite. "We lived in Hor Barching, me, my parents, grandfather, two sister and brother." She spoke slowly, rhythmically, her eyes boring into the fire as if the image of her former home was to be found inside of it. "We lived in a tent mostly, but when warm, when animals ate on mountain side, we did too. Dorjee, my brother, I miss him. I miss Dorjee. He left to monastery early. He was a good boy."

"He became a monk?" Skye asked, passing me the rest of the fried rice.

Choden nodded. "I think so. I have not seen him. They came and took Hor Barching area, but we know they coming, we leave early. We were not rich. We had animals, but no money. My father come into room at night." She laid her finger against her lips in imitation. "Like this he did. I remember his eyes." Choden paused and took a bite of her dhal as the embers popped in the fireplace. Swallowing another mouthful, she went on. "We live in mountains for many months. Many people live in mountains then. All people running from Chinese. But we get caught and they take us away. My sisters and me separate from family. We were young, useful. My parents and grandparents, no. We have to work, we have to work very hard. But one night, I escape."

I placed my empty plate as gently as I could in front of me. Choden's eyes flicked to the dish and was about to stand to gather it, but Skye stretched an arm out to meet the old woman's. "What happened then?" she asked softly.

Choden inclined her head towards Skye, eyes closed for a moment. Opening them again, she continued. "I live in mountains. Many months in mountains. I remember Lama say to India, walk south west. Many times I repeat, many times."

"You walked to India?" I asked, astonished.

Choden nodded. "Lama say, to go to India, walk south west."

"What about your family, Choden? Did you see them again?" I asked. I felt Skye's leg brush against my own, whether to admonish my question or for some more intimate reason, I wasn't sure.

Choden put her head down and went quiet for a full two minutes. Her silence was all the answer I needed. Lifting her head slowly, she looked to Skye and said, "Five years I stay in India. I meet Lama, I meet husband, I learn English." She smiled at us before nodding yet again, as if this marked the natural end to her story. She stood and cleared the dishes, leaving Skye and I alone by the fire with the weight of this story sinking into our bones. Condensation was building up on the windows of the tiny dining area, and the moonlight that managed to penetrate the room was quickly lost in the amber glow emanating from the fireplace.

As Choden showed us to our room later that night, I finally mustered up the courage to ask about the gunshots that had awoken us in Bagarchhap.

"Bagarchap?" she replied. "No, I have heard nothing. But I have no radio. I see no problems here, though."

It wasn't the most resounding of encouragements, but I told myself Skye was right and that we'd be OK for the night.

Chapter 9

Choden's life story, as well as our debate on whether or not to push on and ignore the acclimatization day prescribed by the guidebook, were the main topics of conversation the following day. If we decided to ignore all scientific research pointing towards the rather obvious need of the human body to adjust to new altitudes, we risked becoming violently ill, necessitating an extra few days to recover before setting off again. The needs of our fragile human bodies won out in the end, Maoists or no Maoists.

We had to walk an extra five minutes or so off the path to find a decent spot to camp that night. The trees had thinned out almost to the point of nonexistence, but bushes still sprouted up erratically, offering a bit of cover. From here on out, we decided, it would be best to stay in bhattis, at least until we got over the Thorung La Pass. Nights were getting a lot colder, too, an annoyance that ended up working to my advantage as it forced Skye and I to sleep closer together.

Guesthouses the size of hotels popped up on the skyline as we drew closer to Manang a couple of days later. Everything in these parts was brown: the buildings, the streets, the hills, the villagers' clothes. It was as if everything in the village had literally been carved out of the surrounding mountains.

Just behind the more glamorous and upmarket Himalayan Inn, we found the Glacier Hotel. A young man looked up from behind an old school desk, a look of surprise on his face.

"Namaste," he said with a heavy accent that sounded more Indian than Nepalese.

"Hello, my friend," I returned. "How much for a room for the night?"

He mumbled something incomprehensible, then asked, "And how did you find Braga, if you don't mind me asking this?"

"It was lovely," Skye said, shooting a concerned glance in my direction.

"Yeah, lovely," I broke in. "Listen, we just need to know how much one night would cost, as we seem to have slightly miscalculated the cost of our trip."

"No problem for two such wonderful peoples as you. My hotel is the most cheapest of all hotels in here Manang," he said, the same broad grin still pasted on his face. "One hundred rupees for two peoples. It will only be one night, that is correct?"

"We'll take it, and yes," I told him.

"Ah, very good then, very good," he said with a decidedly Indian wobble of his head. "My name is Mandar." He walked around the counter to greet us. "I will show you to your room now, if you good peoples want?"

"Yes, us good peoples would love that, please," Skye said.

Behind the main building of the hotel were six wooden rooms built side by side. "My father, me, and my good mother have built all of this," Mandar said with a grand sweep of his arm. As a reminder of just how far away from a paved road we were, as I looked back to the south the path seemed no wider than a pencil's width, winding its way down the mountainside like an ancient serpent.

"You like this room?" he asked. At least I thought it was a question; it was hard to tell with his accent. Not waiting for our response, he continued, "And when you good peoples will be wanting your food, please come and see my eating." He shut the door behind him and the room fell into complete darkness.

"Wow. That'll keep the wind out tonight, eh? I can't see a damn thing," I said, grasping along the wall for a light switch.

Skye opened the door a crack, flicked on the single bulb, and then shut it again. I flung my bag onto the bed, where it bounced once before rolling off to land on the floor with a soft thud. Smooth, Joseph. I sat down on the edge of the bed and Skye joined me. We both lay back, sore, hungry, and with the weary knowledge that another two weeks lay ahead of us.

"Beds seem like a luxury now," Skye said, stretching lazily.

"Are you tired?"

"Bloody well am." We lay staring up at the ceiling, and after a short pause she asked, "Joseph, how did you know what he said? Mandar, I mean." I turned to look at her questioningly and she continued, "When we walked into the hotel, you answered his questions without missing a beat. He asked in Nepalese."

"Really? I'm sure I just guessed." My mind and body were more travel weary than they ever had been, and my head was spinning. "Well, let's go eat, then I'm gonna take a shower and do a little laundry. If you want me to wash something for you, just give it to me." I tried pushing myself up, but gravity won out and I fell back with a thud, closing my eyes.

"All the commotion here was shocking. What the hell is everyone doing?" Skye sounded worried and had propped herself up on one elbow, looking at me intently, but before she had even completed her sentence, I had already began to slip out of consciousness.

In almost complete darkness, I saw an object coming towards me. The moon shone off bright-colored clothing, the colors of the garments becoming increasingly visible and more real. Light above, artificial and multicolored, shrouded the path ahead of me. A small, lean figure bouncing up and down as if skipping. "Joseph!" I heard someone call out, and I tried to call out in response, but my mouth didn't seem to be working properly.

"What? Joseph! It's me." It was completely dark again, and I couldn't tell where the voice was coming from. "Joseph, it's me," the voice repeated, more urgent now, closer.

I felt something brush against my shoulder. My eyes burst open with such force that my heart jumped, commanding my body to follow suit. Skye was leaning over me in the dark.

"Are you OK?" she asked, laying her hand across my forehead, which I realized was drenched in sweat, much like the rest of my body.

"What just happened?" I asked groggily, looking around blankly.

"You fell asleep, then you started mumbling something. At first I thought you were talking to me, but when I asked you who you were talking to you just ignored me. I let you sleep, but a few minutes later you were almost shouting, and not exactly coherently, either."

"Really? How long have we been lying here?"

"You were asleep for ten minutes, tops," she said, suddenly agitated. She leaned over the side of the bed and grabbed her bag from the floor. "Look, you probably just need some food. What do you say? I'm heading back to the hotel now."

I told Skye to go on without me and that I'd join her shortly. After a quick change of clothes, I stood with my feet planted wide in front of a sink with no drainage system to speak of, which was propped up with a piece of plywood outside of the main building. With the lack of plumbing underneath, the water dripped to the ground, dampening my shoes. Leaning over the basin, I splashed the refreshingly cold water down my sweaty back. The sun was out and shone directly above me, the heat of the rays intensified by the altitude but balanced by a sharp chill in the air.

"Feeling better?" Skye asked as I entered the restaurant. Mandar was back at his post behind the counter, engrossed in his radio.

"Were you feeling not so well, Mr. Josep?" he asked, jumping right into our conversation. "If there is anything I could do for you, my good friend, please do not be hesitant in your asking me."

"I'll be sure to do that, Mandar. Right now, though, I was hoping I could get a drink? What's the local drink around these parts?"

"These parts, sir? I know only one part to drinking sir and that it goes here." He pointed to his stomach.

"What do you drink when you want something strong, then?" I asked.

"I only drink Khukuri rum, Mr. Josep. Very delicious it is, too, and very cheap, sir, even here in Manang."

"OK then, Mandar. Could I please have a glass of Khukuri rum?"

"Certainly," he answered, reaching below the counter with a grave nod.

"That's probably a good idea," Skye sighed as she looked up at me from behind the guidebook.

Chapter 10

Climbing the steep hill that lay ahead of us, after two larges glasses of Nepali rum each, wasn't exactly my idea of acclimatizing. Before we even reached the top, I could see a huge smile spread across the face of our guide, a local priest, who shouted encouragement from the summit in Nepali as we trudged along.

"I don't think he's seen anyone for a while," Skye shouted to me over her shoulder. I was moving at a considerably slower pace than Skye; by the time I reached the top, they both had been standing there for quite some time. The priest's smile must have been contagious, because Skye was grinning just as widely as he was.

"Look at this!" Skye pointed to a small temple carved into the rock face.

The priest greeted me with several Namaste's punctuated by profuse bowing, not once letting his smile waver. I'm not sure who grabbed whose hand first, but somehow the three of us ended up with hands locked, walking side by side into the temple. The central prayer hall was only a few feet into the cave. At the back, an ornate golden Buddha shimmered in the candlelight, a wooden bench set at its feet. Temple incense lingered in the air, forcing all who entered into instant contemplation.

"Where do you sleep?" I heard Skye ask as I let myself be enveloped by the mystical aura of our surroundings.

Kneeling self-consciously before the golden Buddha, I thought about the way in which our priestly friend had chosen to live his life. I realized I envied him, which was wrong; in the end, there was nothing in the way of me being him and him being me.

For one hundred rupees each, the priest performed two blessings for us early that afternoon. The whole ceremony took about twenty minutes, and before we knew it we were exchanging our farewells with our guide and wandering back down the precipitous hill.

"Skye," I said, pointing down the slope. "If you squint hard enough, you could almost imagine that was Trev coming towards us." Two figures were coming up the hill, still a long way off. When we had met the two Australians a few days earlier, I couldn't help but notice the large, wide-brimmed Akubra perched atop Trev's guitar case.

"I noticed it when we were changing by the hot spring the other day. My eyes may be a bit off, but it's hard not to notice something like that. I mean, look at the size of that fucking thing."

"Do you have to swear, Joseph?" Skye let out a disgusted sigh. "We just left a temple and a blessing and all, then you have to...never mind." She sauntered ahead, annoyance still dripping from her voice as she continued, "Well, I guarantee that if it is an Akubra, there'll be an Australian under it. We're the only people in the world who would dream of wearing such a thing."

"G'day guys," Trev yelled from twenty yards below. I mustered a smile, weary from the morning's rum, the steep climb, and Skye's sudden ire. A notch more enthusiastic than me, Skye managed a friendly wave. In the space of a couple of minutes, we came together at the halfway point of the slope.

"Well, hello there," I said, shaking hands with them both. "This is a nice surprise."

"We didn't think we would see you guys again," Skye added.

"The good Lama still up there?" Jacqui asked with a nod of her head in the temple's direction. Now that we were dry and not sitting in a hot spring I was able to see the both of them standing together, and I noticed that Trev was a good ten inches taller than Jacqui. I also noticed that they both had their noses pierced with small silver hoops, and Jacqui's ears were adorned with what looked to be seven or eight piercings each, a mix of simple silver studs and smaller hoops. Trev's hair was shorter now that it was dry, and very curly. Now that Jacqui's wasn't tied back, it tumbled straight down to her shoulders, a few braided locks falling loosely in front of her face, adding to her mystic appearance.

"Yeah, he's up there smiling away," I answered.

"Good. I told you he'd still be there, Trev."

"So why the rush all of a sudden?" Skye asked.

"Well, it's a long story actually," Trev started.

"No, it's not," Jacqui jumped in. "We were staying at a little place the day after we met you guys, and during the night the entire village fled into the mountains. Apparently, they heard on the radio that a band of Maoists were coming their way." Her hair swished in and out of her field of vision as she spoke, but she seemed not to notice. "Actual fighting has been going on, guys, and has been from the beginning of the trek. Besisahar is finished. The villagers wanted no part of it and people have been killed. It's completely fucked."

"You mean they just left you there sleeping while they all fled?" asked Skye, shock and fear in her voice.

"Yeah, we were scared shitless. We've been moving along as quickly as we can ever since," Trev said, though the cheerful lilt to his voice sounded forced.

"Shit," was the only thing I could say.

"Yeah, you could say that again," Skye replied, and so I did.

"Are you guys staying in Manang?" I asked, attempting to bring the conversation back to easier ground.

"Yep, we're staying in a place called...uh...what was the name of Mandar's place, babe?" Trev asked Jacqui.

"The Glacier Hotel," she told us.

"That's where we are," Skye answered, grabbing Jacqui's hand and giving it a friendly squeeze.

"Honestly, honey," Jacqui went on, "if it was up to me, we wouldn't be staying anywhere. We would have skipped acclimatizing and just kept moving, but this is a must if we're going to reach fifty four hundred metres."

I glanced at Trev; now that we were close, I noticed how red his eyes were. Definitely stoned. We made plans to meet up with them later on at the hotel, then they set off on their second pilgrimage while Skye and I continued our descent.

Once we were back in our hotel room, I immediately lay down on the bed and closed my eyes. Skye announced that she was going out for a walk and didn't ask if I wanted to join.

By the time I awoke it was completely silent; it seemed the entire town had shut down for the night. I reached over thinking, and hoping, that Skye might be next to me, but the bed was empty. I stumbled the few paces to the door and flipped the switch. Nothing happened. Swinging the door open, the brightness of the moon hit me full on; it always seemed to be brighter at this altitude. I thought of the old priest sitting up on the cliff, probably meditating, watching the stars, hearing the wind whip through his little hut, but not feeling the chill at all. "It'd be another story in winter," I said aloud.

I found Skye, Trev, Jacqui, Mandar, and another man I didn't recognize all sitting around two tables that had been pushed together in the middle of the hotel restaurant. A small radio rested on another table in the far corner blaring something, but the heavy static made it difficult to recognize whether it was meant to be music or a news broadcast. On the table in front of the small party was a large, half full (or half empty, depending on how you chose to see it) bottle of Kuhkuri rum, one empty glass, five full, a chillum longer than any I had ever seen and a block of charras the size of a small dinner plate. The room was completely shrouded in smoke, and it reeked of booze.

"Ah, Mr. Josep. It is so lovely to see your good face," said Mandar through a smile almost as wide as the priest's had been. "We have been much waiting and wondering, or wondering and waiting...which is better, Mr. Josep?"

"It doesn't really matter which goes first, Mandar," I answered, returning his smile and coughing a little as I adjusted to the sharp change in air quality from the clear alpine air outside.

"Ah, well, then we want you to join us now. You will be joining our good party, no?"

"How you feeling, hon?" Skye asked, dropping the term of endearment as casually as if we always used such words with each other. Waving the smoke away from my face, I managed to make eye contact and saw that her eyes were completely bloodshot.

"I'm feeling fine, thanks," I laughed. "How long have you guys been up here?"

"About an hour, mate," Trev offered in a lazy slur.

As I sat down, Skye reached out and rubbed slow circles into my back, giving me a languorous smile.

"Would you like drink, Josep? Jacqui asked, with what was meant to be a sly glance in Mandar's direction. This got a laugh from everyone, including Mandar and the unknown man sitting next to him.

Jacqui picked up the empty glass and handed it to Mandar, who poured the rum nearly to the rim of the glass before sliding it across to his neighbor, who then passed it to Skye before it finally made its way on its circuitous route to me. A hush descended on everyone throughout the whole procedure, as if some sacred ritual were taking place; when I finally reached for the glass, the entire table once again burst into laughter.

"Mr. Josep," said Mandar once the cackling had died down, "this is Kumar. He is my cousin from Ladakh."

"Nice to meet you, Kumar."

Kumar sat staring at me, eventually wagging his head and smiling drowsily. Finally he said, "My peace to meet you." Laughter rang out yet again.

"I am sorry for my good cousin, Mr. Josep. He does not understand the English so good. He is here with me helping, as my good father has had to travel back home to look after his good brother."

I took a sip of rum. "And how long will you be staying, Kumar?"

"He will be staying until we return, sir," replied Mandar with a wobble of his head. Kumar's head swayed what looked to be agreement.

The giggles had finally dissipated and a heavy silence settled over the table. I took another sip of rum. "So, what's your take on the Maoist situation?" I asked, directing my question at Mandar but hoping anybody at the table would offer some kind of answer.

Skye grabbed my arm. "Joseph, remember all the commotion we saw when we got to the village?" I nodded, looking down at the white patches forming where she gripped my forearm. "Well, apparently everyone's leaving."

The room went completely quiet, the silence immeasurably heavier than the preceding one. I could make out a faraway voice speaking in Nepali over the static from the radio. 'This can't be happening,' I thought as I looked at everyone's face in turn.

"What do you mean, leaving?" My voice was barely louder than the crackling radio, an embarrassing tremor at the end of the sentence.

"Mate," Trev said through the smoke and static. "All these guys," gesturing towards Mandar and Kumar, "they're leaving. The Maoists are coming and they don't like all the enterprise that's going on, especially in Manang. It's bigger than the average village."

Mandar and Kumar sat motionless, eyes fixed on their drinks. Fear was clearly distinguishable in their bloodshot eyes. "What's with the party then? Shouldn't we be getting our asses out of here now?"

"It's OK, Joseph. Everyone's going tomorrow." Skye squeezed my arm tighter, her fingernails digging in. "Remember the gunshots? Well, they were coming from a two-day walk behind us. And the army will be intercepting them before Manang, probably back in Bagarchhap." Skye looked towards Trev for confirmation; he nodded once, slowly. "We're gonna have to cross the pass as fast as possible now."

Well. We were even more fucked now than when we'd woken up that morning, and yet here we all were, smoking, drinking, and carrying on as though we were veterans with dozens of conflict situations under our belts. I downed my rum in one shot and pushed the empty glass across the table to Mandar. He smiled, his yellowed teeth poking out from lips that looked like they would crack. The room shook with laughter, although not as loud as it had before.

"So, everyone is really leaving?" I asked, watching Mandar refill my glass, right up to the rim again.

"Yes, we have to leave," Mandar said as he slid the glass back across the table to me. "Stop the rough tough, no rough tough I say." He swallowed the rest of his rum in one swift gulp, then slammed the glass down on the table. His lips glistened with the liquid as he continued. "If the Maoists want to enter our politicians, then these people should be allowed, but no fighting. Look at my hotels, look on the street. No one, no peoples like you. No peoples like you, no money for us."

The mood in the room had turned solemn and I realized that nobody wanted to discuss the conflict any further. I had started it, so I was delegated to come up with something to lighten the atmosphere, although they all seemed to be doing a fair job of self-lubricating the screws of panic and confusion.

"Mind if I have a smoke off this thing?" I asked. "This is by far the biggest chillum I have ever seen."

Trev was clearly impressed too. "Yeah, she's a thing of beauty, ain't she?"

Kumar, although lacking in the English department, quickly picked up on the thread of our conversation and, as if he was being paid by the hour, went to work breaking up the soft, coal-colored, extremely fragrant hash.

"Have you guys already eaten?" I asked, turning towards Skye.

"No, not yet. Mandar said he was going to cook us up something special a bit later."

"Yes, my good friend," our host confirmed. "I want to finish with my things today. The army or the Maoists will be taking what they want when they come here, and I don't want to leave to them anything."

Everyone at the table took in a lungful the first time the chillum went around. The girls declined on the second go, and again on the third. The chillum was a two-man operation. It had to be supported with two hands and lit by a second person. Plain as a window, it bore no carvings or markings of any sort. The exterior of the pipe was jet black, and I was sure the inside was as well. Once we had finished with the chillum, Mandar refilled everyone's glasses, said something hushed to Kumar in Nepali, then slowly pushed himself up from the table. Without saying another word, the cousins stumbled off to the kitchen.

"So what are your plans, then?" I asked, looking at both Trev and Jacqui, noting with no small amount of interest that Skye's hand had migrated from my arm to my back.

"Like we were telling Skye earlier, we're just gonna keep going. We can't turn back now. Just get as far as we can, as fast as we can," Jacqui said, looking at me, then back to Trev. "Pretty stupid of us to do this in the first place, though."

"No it wasn't, Jac," he said defensively. "We were told it would all be fine and that we would be safe." Great choice of conversation topic, Joseph. I felt Skye's hand leave my back as she shifted in her seat, distancing herself ever so slightly from the dickhead who kept putting his sandal in his mouth.

Trev and I shared a look, then he suddenly jumped up and left the room with no explanation. I sat in apprehensive silence, sipping my rum.

My sense of self-preservation and sanity needed lubricating. Trev returned, strumming his guitar, a halfhearted, goofy smile on his face.

He serenaded us with a few songs of his own, missing a few lines here and there (or so we were told afterwards), and then took a few requests. Our hosts returned from the kitchen laden down with three large plates of food. A different curry was piled on each one, a huge pile of rice and pickles surrounding them. An enormous bucket of dhal was served up with a long wooden ladle. All conversation immediately ceased as the aroma pierced through the clouds of chillum smoke and we attacked the meal like we hadn't seen food in days.

***

Trev and I studied our surroundings. Standing at a junction in the path, one trail went up and wrapped around the mountain to the right, while another zigzagged down to the Marsyangdi, stopping in front of an unstable-looking bridge before making its way back up and over the mountain on the other side of the rough-flowing river. Villagers were dispersing in all directions.

"It'd be nice to know where everyone is going," Trev said to no one in particular.

"I am officially fucking scared," Skye said, dropping her bag to the ground. Jacqui followed suit, and I sensed a joint panic attack about to ensue.

"Excuse me," I said to a woman with a sleeping child harnessed to her bosom. She gave me a passing glance as she continued along the path. The 'don't even bother' was pretty clear.

Trev kept pace next to an old man with one yak and a radio. Turning left at the path's intersection, I watched as their heads slowly slid downwards as though on an escalator. I waited and watched as people passed, trying to find the right person to ask. Four people later and still none the wiser, I was about to give up when I heard my name being called.

"Mr. Josep! Mr. Josep!' The voice echoed through the valley. I watched as a jubilant Mandar and Kumar came running up to me.

"Mr. Josep, so nice to meet you," said Kumar. I laughed, mostly to sublimate the fear.

"Mr. Josep," Mandar said, grabbing my hand. "Where are all your good peoples?"

I turned, pointing to the girls. "And Trev is up ahead getting information from someone," I added, nodding towards the river.

"Where are you peoples staying tonight?"

"Well, we're thinking of going all the way to Thorung Phedi. Where are you going? And how come you're here already? I thought you said you were leaving later tonight."

"This is true, Mr. Josep, very true this is, but the army has lost many since Besisahar. The Maoists were too close for us to be staying there any longer." Kumar smiled, nodding in agreement. "We will be staying in Manang Darsa, Mr. Josep. Very close this place is."

"How far is that?" I asked, thinking maybe it would be safer to stick with a large group.

"Over that pass, sir. Four hours, maybe five. Very cold it is, though."

Looking up, I couldn't even make out where the mountain pass was.

"Mandar, how long will it take to get to Thorung Phedi? And why is everyone turning right or left instead of continuing on straight ahead?"

A little girl appeared from behind an old woman's legs. She looked up at me and her despondent eyes met mine. Racing towards me, her oversized jogging pants flailing in the wind, she wrapped her little arms around my legs. "Well, hello," I said, looking down to her in surprise.

"Mr. Josep?" Mandar said, as I laid my hand gently on the little girl's head, at a loss as to what else to do.

"Yeah?" I mumbled, more in the little girl's direction than Mandar's.

"Mr. Josep, we have already finalized our pleasantries." What was he talking about?

"I know, Mandar. I was just making a new friend, apparently." I gingerly laid my hand on the little girl's shoulder as she looked up at me with bright, almond-shaped eyes.

"Six hours, Mr. Josep." Mandar continued. "Thorung Phedi is too very far." He looked over at Kumar, who smiled in agreement.

"Why is everyone going in different directions? How come no one is taking the Thorung La pass?" Realizing I was holding my hand awkwardly in front of me, thin air taking the place of the little girl who had been there just a moment before, I looked around in search of her.

"It is much too far, Mr. Josep. No shelter for us peoples that way. We must be still close to our homes. More army is to come from Thorung Pass. You good peoples going best way, Mr. Josep. Best way, indeed." After an uncomfortable pause, he added, "We be going now, Mr. Josep. We must see to going."

I shook hands with Mandar, then Kumar, thanking them both.

"Mate, apparently people don't want to cross the pass because it's too far. They reckon they'll be safe just over this pass or the next one." Trev said, coming up behind me, pointing frantically in all directions. "I still don't really know what's going on, though. I did my best with that old guy I talked to, but..." he said, still panting slightly from the steep climb.

"Good job," I patted his back. "That's Mandar and Kumar up there. They told me what's happening."

"So that's it, then. We walk all the way to Phedi," Skye said, sounding resigned but sticking her chin out.

Halfway to Thorung Phedi I began to worry. We had been walking for over nine and a half hours already and still had at least another two to go before we reached our destination. It was past three o'clock and the sun was already well on its way down, and the temperature was dropping fast.

At six thirty, we were walking by moonlight. Trev and I stopped, waiting for the girls, who bounced up to us, smiles on their faces.

"What the hell are you two so happy about?" Trev asked, visibly annoyed.

"Oh, nothing. We were just talking about how fucking stupid we all were for thinking we could walk this far in one day," Skye giggled. Jacqui laughed along with her like they had just heard the world's funniest joke.

"Have you two been smoking?" I asked.

"What? No, of course not. You guys always carry the hash. Have you ever noticed that, Skye? How it's always the guys who carry smoke?" Jacqui turned to Skye, and they both burst into a fresh round of hysterical giggles. Trev and I stood watching them with equal parts amusement and annoyance.

"What do we do with these two, mate?" he asked, jerking his thumb in their direction.

"No clue, man. Let's keep walking for another hour, and if we don't come across this fucking place, we'll have to set up camp. We'll wander off the path a ways, and it'll be easy to find it again in the morning since there's no vegetation. I mean, look around; there's fuck all. It's like the bloody moon, and I'm freezing, these two are going bonkers, we have no idea if we're going the right way. And the really funny thing is that I'm finding it hard not to burst into laughter myself at this point." When I had finished, Jacqui and Skye laughed so hard they almost keeled over. Trev joined in, but it sounded forced. I managed a half-smile.

Trying to be serious, I said, "You never know, eh? It could be right over that hill."

Jacqui lost it and dropped to her knees. A minute later she completely fell over, lying on her side. There we were, four strangers, fifteen thousand feet up and running from a war we could hear taking place only a day's walk away, altitude sickness clearly setting in, with only the moon as our guide, with one small tent and two sleeping bags between us.

"Right, that's it. We have to walk back," I said once they had collected themselves a bit.

"What? Are you serious?" Skye asked, trying to pull herself together.

"Skye, we have to." I snapped. "This is not the time to be enjoying ourselves. We went too high today. We need to go back down, just enough so that everyone is under control."

"Joe, I think we're OK," Trev said as he helped Jacqui back up to her feet.

"I think we'd be wise to descend for half an hour. Why take the risk?" I couldn't believe nobody was agreeing with me. "If something should happen and we get sick, we're fucked, man. We can't go back that way, and the only way out is up. Look!" I pointed in the direction we were headed, indicating the steady incline. "It's the smartest thing to do. We'll have to camp. That's it, we'll just have to." I started walking back. Damn them all.

"It's possible we just walked slower than everyone else." Jacqui was the first to speak ten minutes into our descent.

"Probably. I'm absolutely beat. We've been walking for a very long time. Fucking ages. We should've been there more than an hour ago, hey Joe?" Trev was up in front, searching for a place to camp.

"What about last time?" I asked. "How long did it take you from Yak Kharka?"

"We didn't take this way, mate. We stayed in Muktinath and walked from there to the Base Camp at Thorung Phedi."

Trev found a spot several feet above the path. The mountain leveled off just enough to pitch our tent with a yard to spare on each side. It was extremely tight; sleeping on our sides was the only way the four of us could fit, and we had to leave our packs outside. Trev and I slept on the outside with the girls in the middle. We lay in silence, fully clothed, jackets on. The wind raged against the tent, pushing it to one side, howling like a pack of starved wolves. Before sleep overtook us, I heard one of the girls start crying softly.

Chapter 11

As dawn approached, the fierce wind pushed the tent to the point of no return, warping the poles. Tired of the fabric flapping in my face, I had turned over during the night, putting me about an inch away from Skye's nose. Awake before the sun, I lay listening to the wind and watching her, enjoying the way her breath ghosted over my lips. The sun was up before five, peeking its early morning head around the crown of Annapurna II, and we were all wide-awake shortly after.

"Don't you have any other gloves, mate?" Trev asked through a mouthful of toothpaste.

"Unfortunately, no. I honestly didn't think it was going to be this cold." I held my hands up and examined my thin wool gloves in disdain.

"Dude, we're climbing to fifty-five hundred metres and you didn't think it was going to get cold?"

"Yeah, well. I've never done this before," I offered weakly.

When everyone was washed, brushed and bundled up as much as possible, we started off and silently climbed for an hour. The wind pushed us back in a perpetual 'fuck off, go home'.

"I'll be damned, guys," Trev shouted over the gale as we came up behind him.

"I can't believe it," Skye replied, looking down. "And yet it doesn't surprise me in the slightest."

A near vertical descent into yet another valley lay before us. My heart dropped to somewhere around my aching feet. The crushed stone path dropped steeply for about two hundred yards, then continued another three hundred or so to a bridge which would get us to the other side. This was followed by a hike of another mile, rising slowly to reach Thorung Phedi, all of which was clearly visible from where we stood at the highest point of the trek on that side of the pass. A collective sigh ran through our group. Hearts dropped, spirits faltered, muscles groaned, eyes watered.

"This makes for a pretty difficult decision, then," I said, breaking the dismayed silence.

"What do you mean?" Jacqui wiped away a tear possibly brought on by the gusting wind, possibly not.

"Well, yesterday we had planned on getting here to save a day on the trek and finish as soon as possible. And now that the day has come, we're still not at the destination, which is over there. It takes the average person seven hours or more to cross the pass, starting from that spot way down there." I pointed to a tiny wooden building standing like a lone sentinel, a long, long way away.

"Shit, you mean we did all that hiking for no reason? What are we gonna do down there for a whole bloody day? Look at the place, there's nothing there. It's just a shack. We're fucked." Skye looked into the gorge, reddened eyes watering from the wind and sheer frustration.

"We could always just go for it. It's past six now; we'll be there by eight. We could make it." I didn't know who I was trying to convince more, the others or myself.

"Joe, we couldn't make the trek yesterday, when we were trying to," Jacqui answered. "What makes you think we can make this?" She and Skye huddled together.

"We have to," Trev said. He turned and sauntered off, and that was that.

The cliff was so sheer that we had to walk crab-like, on all fours. The further we climbed down, the more the anger grew within me. How had everything become so irrevocably fucked up? This was supposed to be some golden experience that I would look back on in years to come and think, 'yeah, I want to relive that.' Instead, it had turned into a 'run for your goddamn life or your screwed' kind of situation.

"This is bullshit," I said aloud, ducking to avoid a falling rock that tumbled down from above, picking up deadly speed.

"Sorry!" Jacqui yelled from above.

The proprietor of the small guesthouse at the bottom of the valley was a short, round man (rare in a country with limited provisions), who informed us that two other trekkers had left early that morning. They'd had a run-in with the Maoists, he added, and were in a hurry. When we asked him whether he was planning to leave the village or not, he told us he would be safe either way; he was on his own and living so remotely that nobody would bother him. We bought some chapattis and cheese, divided it amongst us, then left him there.

At eight thirty, three to four hours behind what was advised as the absolute latest starting time, we began our ascent of the Thorung La Pass. The long and torturous climb zigzagged its way up the mountain path. Slowly and methodically, one foot was placed cautiously in front of the other, we made our way towards the top of the first ridiculously steep climb. By this point my hands and face were almost unmovable from the cold, and I was sure frostbite would set in at any moment. The two shirts and jacket that I had been wearing were now fighting a useless battle against the gale-force winds of the Himalayas. Ahead of me marched Trev, warm and cozy in his thermals and earmuffs, and just behind him was Jacqui, who looked equally snug in her down-filled jacket. And then there was Skye, who had on her big, thick ski gloves and a thermal body suit along with two or three thin layers of clothing beneath it, keeping her enviably warm yet mobile.

"I am such a fucking idiot!" I shouted, my torment going unheard as it got tossed in with the wail of winds.

At the top of the climb was an empty lodge. Running behind it as quickly and inconspicuously as I could, I pulled at my bag in quick, jerky shots like a snapping turtle, my hands so cold that only slivers of exposure were bearable. Eventually prying the bag open, I yanked out a tank top, a t-shirt, and another jumper, which I threw on under my jacket as fast as my cold-bitten fingers would allow. The first herculean task done, I reached down into the deepest recesses of the bag and retrieved two well-used pairs of socks and pulled them hastily over my hands. Next came a pair of Skye's track pants that were bunched into a corner at the bottom of the bag, which I proceeded to wrap around my face, tying the legs in front of me as if it were a scarf. Zipping up and putting my bag back on, I clenched my socked fists and walked back around the lodge to meet the others, who stood watching me with mouths gaping open. They were either too tired or too cold themselves to bother commenting.

The summit housed a very small wooden teahouse that, in better times, would have been a marvelous place to stop for a hot drink brewed over the fire pit. At the top of the pass, a large sign surrounded by hundreds of prayer flags read:

THANK YOU FOR VISITING MANANG
THORONG LA PASS
5,416 M.
CONGRATULATION FOR THE SUCCESS!!!
HOPE YOU ENJOYED THE TREK IN MANANG
SEE YOU AGAN SOON!!!

With no time for celebration or ceremony, we walked right past the sign; no pictures, no hugs, no tea, no hellos, no goodbyes. Nada, zilch, nothing. Our daylight was no doubt going to run out soon, and sleeping in the tent again was not an option, unless of course a suicide pact was drawn up in which we all agreed to freeze to death together.

Looking up just in time to see the sign, I said, barely audible through my makeshift scarf, "We'll need all the prayer flags we can get," before burrowing my head into my chest against the cold.

The trek begins its initial descent just past this sign with the prayer flags. Gradually, at a snail-on-pot pace, we continued to traverse the pass. With every step, I fell further and further behind the others.

"What's going o-" I began, about an hour later, just before I walked smack into the back of Skye.

We all came to a halt. Trev, at the head of the pack, had stopped in his tracks. The four of us were standing one behind the other, only inches apart.

"Trev," I shouted, before realizing why he had stopped. Green-uniformed, gun toting and marching in unison were two lines of soldiers, coming up the other side of the mountain. We stood in mute shock as they inched their way towards us. The path itself is not very wide on the pass; hundreds or perhaps thousands of years of all kinds of animals crossing it, mostly in single file, had carved out a narrow stretch of land, the middle of which we were standing on. I felt something pull at my arm. Trev was pushing us to move aside.

A strange sympathy replaced the anger and some of the fear inside me as I watched the poor buggers advance. They had been chosen, they had not volunteered. As bitterly cold as it was, they were not wearing down-filled jackets, they were not wearing the warmest gloves money could buy, and their ears were uncovered, as were their faces. I counted twenty-five men in the row closest to us; two rows of them made up a total of fifty soldiers. Marching past us, only a handful bothered to look in our direction. They were on their way to stop the Maoists who were advancing from the Besisahar side of the Annapurna Range, the side of the range that had lost its ability to make a living. The side where the villagers ran and hid at night, fearing violent retribution if they chose to resist. The side where entire villages had been deserted rather than be forced into a situation they did not, could not, support. These men, these fifty cold, hungry, weathered men, were being forced into a situation many may not have believed was worth fighting over, but they had nowhere to run. When the last of them had passed us, our little group stood watching them march onwards and upwards, some of them undoubtedly to a very lonely, cold, and certain death.

"Things might not be going so well," said Trev, pulling his sweater down from his mouth to speak. I looked towards Trev as if he had just told me how to breathe.

Looking down towards Muktinath from the pass we took in the majestic view, and for a few moments allowed ourselves to pause and take in what lay before us. Row after row of glorious mountains rose and fell, the valleys continuing downwards into an abyss whose depths we could not see. At that height, many of the mighty peaks were below us. I knew we weren't exactly on top of the world, but it truly felt as though we were, that there was nowhere to go but down.

Without a word passing between us, we began another agonizing descent. After three hours of walking down the near-vertical slope, we came to an abandoned shack that had once been a teahouse. By the looks of it, it had recently been converted for military purposes. Signs warned us to keep away. We discussed a rest period, albeit a short one, and agreed a moment to gather our forces was needed.

"Here comes some more, mate." Trev was standing and stretching, peering down the slope. I stood up too, and, sure enough, spotted another group of soldiers coming from below.

Skye and Jacqui stood up to take a look. "Fucking hell," they responded in near-perfect unison.

We walked steadily on until the sun was just about to sink. Standing as far away from them as possible, we watched thirty more soldiers march past, the thirtieth stopping in his tracks as he reached us. Looking over in our direction, he leered as he raised his hand. For a split second I thought he was about to raise his gun. A blinding white light shot through my entire body and for one-tenth of a nanosecond I was not Joseph Conrad Blaze Dixon, I was no one, I was not even a sentient being. I was nothing but that flash of white light that inundated my entire self. The soldier pointed at me, not with his weapon but with his outstretched hand, which somehow was just as threatening.

"You, come here," he shouted by way of a command.

"Shit," I murmured. "What do I do, Trev?"

"I'll come with ya, mate," he said stoically. The two of us approached the waiting soldier. The rest of his troupe had continued on their march.

"Yes, sir," I said when only a few yards separated us.

His eyes were red, not stoned red but wind-ripped red, and they bulged slightly from the dark brown skin of his face. Shorter than both Trev and I, he was only able to look us both evenly in the eye as he was standing on an incline. He was old, older than I assumed any soldier should be. His nose was bulbous, a trait not seen on many Asian people. I noticed with a shudder that he was wearing the same uniform as the dead soldier.

"Where coming from?" he barked.

"Thorung Phedi," Trev replied with admirable evenness.

He looked us up and down, then shifted his gaze over to the girls. "How is that side? You see trouble?"

"No, sir, no trouble," I answered. "We saw other soldiers earlier today, up on the pass there." I wanted to tell him that villagers were fleeing, but I couldn't force the words out.

"But yesterday, mate," Trev said, taking a step forward, "we were with some Nepali folk who were going into hiding."

The officer looked towards the pass, keeping one eye on his troops. "These peoples, these runaways, from which village they come?"

"Well..." Trev said, "from Pisang. They were crossing the other passes out of fear of violence, mate."

The soldier stared at him, then shifted his glare to me. "Maoists?" he asked, looking me in the eye. I could see the red veins branching out around the whites of his eyes, rheumy mucous caked in his lashes.

"Haven't seen any," I told him. "But we did hear gunfire a few days ago."

Turning to face his troops, he declared, "We must go." He turned back to us, nodded curtly, then jogged away to join his troops.

Chapter 12

Day fourteen of the Annapurna Circuit Trek is a six-hour struggle, a death-defying descent of almost five thousand feet. Having pushed ourselves due to the Maoist thing, not to mention the strapped-for-cash thing, our legs and knees had had time to adapt to the constant pain, and a sheer mile and a half descent no longer brought on an instant panic attack. Helping to ease the pain, for Trev and I at least, was the sweet hash, of which we still had a healthy amount. A light drizzle helped cool us off after an hour of walking, and for the next five hours we trekked back and forth over the Kali Gandaki River a total of four times. Walking into Tatopani, a sign announced, 'Tatopani- The resort village of the Annapurna Circuit'.

We stopped at the Trekker's Lodge, behind which was a hot spring of the finest order. Despite all the turmoil around us, Tatopani was definitely the resort village it claimed to be.

"So, only another two days to go and we're done?" Skye said to no one in particular as we soaked in the gloriously hot water of the spring.

"It went by pretty quick, didn't it?" Jacqui answered, scooping some water over her shoulder and wincing slightly.

It was a matter of minutes before I succumbed to the lull of the hot water and fell asleep in the spring. I dreamt I was in a small room; it was bloody cold and I stood shivering, my knees clacking together violently. I couldn't make out the faces of any of the many others in the room; they were completely indistinguishable. The shapes of their bodies were as clear as day, but their faces were warped and hidden. I couldn't speak to anyone, not only because they didn't appear to have eyes or ears, but because I couldn't seem to move my own mouth. Frantic movement surrounded a lone figure at the center of the room. Suddenly, I was violently shoved by the faceless entities towards this figure, my outstretched hand piercing through its body. My fingers closed around cold entrails, the sticky goo covering my forearm. I looked up into the face of the dead soldier. He smiled at me, his mucous infested eyeballs dangling out of his lopsided, half-rotted head.

Three pairs of wide, questioning eyes met my own.

"What?" I blurted out, slightly irritated by the unwanted attention.

"You were dreaming again, honey." Skye sat beside me, the water just covering her nipples. She leaned against me, one breast against my shoulder. "I tried to make out what you were saying, but I couldn't get it. You seemed to be asking questions, though."

"But I couldn't open my mouth."

"Huh?"

"Nothing. Um... how long have I been asleep?"

"Not long. Half an hour or so."

Trev strummed absently at his guitar, perched on the edge of the spring. Maybe I was being paranoid; maybe they weren't all overcome with curious concern (although the continued pressure of Skye's left breast against my arm said otherwise, not that I was complaining).

It was getting late before we'd had our fill of the hot spring. Skye and I left the other two soaking in the water with a promise to reconvene in about an hour for dinner. Walking with Skye, I felt a chill pass through my entire body, brought on not by the outside temperature but from somewhere within myself. I paused in my tracks to dig a sweater out of my bag.

"You cold?" Skye asked amiably, putting an arm around my shoulders.

"Yeah, a little." I didn't want to tell her how the feeling seemed to stem directly from the weird dream I'd just had in the hot spring. I tried shrugging it off as we kept walking, but even Skye's touch didn't feel right. Something was missing. Not from her, but from me. I began an internal sanity check.

We pitched our tent in a clearing not far from the path. As it had rained for most of the day, we were able to find a good spot almost entirely covered by the forest canopy. The ground was still moist, but it would have to do. After tying a piece of an old t-shirt to the largest tree we could find, we set off to meet up with Trev and Jacqui. I still had the chill. I kept my sweater on with two shirts added underneath. My dreams came back to me, cobbled together in no particular order. The cold feeling snaked its way under my skin. Skye was talking. She was mere inches away from me, but I couldn't make out anything she was saying. I turned to look at her; she had no face. Somehow she was talking without a mouth. I could see her long brown hair pulled back into a ponytail, her scarf wrapped high around her neck, but I couldn't make out any of her facial features. I shook my head and looked again, squinting slightly and swallowing back panic, but as I did she turned her head to look into the forest, her movement timed perfectly with mine. Was this another dream? Maybe I was still asleep in the spring. But I could feel the wind, could hear it moving in the trees, and I was sure that if I reached out, my fingers would close around Skye's very real scarf.

We weren't far from the spring now. To my immense relief, Trev and Jacqui's tired faces were perfectly distinguishable above the reflection of the water. Shake yourself out of it, Joseph.

"They're still here," Skye said, turning to face me. I could clearly make out the little wrinkles around her eyes, her perfect lips pushing her cheeks upwards for a few seconds as she grinned at me. She held her stare a split second longer than what would be considered normal after making such a mundane comment. I smiled back dumbly. She pulled me towards her and slowly let her lips take mine. I tried to kiss her back but it seemed as if my mouth wasn't functioning. My lips were making some attempt at motion, but my tongue remained limp and numb in my mouth. I could hear a voice in the distance; it was Trev, crooning the song he'd sung when we'd first met in the other hot spring not so long ago.

Half an hour later, we were sitting down to dinner at the local guesthouse. Skye and I ordered the usual, two thalis with some roti. The restaurant offered a surprisingly large selection of malt whiskeys, bourbon, and vodka. I skipped the western stuff for monetary reasons, opting instead for two glasses of the cheap Kukhuri rum I had grown accustomed to. Two glasses was enough to make my head spin, so I said very little during dinner. There was excitement in the air as the knowledge that the trek was coming to a close overtook us, and we were all a little giddy with the realization that we had almost made it, alive and in one piece, so we drank to that, toasting with more Kukhuri rum.

Skye and I left to head for our tent just after midnight, our inebriated state proving to put our navigational skills to the test. With only a flashlight to guide us under the clouded-over sky, we made our way through the moist Himalayan night clinging to each other like two drunken sailors on leave in Shanghai, stumbling forward every few steps, once even falling right over with uncontrolled laughter.

We somehow managed to find our way back to the tent (by sheer luck, as neither of us spotted the marker we'd left on the tree), where we promptly collapsed. I knew that trying to do the right thing was going to be difficult, like building a skyscraper single-handedly difficult. The sloppy, drunken kissing started as soon as we found ourselves horizontal. Skye eventually rolled onto her back and took her sweater off, leaving only the thin fabric of her tank top separating her skin from mine. It took every ounce of my self control, and probably shaved four years off my life expectancy, not to immediately move my hands to those gorgeous breasts and massage, kiss, rub, lick and generally do unspeakable things to them. The moment I thought I was going to scream with anticipation, she pulled the flimsy and annoying piece of fabric up and over her head.

She slowly removed her bra. Our plastic boudoir began to spin as she grabbed my left hand, pulling it down to its rightful spot on her right breast. I repositioned myself, licking my way down her neck, reminding myself to go slowly, not to ruin everything. Then she asked if I had a condom. I hadn't had the need for one in ages. Cursing my stupidity with every fiber of my excruciatingly wound-up being, our lips slowed. It was all over, unlike my erection.

I kissed her cheek and she let out a frustrated sigh as I reached down to grab her jumper.

"It's OK," she said, grabbing hold of my wrist. "It's warm enough tonight. Just stay close to me."

Shocked at this new development but not willing to question it, I pulled the sleeping bag over us, tucking myself in right behind her. She rolled on her side and took my hand, placing it underneath her breast. Still standing to attention, I thought would take weeks to go limp, she wiggled into me with a soft giggle. I wanted to cry.

***

The next day began with a fierce hangover. Ghorepani, the day's destination, was located at the end of a six-hour ascent of over five thousand feet. At just past six o'clock, we were bombarded by all of the hotel options in the village. Skye and I decided we would eat first before heading on a little further to find our last camping spot of the trek. We followed Jacqui and Trev to their guesthouse and headed straight for the restaurant, where we found a suitable picnic table and ordered our last meal together.

It started to rain before we left the restaurant. Memories of the night before were vivid in my eager mind. The protection situation obviously hadn't changed, but what about Pokhara? And Kathmandu? We could easily find the requisite supplies there. Was I supposed to expect that we would? I caught myself nearly wishing it hadn't happened, grumbling internally about how sex often fucks up a good thing.

"Good spot, don't you think? And look," Skye shone the flashlight upward to the canopy of trees, "our own roof again. Ground's a bit wet, though." When I offered no reply, she shone the light directly in my eyes. "Something wrong, Joseph?"

"No, not at all."

With the tent up and ready to go, I went off to relieve myself a little further down the path. A few minutes later I returned to the tent, giving my teeth a quick brush with my remaining water supply, then unzipped the tent and crawled in. Skye was already sound asleep. I crawled underneath the sleeping bag and pulled her towards me.

Chapter 13

I awoke with my face pushed up against the side of the tent. I lay there, moving my head just enough so that it wasn't actually touching the damp wall of the tent, but not enough to disturb the beautiful woman sleeping next to me. This was it; a few days from now and I'd be saying goodbye to Skye, and a day after that I'd be heading home. I felt Skye stir behind me.

"Morning, sunshine," I murmured.

The path from Ghorepani to Birethanti covers a descent of six thousand feet, one final hurdle before the trek sends you on your merry way with a slap on the ass. All the effort we'd put in the day before to reach the Ghorepani Pass would now be handed back to our overworked knees, threefold.

Heading into Ghorepani after packing up our campsite, Skye took hold of my hand.

"Looks pretty dead around here, hey?" she asked as she eased the door to Trev and Jacqui's hotel open.

We were greeted by a local woman sitting at the picnic table where we had eaten dinner the night before. "You should go," she said her face pursed with fear. "Everybody go," she added with greater force, pointing outside. Skye's bag slipped to the floor and she ran up the staircase in search of our friends.

"Nothing," she said upon returning to the landing a minute later. "There's no one in any of the rooms."

Without thinking, I dropped my bag next to hers and made for the door. "I'll be back in a few minutes, just stay here," I shouted over my shoulder. Skye stood in the doorway, looking perplexed but saying nothing.

Rounding the only turn in the village road, I saw flickers of light dancing in the window of a nearby bhatti, smoke rising lazily from its chimney. Starting towards it at a jog, I suddenly froze mid-stride. I had heard someone approaching from behind; with a quick turn of my head, I saw three men rounding the corner herding nine yaks, one man in front of the pack and two behind. They all smiled at me in passing, their betel-stained teeth giving them a sinister look. Puffs of chilly early dawn air escaped the yaks' nostrils, clouding their furry bovine faces, the bells hung around their necks clanking into the distance.

Neither the herders nor their animals seemed particularly panicked. Maybe the danger in the air was nothing but my own paranoia. Peering around the corner again, I had almost worked up the courage to approach the occupied bhatti when the door suddenly swung open and two men appeared. Familiar men. My brain clicked in recognition as I placed them; I had met them on the other side of the pass. They had taken my money while Skye searched for a camping spot in the woods. I then felt a sharp pressure stab my shoulder.

"What you do?" shouted an angry voice from just behind my ear.

In my peripheral vision I saw the muzzle of a gun resting inches from my left ear. My hands shot instinctively skyward.

"Nothing," I said, my voice cracking on the first syllable. The muzzle of the gun tapped my shoulder a few times before withdrawing from sight. I turned, hands still up around my head.

"What you do?" repeated the man with the gun. He came up to my shoulder in height, but the AK-47 made his stature infinitely more impressive. He wore a long green coat, a red sash wound tightly around his left arm. His thick dark hair protruded out at the sides from underneath a plain black baseball cap. A long scar raked its jagged finger along his left cheek.

"Nothing," I repeated, barely a whisper, then cleared my throat, which had grown achingly dry. "I was just looking for my friends."

The soldier eyed me suspiciously, reaching into his coat. I froze. He watched me with a hand on his gun as he extricated an old wallet, waving it around in front of my face.

"Money?" I asked. "You want money?" He jiggled the wallet even closer to my face. The muzzle of the gun was now sticking into my ribs. I was seconds away from pissing myself. "OK, OK, I have some." I nodded my head vigorously, keeping my hands raised in supplication. The soldier took a step backward. My heart pounded against my ribs, sweat forming on my brow and threatening to spill down my face. My hand was shaking as I reached into my pocket and took out my wallet, holding it out for him to take. He pointed at the money sticking out of it. He just wanted the cash. Handing him all the remaining rupees I had, he stuffed them unceremoniously into his breast pocket before brushing past abruptly and making his way back towards the bhatti I had seen the other two men exit. No receipt this time, I thought, a strangled half-chuckle bubbling up through my lips. Doing my best not to break into a full-out run, I returned to the hotel to find Skye.

"What happened Joseph? Did you find Jacqui and Trev?" She asked as she stood up from one of the picnic tables. The woman was still sitting there, the same look of foreboding creasing her brow as she stared vacantly out the window.

"Nope." I grabbed my bag and slung it over my shoulder. I was out the door again before she could ask another question. She grabbed her own bag and followed suit.

The bus stop out of Birethanti is actually located just above the village, in a town called Nayapul. There was a mad rush to board the bus, and Skye and I joined in the anarchy, all thought of politeness abandoned as we elbowed our way onto the vehicle. Skye squeezed her way through the crowd, looking frazzled. "Joseph?" she called out, pausing to catch her breath. "What are we going to do now?"

"Don't know."

The bus was loaded, Asian style, people packed inside and on the roof, a few on the floor, and some hanging out the open windows. The two men behind us were engaged in a heated argument that was peppered with occasional English words. I waited until there was a lull in their conversation before turning around in my seat, hands clasped together in the traditional Namaste gesture.

"I'm sorry to bother you, but my girlfriend and I just jumped on the bus. How much is it to Pokhara? That is where we're going, isn't it?"

The two men exchanged surprised glances. "We will pay seventy-five rupees," one of the men replied, his emphasis on the word 'we' seeming to indicate my companion and I could expect to pay more.

I turned back to Skye. "OK, seventy-five it is. Do you have the cash?"

"I think so." She reached into her pocket and pulled out two hundred-rupee notes. "This is the last of it."

"When the guy comes around, don't say anything. Just look out the window. I'll hand him the money, and that'll be that. He won't give us change, but who cares at this point."

The ticket inspector eventually rose from his seat and made his way towards the back of the bus. Skye, who had closed her eyes and rested her head on my shoulder, safely avoided any potential confrontation; the inspector looked me dead in the eye when my turn came but said nothing.

"Pokhara," I said, pointing to Skye and myself. I handed him the notes, quickly averting my gaze to look out the window and down into the valley below. Out of the corner of my eye, I saw a hand reaching out. Thinking he was going to shake Skye awake and ask her for two hundred rupees as well, I turned to face him, ready for battle. Instead, I saw that he held one fifty-rupee note and two small pieces of paper in his outstretched hand. I couldn't believe it. I took the notes and receipts and looked up to thank him, but his attention had already shifted to the men sitting behind us. Skye started to snore gently against my shoulder.

Chapter 14

Leaning against Skye's doorway, I watched her rummage through her things, preparing for the next day. The last day, I corrected myself.

"Ah, fuck it. Only one more day, anyway." She threw the handful of wadded up clothes she was holding onto the floor, then dove face-first onto the bed. A total lack of good judgment under such circumstances, coupled with an overall absence of tact and consideration with how to deal with the situation, I left the room and succumbed to my own bed in the room next door.

*****

The sound of screaming was almost unbearable. I lost my equilibrium as I was jostled and pushed. I tried pulling my hands up to my ears, but couldn't seem to release my arms that were pinned to my sides by the mass of bodies crushing in on me. Towering over everyone else in the room, a sea of heads surrounded me. In a frantic bid to save my sanity, I continued searching for a way to free myself; tried jumping up and down to squeeze myself free from the mass of close-packed bodies, and it was then that I noticed that I wasn't wearing any shoes. The ground beneath me was soft, but prickly. Gradually, through no force of will of my own, I was shuffled towards a corner of the room where the press of bodies thinned out considerably, as if some invisible barrier demarcated that section of the room. The unbearable scream continued to pierce the air and my eardrums.

My body was shaken by an unknown force, rocking uncontrollably back and forth. The sea of heads around me grew blurry as I focused on a mirror hanging on a wall reflecting shimmering sunlight like water. Suddenly the space around me was clear.

I shot straight up in bed, sweating and out of breath. Skye was sitting next to me with concern furrowing her brow. "I know this room," I murmured, still half-ensconced in the dream.

"Of course you do, Joseph," Skye sighed, her concern cut with impatience. "It's the same room you stayed in the last time we were here. My room's the same, too." She reached over and knocked on the wall next to me.

"I mean, I..." I couldn't think of anything to say. "Was I...shouting something?"

"No. You were lying like the dead. You had your arms crossed over your chest and everything, but you were breathing heavily. I'm starving and I'm not leaving this hotel alone, so I nudged you awake. You nearly knocked me out with your forehead in the process," she frowned.

***

"You don't have to come all the way to the airport, you know," Skye said, stuffing the last of her rumpled, unfolded clothes into her bag. We'd just returned from an Internet café where she'd sent off messages letting those back home know when to expect her to arrive.

Our last day had been spent wandering around the streets of Kathmandu. Betel-stained teeth, all smiles as we passed their tiny shop doors; men with no shoes pushing carts ten times as large as their skinny yet toned bodies; alluring young women with glossy black hair tied in a single braid whooshing past in colorful, no doubt self-made, costumes; the enticing smells of Asian spices roving through curtained doorways to the ramshackle streets, mixing with the scents steaming off the food carts.

I was the makeshift tour guide, making everything up as we went along. Durbar Square, the religious and cultural heart of old Kathmandu, was transformed into an ancient chessboard used by the gods. Skye smiled after listening to my theatrical musings. I started again. The historic Hanuman Dhoka gate and its wooden carving of Vishnu incarnated as the monkey god was actually a replica built around the nineteen forties, I told her. Thousands of years ago, I continued, the Himalayas had been the playground of ancient, god-like monkey children who would pack the tops of the mountains with snow to blunt the impact when they inevitably fell on top of them. The most popular game at the time for god-like monkey children was a variation of contact croquet. When first discovered in an undisclosed location high above the tree line of the Himalayas, it was obviously mistaken for a simple gate, but after careful excavation and extensive deciphering of the markings carved into it, scientists were now almost completely certain that it was from the ancient game the god-like monkey children had played so long ago.

"OK, Joseph, that's enough." There was no smile this time, like when I had spun the tale about the ancient chessboard. "I've really got to get going."

Trying not to hover over her an hour later at the hotel, I tried not to appear crushed when she stressed for the second time in as many minutes that my presence at the airport was not needed (or wanted, a voice inside me reminded me). "Of course I'm going with you." I answered, watching her adjust the frayed straps on her bag. She didn't look up, but continued to fiddle with her bag. I remained in her doorway watching her, trying to think of what to say next. "You know, everything is going to be OK, Skye. Really. Don't worry."

The words hadn't come out as strong or reassuring as I'd hoped, but something in them made her turn from her bag and look up at me expectantly.

"I want to believe that, Joseph, I really do. I'm just having a hard time of it at the moment." She gave me a piercing look that I couldn't quite decipher before turning her attention back to packing with a sigh.

I was suddenly overcome with the need to see her smile. You spend years traveling around the globe, and then just when you think you may have found something, you can't hold onto it. "There's nothing stopping me from coming to see you in Australia, you know. I'm still young enough to get a year's visa." She didn't say anything, so I sat down on the bed beside her. I didn't really know what else to say.

***

Kathmandu has a surprisingly modern airport, considering most of the country lives off less than two dollars a day. We sat near her departure gate, me casting quick glances in Skye's direction, realizing I really had only skimmed the surface of her. I didn't know her favorite color or her favorite movie. I hardly knew her at all but, then again, I did. We had shared experiences in this bizarre, troubled corner of the world that we hadn't shared, couldn't share, with anyone else. I knew the smell of her hair in the early morning. I knew how when she was really tired she would zone out and fiddle with her piercing. Yet there was so much more; there were things that I might never know, and this angered me. I had told her not to worry, but that's exactly what I was doing now.

"Before you go, I have to ask you a few things," I murmured in her ear, my lips gently brushing her hair. She remained facing stiffly away from me.

"What are they?" she asked.

"Well, what's your favorite color? What's your favorite season? Favorite movie?"

She stood up abruptly and started slowly walking backwards, her eyes clear, not even slightly pink with unshed tears. "Blue. Spring or fall. A Perfect Romance." Each reply was punctuated by another backward step. She was nearly through the doors. Finally reaching the gate, she made eye contact and blew a halfhearted kiss, then another. The metal doors were closing. She gave me one last wistful smile and the doors slid shut.

I left the airport immediately with an awful pain in my stomach. I wanted to be outside when her plane left, to see it fly off into the distance. When I did finally leave, I headed straight for the hotel, taking the bus back as it was much cheaper. The first thing I did was grab the chillum. I wasn't getting stoned to block the pain; there wasn't any. I just wanted to get stoned, listen to music on the roof, and clear my head. And that's just what I did, eventually falling asleep up there, waking up sometime later in the empty dark night.

It was just past ten when I ventured out for my final dinner in Kathmandu, by which point I was starving as I had neglected to eat since seeing Skye off at the airport. In honor of her departure, I decided the most appropriate place to dine was the restaurant where she and I had first talked about camping the Annapurna Circuit.

"Namaste," the waitress greeted me, the same one as last time, as she placed a dish of momos on the only other table that still held patrons at that late hour. "Would you like drink?"

"Yes, please. A glass of Khukuri rum and a tongba."

Nearly two hours later, I was still sitting there drinking tongbas and feasting on momos and a never-ending thali. The streets were empty when I finally left; the only other souls I came across as I made my way back to the hotel were three pushbike drivers huddled around a small fire burning away on the curbside with nothing to contain it. I stopped to warm my hands and the eldest member of the little group reached out and handed me a large bottle of rum. I took a large, indulgent swig from the bottle before handing it to the young man beside me.

"You shouldn't be out late," the elderly man said, snatching the bottle away from the young man I just handed it to.

"Yeah, I know. But I leave tomorrow and I needed a walk."

"The military's tonight," he added, encompassing the night in a sweeping gesture with the bottle of rum, the liquid glowing amber in the firelight.

"I haven't seen any military," I told him, looking around carelessly. "Hey, is that your rickshaw there?" The young man beside me nodded. "Would you mind if I took it for a spin?" When he didn't respond, I added, "I mean, can I ride it? Just down the block?"

The older man let out a laugh. The man next to him followed his example, not taking his eyes off the fire. The young man beside me made a gesture with his hand as if to say, 'Go ahead, I don't give a shit. No tourists around now, anyway.' At least, that's what I took it to mean.

It turns out those bikes are a lot harder to push than one would think, but after the initial step is over, it's pretty easy sailing. I peddled back down the street from whence I had just come. It felt good to be in Nepal, in the dark, half drunk and riding some stranger's three-wheeled rickshaw. Towards the end of the block, I noticed a figure in the shadows up ahead of me. My heart jumped and I slowed the bike to a crawl so slow that it would have been quicker to get off and walk. The figure came towards me. I maneuvered the bike to the left-hand side of the road, feeling my grip becoming unsteady on the handlebars. A sigh of relief left my lungs; it was the woman from the restaurant.

"Namaste," I greeted her.

"Namaste," she answered. It was so dark I could really only make out the white gleam of her teeth.

"Can I give you a lift?"

She stopped and turned around. "A lift?"

"Yes. I could drive you to where you're heading."

"Oh...OK."

Hot damn! Surprised, I turned the bike around, which required me to first dismount, as I was neither strong nor sober enough to reverse it without it tumbling into the gutter. She laughed aloud watching my clumsy struggle, but I didn't care. Giving the seat a quick brush, I motioned for her to jump up. She did so with such grace it turned the ratty old rickshaw into a stretch limo.

I began peddling tentatively back up the road. "How far?" I asked, turning my head slightly.

"No far," she answered, but said nothing else. I had no idea where to go but copious amounts of rum flowed freely through my veins. Just before we reached the group of drivers still huddled around their fire, she leaned forward and touched my shoulder. "Right there," she said, pointing across the road from the group. I eased the bike up nice and slow to the alleyway, then leapt off the seat and held my arm out for her to take. Surprisingly, she obliged as she stepped down delicately from the bike.

"Thank you much," she said, her smile once again gleaming in the pitch dark, then turned to make her way down the alley.

Pushing the bike back to its owner, the old man smiled and held out the bottle of rum once more. I took another swig, handed it back, then patted the young man on the shoulder. "Thanks for the bike, my friend. I needed that."

Twenty minutes later, I was back at the hotel and in the beginning stages of a comatose sleep.

Chapter 15

A pounding headache greeted me the next morning with a kick to the cranium, screaming, 'Get the fuck out of bed, you wanker!' I was incredibly parched and a sticky white film took the place of anything resembling saliva. Rolling over to check the time, I half expected to find Skye lying there as I stretched my arms.

I lay there trying to collect my thoughts, something you tend to do when you wake up alone in a strange bed, in a foreign country, with a hangover that could swear a raging alcoholic off the sauce. An unfamiliar noise rattled the window by the bed. Taking a few breaths to prepare myself, I finally stood up to have a look. People below busy at their work, gathering the little bits they would need for the day for the few tourists they were expecting. Something was different, though; the unfamiliar noise grew louder with every passing second, and then just as fast as it had intensified, it would fade away again. It took me a full two minutes standing there at the window to classify the now increasingly familiar sound: helicopters.

It was just past eleven when I clambered into a taxi, taking up the entire backseat with my large bag and removable backpack, plus a cotton shoulder bag I had purchased in India. My driver that day was no different than any other I had seen during my time in Nepal; no older than twelve by the looks of him. I wasn't overly worried about his age, as he agreed to take me the ten miles or so to the airport for the low price of one hundred and fifty rupees. I watched Kathmandu zoom by through the dusty window, wondering when I would return to this place. The helicopters still hovered above, seemingly multiplying in the cloudless sky.

'Kathmandu Hearty Welcomes Members of SAARC,' read one sign hanging from a pedestrian bridge over a roadway. I smiled as it brought back memories of the numerous spelling errors I had seen over the past five months. What the hell was SAARC, anyway? I had no clue.

"Hey, what exactly was that sign?" I asked, leaning on the seat in front of me, almost taking it off its hinges in the process.

"Nepal is most welcoming Presidents, Prime Ministers and members of Royal Families. South Asian Association for Regional Co-operation," he answered in between a couple sharp jerks of the steering wheel that sent me tumbling across the back seat.

"That can't be easy when the whole country is in a state of emergency, huh?" I asked from a half-horizontal position, struggling to pull myself up. He glared at me through the rearview mirror, from which hung a rather sizeable photo of the king, but said nothing.

Although young and inexperienced with pricing, my chauffeur had already acquired the requisite physical instincts to drive in such a chaotic country. We sped through traffic, weaving, honking, U-turning, basically performing every illegal activity possible to accomplish in a moving vehicle. We had just turned off a main road to take an apparent shortcut when we met a long line of cars all crammed into one back alley, all apparently trying to use the same 'shortcut'. We waited a few minutes, just long enough for my driver to unleash a few tirades of multiple obscenities worthy of a much older man about everything that was wrong with Kathmandu, Nepal, Nepalese people, people in general, and global warming. I tried to assure him that I wasn't in much of a hurry, that for once in my life I had given myself plenty of time to get to the airport. He either didn't understand or just didn't care, bouncing and hopping the little hatchback into reverse, narrowly missing another taxi and ricocheting off a concrete wall, all while trying to find some miraculously placed portal that would lead to the airport.

Discussions with other drivers through rolled-down car windows revealed that the military had completely sealed off access for any vehicle within a three mile radius of the airport. Informing the public of the situation beforehand must have proved too difficult, or else just not important enough. I contemplated my situation over a cigarette, as did many of my vehicle-bound neighbors. The man beside me enjoying his smoke informed me it was about three miles to the airport. Deciding there was no point in sitting around watching my driver work himself into a frenzy, no matter how amusing it was, I grabbed my bags and told him I was walking.

"No, no," he replied, shaking his head emphatically. "Much too far, sir. Much, much too far."

"How much do I owe you?" I asked, expecting a discounted price since I clearly had not reached the agreed-upon destination.

"One hundred and fifty rupees, sir."

"What? But I'm still three miles away from the bloody airport."

"Sir, I cannot be responsible for governments. I take you to airport as we agreed, it take some time, sir."

'You're kidding me,' I thought. My final haggle of the trip, and it had come to this. I had neither the time nor the patience to continue the discussion, so without another word I handed him the requested sum and started walking.

It was a brilliant day, all things considered; bright and sunny with just a few billowy white clouds gracing the azure sky. Under normal circumstances, a damn fine day for a walk. A few hundred yards and the alcohol sweat of an eighty year old drunkard began pouring out of me; I could practically smell the tongbas. I managed to drag my belongings down the street and into the junction of Airport Road, where I joined many other hopeful flyers who had also decided that the only way to make takeoff was to ditch the cabs and set off on foot. Much to our collective dismay, we were told by a group of large Nepalese soldiers that we would have to continue our journey through the ditches on the side of the road.

"Nobody allowed walking on or near Airport Road," the biggest said aloud in Nepali before translating into several other languages. Soldiers guarded the entire length of the road to the airport proper, stretching a good mile or more in the opposite direction, too. They stood, guns in hand, visually dissecting everyone who walked past. The ditch where we were made to walk was downright grotesque, as any ditch in a country like Nepal would be. Further away from the soldiers, the ditch transformed into a patchy strip of land travelling the length of the road. Most of the pedestrians, myself included, chose to take this route. Still muddy, but at least you didn't have to worry about stepping into a shit-filled hole a yard deep.

An elderly man followed close behind my group. So close, in fact, that I started to convince myself that he was following me. I turned once and smiled, which he returned with a wide grin, his upper lip curling. Had we met before?

Fleets of limousines and military vehicles passed us on the forbidden road. With each passing vehicle, I could feel the tension and anger mounting in the crowd around me. Constantly trying to rearrange my bags to a more comfortable position while avoiding as much of the dirt and shit as I could became my main priority. Traipsing along the dirt road, I must have looked like a white porter hired by my fellow ditch-dwellers to transport all their belongings to the airport. In a country famous for their porters, I must have looked quite the sight.

Several pints of tongba-flavored sweat and an enriched understanding of Nepalese curse words later, I finally found myself a few hundred yards from the main gate of the airport, where a huge crowd waited not so patiently to get in. The military buildup grew closer towards the main gate; the soldiers there stood next to each other, looking less than pleased.

Now that the trek was over, the old man behind me had grown visibly furious, letting the soldiers know exactly what he thought of them, both orally and physically. He repeatedly attempted to cross the barrier of soldiers and make his way onto the road, each time in vain. With every procession of limousines, Hummers or military vehicles that passed, a great satirical cheer rang out from the crowd. Everyone smiled, waved, and muttered what I presumed to be 'Fuck off' in their respective tongues. Others raised their fists in anger.

It occurred to me that I still had some hash on me, a few little nuggets the size of deer droppings jammed in my cigarette pack. My heart leapt at the thought of it, forgotten amongst all of the day's excitement. Looking around surreptitiously, I noticed that this was likely the worst spot to dump the stuff. There were soldiers everywhere and thousands of eyes staring at the pasty-looking foreigner who was already sweating like he was guilty of something truly heinous.

Setting my pack down on the dusty ground, I rummaged through it to locate my beedis. I took one unwanted smoke out and put it to my lips, then reached into my pocket while fiddling with the hash inside the pack, making it look as though I was searching for a lighter. Breaking the hash up into smaller pieces that I could get rid of more easily, I pushed some up towards my wrist. When I pulled the lighter out, I dragged the smaller bits of hash along with it. This took a few attempts, and involved one extra beedi that I really did not need with my hangover, but I managed to complete the job.

Despite myself, I began to feel compassion for the soldier who had become the sole target of the stubborn old man's diatribe. Again I asked myself if we had met before; we made eye contact and he grinned that same sardonic grin. The soldier stood upright, taking the abuse without retaliation. After each volley of abuse, the elderly man would eventually get tired of yelling at the soldier and slowly make his way back towards the crowd, kicking, spitting, and cursing the ground. On his final attempt at showing his disapproval for the whole situation, he went down the ditch once more and up the other side towards the road. The soldier once again blocked his way. He said in English, tiredly, "Sir, please stop trying to make your way to the airport. You will be allowed to cross shortly."

To which the old man replied, "No, my brother! I am not moving! Shoot me here if you wish!"

The ever-gathering crowd strained to hear the soldier's answer. There wasn't one. A large military officer wearing a sports coat emblazoned with medals and other useless pomp, who was carrying an even larger gun than the soldier, made his way over to the elderly man. Grabbing him by the arm, he dragged the ancient back to the side of the road. The officer gave him a shove and the old man tumbled into the ditch, landing in the dirt and shit and God knows what else.

"No compromise, then?" yelled the old man, sitting on his knees, wiping the shit from his face.

"There are no compromises in security! No compromises!" barked the officer. A few travelers rushed to help the old man to his feet. He said not a word after that, nor did anyone else in the crowd.

One last limousine procession went by and we were finally cleared to go. The soldiers remained silent before at last departing in a fleet of four by fours and an assortment of other military vehicles. Only the helicopters remained. As most of the crowd dashed for the airport entrance, making it impossible to move for at least a few minutes, I stood still and kept an eye on the old man. He didn't show defeat as one might have expected; rather, he seemed calm and stoic, as if he knew he would be victorious in the end. The deep, dirt-encrusted lines in his face showed a life that was tough, brave, and patient. I watched him for as long as I could before he was swallowed up by the crowd.

Chapter 16

The plane touched down through the early morning sky, and ten minutes before the scheduled landing time to boot. I sat next to a rather large American whose name was Mark, "Mark from Seattle," he specified emphatically while shaking my hand in his much bigger one. Mark had the window seat, leaving me to squeeze into the middle, as a little old ancient who had her eyes shut and her mouth set in a firm line, announcing an all-too-clear 'don't talk to me', occupied the aisle seat.

"So, what brings you to Toronto, Mark?" I ventured after allowing a few moments of silence to lapse in the wake of his initial bombardment of information.

"Headed to a convention. Vacuum convention."

I honestly thought he was taking the piss. "I had no idea such things actually took place."

"Yep. It's an annual event. Seattle and Toronto rotate yearly to host it." Taking in my incredulous look, he pressed on. "They're good fun. The vacuum world's a lot more exciting than you might think. And you boys in Toronto really show us Americans a good time."

"Well, happy days then."

"Yeah, this year should be good," he said, using a worn handkerchief to mop away the sweat that glistened on his brow, trickling down into his greying sideburns. "New product coming out this year. Our designers over in India have come up with something that will revolutionize what we think of when it comes to vacuuming."

"India?"

"Oh, yeah. Them boys over there really know what they're doing," he said, punctuating his words with another swab at the sweat on his broad face. "Cheap as fuck as well, if you don't mind me saying so."

"Doesn't bother me," I told Mark from Seattle, wishing fervently that he would simply sit back, close his eyes and fall into a determined nap like the old lady on my other side.

"Yeah, those boys in India," Mark set in again. "Do you realize that the number of university graduates in India is the same as it is in America? Problem over there, though, is that it's still developing. They'll surpass us Americans when it comes to standard of living before I die, you can rest assured of that. America has too much of a masculine mentality, you know, Uncle Sam and the whole bit, whereas other countries refer to their homeland as a woman. Nurturing and giving, all that shit. It's as simple as that."

I pictured him performing a vacuum demonstration in front of a potential client, sweat running down his portly face, the stink of cigarettes wafting off him, declaring, "You see, it's as simple as that."

"I suppose you're right." I didn't particularly feel like indulging in talk of my time in India, lending further fuel to his conversational fire.

"This new thing they've got going is like a controlled tornado, you see. Truly amazing. You know how cyclones suck everything up from the ground and toss it all over the place?" Making a rotating motion above his head with his hands, he then proceeded to flick all ten of his sausage-like fingers in every direction once he couldn't raise his arms any further (which wasn't very high, thank Vishnu). "You see, it's just like that. There's a lot more to it, mind you. Patented technique, too; no one can reproduce this. Going to make us millions."

After a slightly unnatural pause involving more brow-mopping from Mark and some seat-fidgeting from me, I asked, "So Mark, you married?" I wasn't entirely sure why I settled on that of all questions; possibly my subconscious checking up on the state of natural selection.

"Was, two times now. Will be again, too, no doubt. First wife ran off with a co-worker of mine. I was shocked, that much I will say. Heartbroken..." He paused, turning to look out the window. "No," he continued, shaking his head and breaking out into an almost manic grin as he faced me again. "Can't say I really was."

The cabin crew began running through the emergency instructions with all the enthusiasm of a gravedigger nearing the end of his career.

"Second wife, now, she was different. Wonderful woman she was. Loved her to bits. I still recall waking up in the morning to the smells of coffee brewing and vegetarian bacon sizzling in the frying pan. Every morning she made me breakfast, for six years without fail."

"Veggie bacon?" Come off it, now. Next he would be telling me he did yoga.

"Yeah, she was a vegetarian. Fit as a gymnast, she was. Me, on the other hand...Well, let's just say I love bacon, ham, chicken, steak, moose. Hell, I even like snake, but for her I would eat veggies. What I never told her was that every morning after breakfast I would stop at McDonald's on my way to the office and grab two sausage McMuffins. Didn't have the heart to tell her. She was trying to make me better, you know, but it would never work. Women go into a marriage thinking they'll change their man. Men go into a marriage hoping their woman'll never change. It's as simple as that."

The plane reversed, taxied, and readied for takeoff. The seatbelt sign overhead pinged, seemingly marking the end of Mark's spiel. I was glad he'd chosen this moment to be quiet, because the only part of flying that I do enjoy is takeoffs; the way the whole vessel falls silent, everyone absorbed in their own little world, their own good, bad, terrible, brilliant, and possibly horrific thoughts.

I thought about Skye at the moment I lurched back in my seat, head pinned to the headrest as the plane lifted its nose and began its slow climb through the clouds.

"Tracy was her name," Mark from Seattle continued, as if he had only stopped to scratch an itch. "Loved her to bits, I really did. But like I said, she wanted to change me, and I wasn't for changing."

Mark continued his verbal autobiography for the next two hours. The only thing that halted him (albeit temporarily) was when the air stewards came around to serve the meals. The topic of conversation did switch to me now and again, but I kept my distance. I wasn't in the mood to talk, but listening to Mark go on and on kept my mind occupied.

After the pilot informed us that we would be descending in just a few minutes, I excused myself from Mark's thrilling narrative and made my way to the restroom. Giving myself a once-over in the mirror, I figured that for having spent the entirety of the previous night trying to sleep on a plane and most of this day stuck on another, I didn't look half bad.

"Home," I said aloud to my reflection. Nothing stirred inside me. Feeling like I might have just failed some sort of test, I made my way back to my seat. For the first time during the flight, I allowed my eyes to drift shut. Expecting Skye to appear, or some distant memory of home that had found its way to the big screen of my mind, instead there was nothing, just one massive blank. I tried to capture an image tied to some emotion, conjure up some feeling, but I was apparently void of anything. My ears popped from the change in cabin pressure. Peering around Mark from Seattle's enormous girth, I caught my first glimpse of home as the plane glided over Highway 401.

Going through customs proved to be more complicated than expected. There were plenty of forms to be filled out, the questions on many of them eliciting a total blank in my mind. How much money I had made while overseas? What were the names and addresses of my past employers? Which countries had I visited and how long had I spent there? Had I been to Asia? Had I been in contact with any animals while in Asia? What were my plans now that I was returning to Canada? Where would I be staying? Had I been hospitalized or had any vaccinations since leaving the country? Had I fallen ill during my travels? What were the dimensions of my penis? How big were the men's penises in India and in the other countries I had visited? Had I slept with an Asian while traveling abroad? How would I rate the experience? What is the square root of all the whores in Calcutta divided by the amount of gay men giving hand jobs in the theatre toilets of Amsterdam?

I lied in response to most of the questions. No, I hadn't been sick. Yes, I had been to Asia, but no, I never even so much as laid eyes on an animal there. I worked at such-and-such pub and this-and-that restaurant on more than one occasion. Seven and one third inches. Three inches. See previous answer. The entire world revolves around bullshit, so why was I expected to be any different?

The time it took me to fill out all the forms resulted in me missing the last bus going my way. I did, however, learn the valuable lesson that Pearson International Airport is not exactly backpacker-friendly. I considered sleeping in the airport lobby but in the end decided against it. It just didn't seem right somehow, now that I was so close to home. Grabbing my bag, I made for the rental car booths. All of the rental companies had pretty much the same to offer, but the drop-off fee for not returning the car to the same office took the price into digits that I couldn't handle at that point in my worldly wanderings. I gave up and walked over to the hotel reservations kiosk. I found a hotel that was relatively close by and even had a pick-up service. I picked up the receiver of the shockingly clean public phone and pushed the button to connect me to reception.

"Hello?" I asked when I heard the click of someone picking up on the other end.

"Hello?" they responded through crackling static. Clearly a bad connection.

"I was just wondering if you guys have any rooms available tonight. And pick-up service, if it's still going?"

"Oh, well, yes, we do have a room available. But, uh, well, the service has ended for the day. I'm afraid the driver's gone home, eh?" Her Canadian accent hit me hard; I was home. My heart lurched a little in my chest. "But, uh, I could come get you, I suppose. You're at the airport?" she asked. I confirmed that I was, to which she replied, "I thought so. The connection there is horrible."

I smiled, thanking her and letting her know the terminal number where I would be waiting.

"I'll be there in twenty minutes," she said before hanging up.

This wasn't how I pictured spending my first day back in Canada, but I had no choice. I waited outside smoking a beedi and getting strange looks from travelers and airport staff alike. The woman from the hotel arrived in exactly twenty minutes. I threw my bag in the backseat of her Cavalier and jumped in the passenger seat. She seemed older than her youthful voice over the phone had conveyed.

I checked into the hotel, and couldn't help thinking how long I would be able to live off of the cost of one night here if I were back in Nepal. I dropped my bags unceremoniously on the floor of room 203, flicked on the television, and slumped onto the bed. I lay looking up at the ceiling, ignoring the television. It felt strange to be in a room defined by so many comfort features. It seemed like witchcraft that I could adjust the room temperature to exactly my liking and the water in the taps could be dispensed as hot or as cold as I liked. There were more TV stations than could be found in all of Nepal, I was certain, and the bed smelled of laundry soap. More towels than I would ever need hung from the polished racks. An assortment of toiletries, each individually wrapped donned the sink counter. This was the over-sanitized, pre-packaged, high-tech world I had once called home. All I could do was lay there on the bed staring up at the stucco ceiling and wonder why there wasn't a very noisy oscillating fan directly above me, just out of reach of a ratty mosquito net.

I wanted a beer. It had been years since I'd had a good, strong Canadian beer and I couldn't wait any longer. I could practically taste it in my throat, and I couldn't see myself getting comfortable in my room anytime soon. Splashing some water on my face, I went downstairs to see where I could find a drink. The woman at reception told me that the restaurant in the hotel sold beer, but that it was now closed for the night.

"But, there's a sports bar across the road."

I headed outside and looked around. The sky above was clear, and the air was crisp. I hadn't thought of bringing a jacket, but seeing as it was only across the road, I decided to ignore the slight chill. The hotel, being so close to the airport, was on a road built for cars and not for people. The street was wide, wider than some of the villages I had been through on my travels. A divider ran the gut of it, making it impossible to cross anywhere but at the traffic stop. Off I marched to the distant yet beckoning flashing lights.

I opened the door to the sports bar. The place wasn't busy and a sprightly young waitress came over and asked if I wanted something to eat as the kitchen was soon closing. I told her I would, if it wasn't too much trouble. She then grabbed a menu with irritated eyes and handed it to me. I sat at the bar and scanned the fridge behind the barman.

"What can I get ya?" he asked, eyes glued to the television. There was a game on the elevated, illuminated box.

"I'll have a Moosehead."

He dried his hands on a towel and retrieved a green bottle from the fridge. He grabbed from the back, as he must have just stocked up for the night.

"And can I get a chicken caesar as well, please?"

I took a sip from my beer, moving it around in my mouth before swallowing. It was good. Really good. My watering hole danced a happy little jig, shouting in pleasure that I had done well.

"So, who you goin' for then, eh?" the barman asked, nodding to the television.

"I don't know who's playing."

"Hockey, buddy. You don't watch hockey?"

I hadn't seen a game in almost three years and it had never really occurred to me to pay attention to it when I was outside of Canada. "Sorry man, but it's been a while. Haven't really paid much attention lately." And with that, our very short conversation was over. If I didn't understand hockey, then there was no point for him to talk to me. Our meeting would be strictly business. I turned in my chair and glanced up at the screen. I had no idea who the two teams were. Directly under the screen was a large table with six girls who all seemed intoxicated. A round of shots waited on the table, but they too busy drunkenly swaying to the Bon Jovi that was playing over the speakers. With every 'Blaze of Glory' they would mime the lyrics with imaginary microphones while beating and grabbing at their hearts as if in real pain.

My food arrived in record time, as it was obviously the last meal the cooks had to prepare. They had forgotten to put chicken on it, but I didn't care. I ate in silence, looking out the window to my left.

I was home, but it didn't really feel like home. It still hadn't really hit me. Maybe having that back-home feeling would take some more time. I didn't know. I thought about Skye and what she was doing at that moment. I thought of her hands, and her fingers that she always decorated with the most exquisite rings. And her piercing in her chin that somehow accentuated her perfect smile. I thought about how I would wake up every morning with her pressed up against me as if during the night, in order for her to sleep, she had to be as close to me as possible. It made my heart warm thinking of her, and although we were thousands of miles away, I sensed she was thinking the same thing. I smiled at the thought as I finished the last of my beer.

Jumping off my stool, I grabbed my bill from the counter. As I turned, one of the girls from the table behind came over and put her arm around my neck. Her breath smelling like a mix of Jagermeister and cigarettes, and with eyes incapable of focusing on a fixed point, she slurred, "Where you going, handsome?"

"Just across the road," I answered, pointing to the door.

"You staying at the hotel, too? So are we," she said, looking in the direction of her drunken companions, who all stared back at the two of us. "Tomorrow we're off to...uh...shit." She looked again to her friends and slurred, "Where the fuck we going tomorrow?"

"Cancun!" they yelled in unison.

"Ah, that's right." She was swaying now as she spoke. "Cancun. What are you doing over there, handsome?" Again handsome? Clearly more drunk than I thought.

"I'm on my way home, actually. Been gone for a while."

"Oh, yeah? Where you been then?"

I wasn't in the mood to discuss my life story, and she wasn't going to remember any of it anyway.

"Was in Europe, then off around, well, Asia."

She looked back at her friends with a big smile on her face as I spoke. She wasn't listening to me at all.

"So, maybe we should just go back to the hotel together then, eh?" I could see black stains on her t-shirt from a misguided attempt at drinking.

"Look, I'm sorry, but I just need some rest. You girls seem to be doing just fine without me."

"Are you fucking serious?" she asked, her already-shrill voice rising painfully, right in my ear.

"Sorry, I have to get up early, you see, and..."

Her arm tightened around my neck as though she was about to hit me. She leered at me for a moment, looking into my eyes, and for a split second I thought I saw them focus. Then she smiled and let go of me. She didn't say anything. She turned and staggered back to her giddy friends. Relieved, I quickly walked to the register and settled my bill with the waitress, spritely once again now that the bar was closing up for the night. I didn't look up until I was outside the bar.

I fell onto the bed fully clothed. The room was still, not a sound to be heard. Not one hint of life outside the walls of the soulless chamber. It was a tomb of sorts, my tomb, fully stocked with all the comforts of home, yet still it seemed naked, dead. Acclimatizing to the mountain air of the Annapurnas felt easier than slipping back into Western civilization.

Chapter 17

I stood staring at the house where I had spent most of my childhood. It appeared exactly the same, from the color of the door to the patchy flower garden next to the porch. But somehow, it was different. It was simply a house, no longer a home.

It was the middle of the afternoon and the chances of someone being home were slim, but I rang the doorbell anyway. Whatever had happened to my keys? There was no ceremony, no letter of warning, not even a post-it note on the fridge. I was suddenly a stranger, standing on the porch like an unwanted visitor.

Not so much of a stranger that I forgot the spare key hidden rather conspicuously in the mailbox. After dumping my bags in the foyer, I headed off on a tour of the old neighborhood. It was a beautiful, clear day but cold, much colder than I remembered spring in southern Ontario. My father's place was on the outskirts of the city. I started towards the river, where I used to swim as a child.

I had been gone for three years, not the longest of times to be away from home, but enough for the inner mechanism that determines where "home" is to be permanently modified. On the other side of the river began the city proper, where all the homes were basically identical. It was a blue-collar area where everything and everyone had some association with the automobile industry. Before embarking on my globetrotting jaunt I had, much to the disbelief of many family members and friends, quit the steady and surprisingly lucrative job of putting bolts on engines. How I could just pack up and go, leaving behind such a relatively mindless yet high-paying gig, was mind-boggling to most in my hometown, who thought that putting bolts on engines for the rest of one's life was the best thing for any self-respecting citizen to do. Sixteen-plus years of schooling and that was the best the place could offer me.

I bought a large coffee and the local newspaper at a corner store whose prior existence I couldn't recall. The flavorless coffee was disappointing at best after the chai I'd enjoyed in India and Nepal, but the automotive section of the paper served nicely as a seat on the grassy riverbank. I crossed my legs and took in the goings-on of my hometown: some local twins had had their bicycles stolen. The corner of Tennoji and Ouellette was designated as the most accident-prone intersection in the city, tallying a grand total of five, beating out its closest competitor by four. A local politician was seen covertly exiting one of the many downtown strip bars in a state of complete intoxication. Fascinating stuff.

By the time I wandered back to my dad's place, his car was in the driveway and I could make out the faint glow of lamplight from the living room. "Kiddo!" my father bellowed as he opened the door. He then stepped forward and embraced me harder than I had expected. "Three years is a long time," he said, finally releasing me from his bear hug.

"Yeah, sorry about that."

"No you're not." He smirked, his head tilted a bit to the side, as if trying to pinpoint something about me that was off. "I had no idea you were coming home. When did you get back?"

"Just got back last night." I stepped passed him, and he placed his hand on my shoulder. "Changed the color of the walls, I see."

"Yep, twice since you've been away. You know your mother always has to be doing something." He always referred to my stepmother as 'your mother', which I found a little insulting to my real mother, who was very much alive and kicking and inhabiting the same city. "So, what's been happening, kiddo? One e-mail a year isn't much to go on, you know."

"Well, I might as well tell you now. I'm not planning on staying very long. Thinking of heading back to Nepal," I told him as I took a seat on the new couch, doubtlessly part of my stepmother's most recent redecorating rampage. Dad sat down across from me in his favorite old armchair. At least some things remained the same.

"Well, how long is long? I suppose you'll be taking off as soon as we get used to seeing your face around here again." He was irritated and I felt bad for telling him straight off.

"I've got enough money to get me back there, but that's about it. I was hoping to find some work here, save up a bit and then get a move on as soon as possible."

He stood up as fast as he had sat down and, without speaking, made his way to the kitchen. I heard the fridge door open, followed by a dull clink of glass and the hiss of two bottles being opened.

"What's this?" I asked as he returned and handed me a Keith's. "You don't drink beer."

"I started to a couple years ago. One beer at your uncle's place watching the game turned into two, then three, then four. Before I knew it I was calling your mother to come pick me up. It's weird, for fifty-three years I never liked the taste of beer, then all of a sudden I started enjoying it. Now I always keep a few in the fridge for when guests stop by. Cheers." He raised his bottle and I clinked mine against it with an appreciative nod. So now I was a guest. It was official. I knew he didn't really mean it that way, but it still kind of stung.

"So, what's this about going back to Nepal, then?"

"I'm going to volunteer, dad." He tilted his head awkwardly to the side again, and this time I got the distinct impression that he thought something was wrong with me, something he couldn't quite put his finger on. "I'm gonna check out different opportunities online. Might try somewhere else, though. Nothing's set in stone yet." I wasn't about to tell him, my mother, or anyone else at home about the Maoist situation in Nepal. About the dead body I'd tripped over, the uprisings, the abandoned hotels, the military-supervised trek to the airport.

"So why Nepal, if you've been there already? You know, for a minute there I thought you were going to say you were off to Australia to see that girl you wrote about."

"Well, I thought of that. But I feel like I need to do this now, see where it takes me. See if it makes me a better person."

"What's wrong with who you are now?"

"Nothing," I paused, picking at the label on the beer bottle. "Well, nothing really. It's just that I haven't really done anything with myself since I left here. Saw a bit of the world, which is all well and good, but I also saw how shitty things are in some parts of it. I just have this gut feeling that I should be doing something more."

"When did this all come about?" He took a sip of beer, his brow tensed. "You can't solve the world's problems by yourself, you know."

"I know. I have to do this, though, and I have to do it now." I took a swig of beer and glanced out the window at the elongating shadows cast by the still-leafless trees. "Not sure how I'll know when I'm a better person, anyhow." I hadn't phrased it as a question, but I found myself looking into my dad's eyes expectantly, as if the answer was to be found in this graying version of my potential future self.

"Son, the only thing I can say is that you'll never be exactly the person you want to be."

"Yeah, well. I'm tired of being who I've been. What about you? Are you the person you wanted to be?"

"Well, I'm happy, that much I can say. I'm sure as hell not perfect, but who is?"

My father was now staring at me in earnest, his look many times more searching than the one I'd given him a moment earlier. Rather than maintain eye contact, I looked towards the mantle, where four framed photographs that had been there for as long as I could remember stared back at me: one of my graduation portraits from some early year of elementary school (I couldn't remember which one), and clustered around it three other silver-ringed frames housing smiling brown faces, two of them missing teeth, one missing an eye. My father had been sponsoring children around the world since my own childhood. "What about them?" I asked, nodding at the three portraits, not realizing how vague my question sounded. Maybe it was the beer, although, looking down, I realized the bottle was only a quarter empty. Looking at those little faces brought up a surge of panic and confusion, which I did my best to swallow down with another swig of beer.

"Does it make me a better person?" he asked. I nodded. "Well, sure. Any act of kindness helps make you a better person, and I'm not just talking in terms of money, here."

"I suppose that's why I have this feeling now. I can't afford to give with my wallet, so I'll have to give with myself, my time."

"Yeah, well," he said, finishing off his beer. "You gotta do what you gotta do, right kiddo? I had thought this whole travelling thing was going to stabilize you a bit, though, to be honest. Not to mention this People's War business. Is it really safe over there? Looks like you made it out OK." It seemed he was finally tired of all the 'nice' talk. "You look different somehow, though. Not physically, really. Just...different. You are OK, though, right?"

"Yeah, I am. Honestly, there isn't much to say about the People's War. The Maoists leave the tourists alone, you know. For the most part, anyway. But going back to the whole finding myself thing..." I wanted to change the subject, and fast. "That's just it. There's still so much more for me to do."

"Your mother's not going to be happy, you know."

He was talking about my stepmother, Amy, again. They'd been married for about six years, and I'd been gone for three of them. I liked her just fine, and she liked me, but we weren't exactly close. He must have noticed the look on my face as I pondered this, wondering whether Amy would really be that bothered by me taking off again, because he added, "Your real mother, I mean. We've gotten back in touch, you know. I ran into her outside the grocery store one day and we got to talking again."

"What does Amy have to say about all this?" I asked, not quite able to keep the surprise out of my voice.

"It doesn't bother her at all. Hell, she even encouraged it. Said it would be better for you. But, you know, I'm a stubborn old man," he smiled.

Sitting there watching my father, I noticed how the years had changed him. His hair was now almost completely grey. He had put on some weight, too, at least twenty pounds. But nursing his beer in his chair across from me, he seemed more complacent and content than he had ever been. Maybe getting older does that to a person.

We sat for the next hour talking about everything I'd missed over the past few years. I had a new baby cousin, and a distant relative had been sent to prison for robbing a Laundromat (which had made the front page of the local paper, setting the family name back ninety years, according to my grandmother. "She's getting a little confused these days," my father felt the need to mention).

I told him the stories I could tell, and toned down some that I should have probably kept to myself. Not a bad way to spend my first evening back home; by the time I grabbed my bags and headed downstairs to the spare room, I was smiling to myself, partly the slight buzz from the beer and partly because I was honestly glad to be back.

After dinner that night (Amy's homemade pizza and a few more beers), my father settled into the couch to watch the game and Amy went to research her next project, which, I was told enthusiastically at dinner, was a total makeover of the backyard.

I spent most of the night parked in front of my dad's ancient desktop computer, checking out various volunteer programs in Nepal and South America, just for the hell of it. With a few beers under my belt, they all sounded interesting, even downright thrilling. I sent off e-mails to a couple of programs straightaway, the ones that immediately seemed legit. Having yet to pop my volunteer cherry or meet anyone else who had, I was left to my own devices. Some of the programs I was interested in listed personal e-mail addresses of prior volunteers, so I wrote to a few of them asking for any information they could give me. My electronic enquiries finished for the night, I phoned my mother and made arrangements to meet the next day.

The next morning, after eating a solitary breakfast of over-sweetened cereal and orange juice, I decided to try out the treadmill that had been placed in my old room immediately following my departure. The room had been painted, and all of the markings that had once made the room my own had been wiped away, even the remnants of masking tape and sticky tack I thought would be there until the house fell down. It didn't make for the happiest of atmospheres, and after ten minutes or so I didn't have it in me to exercise. I was out of breath anyway, so I took a quick shower and waited for my mother to arrive, transferring some photos onto my father's computer. At half past twelve I heard a car horn outside, two quick bursts that had been my mother's trademark as far back as I could remember.

When I walked onto the front step, I could see that my mother was already in tears, peering over the steering wheel, which she held in a white-knuckled grip.

"Mom," I shouted, waving at her. "Come on in. Have a look at some photos."

"I can't, son. And I don't think I want to, anyway," she said through a hitched sob and the rolled down window.

It hadn't occurred to me that she wouldn't want to enter my father's house. To me, my parents were always Marilynn and Don (never the other way around, for some reason), and whatever one owned was the other's, too. Then one day, just before I graduated from high school, my father came home and told my mother he had quit his teaching position at Henry S. Shallow High School, where he had been a faculty member for twenty years.

Around this time, dad was also a member of the Strikers, a bowling team who had bowled ten-pin together since they were in elementary school. After winning an impressive number of tournaments, he was persuaded by some of his teammates to take it up full time, which he did, promptly leaving behind his teaching career. My mother did not take this news terribly well. After a year on the road, he returned home with the stunning news that he'd taken up with a pretty young scorekeeper on the circuit. Before you could say 'seven-ten split,' my mother had her things packed and was living with her sister, while I stayed on with Mr. Champion Bowler and his new partner. Their time on the circuit didn't last long, though; my father, despite his talent, never made a cent on the tour and Amy grew tired of the constant travel that was a prerequisite for scorekeeping for the PBA. The old man returned to teaching and Amy started a new job as an airline representative answering phones in a call center.

I ran back inside and grabbed the first two photo discs I saw. Mom got out of her car as I locked the door behind me. I walked over to her and she flung her arms around me, practically jumping on top of me. "I missed you, I missed you," she repeated through her tears. Despite the fact that I had been gone for almost three years, I was surprised by all the emotion. After having been away for so long, it seemed everything was bubbling to the surface.

"I missed you, too," I told her, tightening my arms around her. We stood in my father's driveway for quite some time, to the point where I felt compelled to say, "Mom, I think you can let go now."

She pulled away begrudgingly and punched me lightly on the arm. "And you know you deserve that," she said, anger creeping into her voice. "Three years and only a handful of e-mails! No way to treat your mother, you know."

"Yeah, I know mom, I know. Things got pretty crazy over there. I had some trouble with immigration."

"That's no excuse, and you know it, mister." She held my gaze sternly. "What's with you?" she said suddenly, putting her hand to my face, her warm, motherly fingers gripping my cheek and turning my head gently from side to side. "Something's going on with you."

"It's nothing, come on now." I touched her forearm, not quite meeting her eyes. "How about letting me drive?" I asked, moving my free hand towards the keys dangling from her left index finger.

She let go of my face. "Well, you're not exactly asking, now, are you?" she answered, already making her way to the passenger side.

"It's been awhile. And besides that, you're a mess. What would happen if you had another crying fit in traffic, eh? We'd both be goners."

Her Ford Tempo refused to start right away, so I pumped the gas pedal a few times.

"Well, where to first?" I asked, pulling out of the driveway.

"Let's go to my place. I want to see your pictures and talk to you. I missed you, you know."

"Yeah, mom. I know."

I felt like a tourist driving the streets of my hometown. I almost got lost before I spotted the movie theatre where I had seen my first horror movie (and my first naked woman).

As we sat at her kitchen table, having made our way through the two discs of photos in quick succession, my mother bombarded me with questions. Over the course of two hours and as many cups of coffee, I recounted most of my time away. She listened intently and never interrupted. Though she showed great attention in regards to Skye. Upon my mention of the few others that I had met very early on in my travels she said,

"Oh, Joseph. You would have fallen for anything with a pretty face and an accent."

I smiled, realizing how much she really did know her son. For a while, at the beginning of my globetrotting adventures, my mother was always the first to know when I had taken up with someone. At that point, the two of us had stayed in touch on nearly a monthly basis.

Having finally placated my mother with my talk of matters geographical and romantic, I found myself standing in the cramped bathroom next to the front door staring at myself in the mirror. "Maybe it's inevitable," I told my reflection. "Maybe thinking about Skye now is just a waste of time. After all, if you really couldn't live without her you'd be on a plane to Australia right now." After washing my hands, I continued my monologue. "But then again, there are other things you want to do, and you'd regret not doing them if you just throw caution to the wind and go running after her." I was thinking too much, partly due to consuming more coffee than I had in months, if not years. But there was something else, too. I wasn't in the habit of partaking in impromptu soliloquys in bathroom mirrors. A soft knock at the door interrupted my train of thought.

"You OK?" my mother asked.

"Of course," I said, turning the knob and stepping into the hall. "Why wouldn't I be?"

"No reason," she said. "Just thought I heard you talking to yourself in there." She followed me back to the kitchen with a sad half-smile on her face.

Upon my mother's insistence that we not stay cooped up in her apartment any longer, we went across the road to her local pub. I knew at some point I was going to have to tell her I was planning on leaving again, and I wasn't looking forward to it. I thought about waiting and telling her in a week, but then thought the better of it with the realization that she might feel even more depressed knowing our time together was even shorter. At that moment, she just seemed too happy. Finally finished her line of questioning about me and my travels, she began to tell me what was going on with her side of the family. I hadn't been in touch with anyone, apart from my grandmother, who was apparently beginning her slow descent away from this world. The only other news of note was that she, my dear old mom herself now had a boyfriend.

"Get the fuck out of here!"

"Language, Joseph," she said, looking around furtively, although the place was practically empty.

"Sorry. Why didn't you tell me sooner?"

"Well," she said, folding her napkin primly in her lap and fiddling with her hands. "It's all just so recent, I thought I'd tell you when you got here. Besides, you weren't exactly easy to contact, now were you?"

"That's great, mom." My words sounded hollow, but I wasn't sure what else there was to say.

"Now, don't get too excited. We've only been out together a few times, but he's a nice man and we get along well."

"How long have you known each other?"

"A few months. We met at a hockey game. We were sitting next to each other and we got to talking after the first period and, well, next thing I knew we were exchanging numbers."

"Holy shit, mom, you got picked up at a game!"

"I did not get picked up," she said, lowering her voice conspiratorially on the last two words, her eyes once again darting around the room. "I met someone, that's all. That's how we're going to word it."

"He shoots, he scores," I muttered.

I could tell my mother half wanted to reach across the table and slap me and half wanted to giggle. She managed to resist both. "Yes, well...how is your father doing, anyway?"

"He's good. He's started drinking."

"What? What do mean, drinking?" She seemed genuinely shocked.

"Not like that, mom. Just a few beers here and there. I was pretty shocked when he took a couple out of the fridge last night."

"Your father never liked beer." This mundane discovery seemed to shake something in her core, and she looked away.

"I know. Funny, eh? He's looking a lot older, too. Looks his age, I should say. You, may I add, look great. You never gave me the chance to say so earlier, but it's true." I meant what I said; she looked as though she hadn't aged a day since I left. Her hair was shorter than I remembered and possibly a shade greyer, but it had kept its luster. She still had a bounce in her step too, one that I noticed as we crossed the street from her apartment.

"Thanks, son. And as for you, you are far too skinny. You've got to start eating more, and there's no use arguing with me about it." She waved the waiter over and, as if to prove her point, told me to order dessert. I happily complied and ordered a hot fudge sundae, which I hadn't had in years.

As I stepped out of the car in my father's driveway, she leaned out of the driver's side window and told me not to make plans for Saturday night.

"You're going to come over for dinner and meet James. And I'm not taking no for an answer."

"Sounds great," I answered over my shoulder as I walked around the car. It seemed I would not be mentioning the volunteering anytime soon, then. It would have to wait until dinner with James.

Chapter 18

Day three I didn't leave the house. A lethargy that no jet-lag could produce enveloped my entire body. After my mother had dropped me off, I opened the door to my father's house, which was already dark, and slowly made my way to the extra bedroom. In the ride over I felt a sleepy uneasiness begin to grow within me. At first thinking it was a caffeine crash, I tried to ignore it, but soon found that I could not. Starting at my feet, it sprouted upwards in short bursts of life, and by the time I had reached my father's steps it was clear I could not control it. Each step to my room it gained with intensity, an unwinnable battle against the claws of this desire to sleep. Inside my room, I had barely removed my shirt before crashing heavily onto the bed and closing my eyes. Every fiber of my being now having lost, it wasn't long before someone pulled the blinds of sleep down and I entered the other world. For fifteen hours I slept without stirring. My room a sepulcher, the sleep of the dead having crept into it and taken over. I dreamt much. Strange, dark dreams that continuously skipped from one to the other, and at times losing me, one moment a character and playing my roll, improvising, but then falling behind and a burden to the scene, an out of time cast-member. The images sped up when I lagged, and I was fully aware of my misgivings. The dreams sped up when I failed to speak and eventually a force stronger than myself angrily pulled me up and out and then forward. Suspended in mid- air, but not air, not our air, but an unworldly air. A black background with no stars, not space. Just black. I watched as the dreams below me flew past, not on a reel, or anything concrete, just suspended floating memories. The powerful force dragged me along in anger, jolting my body back and forth in a deliberate manner. This went on for what seemed like eternity. Upon opening my eyes, I found myself lying in the exact same spot I had fallen the night before. My left cheek was damp from spit, and my jaw ached. My eyelids caked in sleep, tiny nuggets seemingly hung in mid-air, trapped within my lashes. I lay for another hour fully awake but unconvinced there was any reason to move.

When I finally left my room it was past noon and the house was empty. The refrigerator my only companion, a low lonely hum echoed throughout. I wandered about my father's house, consciously aware it was no longer a place I called home and would never be again. Picking up knickknacks that had meaning to both my father and Amy left me blank. I had no idea where they had come from or what they meant to them. Photos of extended family, joyful re-unions that I had missed with cousins I could not even name donned their walls. It felt like walking through a museum, an elaborate display for me to see, to think of, to wish I had been there but was never a part of. Maybe I was talked about. I pictured my father, sipping his new beverage of choice, awkwardly answering queries about his only son. What did he say? What could he have said? I grew wearisome, my body still ached and my joints burned, my limbs sore deep within my tissue. I made it to the front room and collapsed into my father's chair, the burgundy walls of the small room breathed with me. Outside, the white grey sky lacked any real character, promising not a storm, but a reminder of rain. Coming through the window it shaded the room a dull white. Light, but not sun. Rain began to fall and the initial drops, as if in apology, were first soft, a gentle drip upon the earth. My stomach panged for food but I didn't want to move. Ignoring it, I stared out the front window and watched the rain grow with intensity. A steady rhythm that lulled me back to sleep.

Chapter 19

"Now, this is just an aptitude test," Rachel the secretary said almost apologetically, placing a brown envelope and a pen on the table in front of me. "Take your time with it. It's just something we have to do in order to best match our clients with the right people." I picked up the pen wondering if I was the client or the people. "I'll be back in thirty minutes." I looked at the clock and took a long breath.

"All finished?" Rachel asked as she closed the door behind her.

"Yeah, all done," I answered, pushing the exam across the table.

"Right, now Joseph, we have a few positions open, but unfortunately they are all temporary." I nodded, having fully expected her to say that. Temporary meant that I would be a number and that was it. "We happen to have a client who is in desperate need of warehouse laborers. Looking at your exam here, I don't think it would be a problem."

For the next month, I was gainfully employed with the thrilling task of recycling wooden pallets at one of the local factories. My supervisor Martin introduced himself with a halfhearted handshake; a middle-aged man with a thick greyish beard sporting some of his morning's breakfast (eggs), he wasn't the talkative type. I followed him past the twenty-foot stacks of lumber, dust blurring my vision and the woodchips crackling underneath my borrowed boots. Martin led me to the back of the warehouse, where I met my three co-workers; two young men right out of high school and a third, older man who I presumed suffered from a learning disability of some kind.

I was instructed to remove parts from the stacks of used pallets and replace them with parts from another, slightly more gently used stack of pallets. My two younger co-workers kept mostly to themselves, sneaking out back every chance they got to smoke a joint before sauntering back in with wide grins pasted on their dopey faces. One of them confided that Derek, the older guy, did indeed have a disability of some undisclosed kind. Regardless, he managed to double the amount of pallets I restored on my first day.

I was exhausted that evening as I sat at my father's desk staring at the computer screen listening to the screech of the dial-up modem. It wasn't the bone-tired yet exhilarated exhaustion of the Annapurna Circuit trek, but more a mind-numbing, all-enveloping stupor. I was hoping to find an e-mail waiting in my inbox from a couple I had contacted who had volunteer experience in Nepal. It had been a week since my return and I was still riding a travel high, one that faded every morning I woke up without the knowledge of what I would be doing in a month's time. My inbox was empty. I decided to write to Skye.

Hello beautiful.

How is my favorite Australian? Things here are OK. It's weird adjusting to life after being away for so long. How are you coping? I'm thinking about volunteering in Nepal. But then again, maybe I should just come to Australia. I don't know, too many decisions. I managed to get a job here taking apart pallets, which, needless to say, is incredibly stimulating. I should be able to save up enough money in a month or so to get myself to either Nepal or Australia.

Surprised you haven't emailed me yet. It's been a week already, hard as that is to believe.

Missing you lots. Can't stop thinking about our time together.

Love Joseph

My cursor hovered over the send button as I pondered why she hadn't contacted me already.

Chapter 20

My days quickly fell into a routine. Every morning I would rise just early enough to throw on some clothes and stumble out into the driveway where my father waited. Sometimes he was in the driver's seat, sometimes not. Through the window still with morning dew I could see his frame blurred by tiny droplets and I knew which side to walk to. One of us always steered the car south towards the highway. On his way home after his morning walk, the retired neighbor, who was a widower that lived across the street, never failed to wave as we passed. Neither my father nor myself morning people, we commuted in relative silence.

Driving along the highway the sun teased us just below the horizon. My father would put on the radio and make a comment or two about baseball, of which I knew nothing about. I dropped him off in front of his school, earlier than he had to be there I knew, though he never mentioned it. He smiled, wished me a good day and then gently shut the door. Every day I watched him through the rearview mirror as I drove off and noticed he lingered there, a look of concern on his face. And then every day I drove for another twenty minutes watching the sun come up directly in front of me. The sky's pinks and yellows a daily reminder of Nepal. I always stopped at the coffee shop out near the warehouse where I worked and ordered a large coffee. I then smoked cigarettes while sitting in the car waiting for the dashboard clock to tell me it was time to go.

Most of my day was just a waiting game until it was time to leave. My body in motion without much thought as to why. My co-workers kept to themselves, and this did not bother me in the least. Our simple manual labor did not require any communication, though I sometimes found myself in what could be called a conversation with Derek.

My hands first blistered, but then became use to the work, developing small patches of rough skin that if kept up would mature to full callous. Derek had the largest, roughest hands I had ever seen on a human being. His digits swelled with muscle. And they were familiar to me in a way I could not understand, but spent many a lunch hour trying to figure out why.

At night, after dinner I started taking walks. A time I used to clear my head and think about my next move. However, these simple strolls around the block soon flourished into two hour wanders. At dusk's first early showing   I walked down towards the river and watched the ducks dive into the water only to appear moments later downstream. The meandering river calmed me as its gentle waves lightly caressed the river bank. A stark contrast to the angry flow of the Marsyangdi River I had followed for three weeks in Nepal. But the riverside was a popular area for people doing the same, so after a few days I started out in the opposite direction, south towards the highway.

I often stopped at the underpass and smoked a cigarette as the late commuters drove home overhead. The steady rhythm of the wheels rolling over the bumps and cracks of the highway soothed my ears. People in cars passing on the road in front would inevitably stare out their windows, surely wondering why a grown man sat on the side of the road, smoking cigarettes beneath the underpass. When I eventually tired of this I continued my stroll towards the woods a short distance away.

Here the true countryside started. A large forested park used mainly in mornings for dog walkers was the last sign of the city that began near my father's place. Early evening showers often fell while I meandered through the forest. The tall green trees, the lonely dirt paths, and the sensation of the beads rolling down my face so familiar I often stopped in midstride, certain I would locate the memory, but it never came. Amongst the trees, wooden shacks sometimes appeared and then disappeared as the rain grew then withered. I blinked in disbelief, telling myself I was mistaken.

Twice I got lost, finding my way out of the woods just before the sun said its nightly goodbye.

***

With still no light at the end of my proverbial tunnel and the day's last pallet reconstructed, I left work a few minutes early, not finding it in me to care what the time card would read. Derek stuttered something, pointing at the time clock, like it was a bomb about to go off. I left him there watching the clock's long hand tick over.

"You're early, kiddo." My father tossed his briefcase onto the backseat of the car. I had never once seen him open it at home, yet he always brought it with him to and from work.

"Thought I'd take off early. Doesn't seem to matter to them, anyway," I mumbled as I pulled out of the school's parking lot.

"Things at work not going well?" he asked. "This is the second time you've left early this week. Won't they say something?" He craned his neck to scowl at two boys who had just lit up cigarettes on the sidewalk in front of the school. They looked no older than thirteen.

"Dad, I'm fixing pallets, not performing surgery."

"That may be true. But last Thursday you stayed in bed all day playing hooky. Said you weren't even sick. That's not right, you know." I could tell he wanted to push the discussion further, but I didn't think I had it in me. "You know, I could lend you the money to go," he said eventually, still staring out the passenger window.

I was surprised at the offer, but only managed to muster a shake of my head in response.

After a few minutes of silence, he said, "You know, you should call up your old buddies. Go out, spend some time with them. You haven't seen any of them yet, have you?" The thought hadn't crossed my mind.

Two messages waited in my inbox when I got home, one from Ben Tollen, a contact from one of the volunteer websites who lived in New York, and another from Skye. I clicked open hers immediately.

Hi Joseph,

Apologies for not getting back to you sooner, but like you said, it's pretty chaotic adjusting to being back home.

Volunteering sounds like a good idea. You seemed pretty at home in Nepal, like you knew so much for having been there such a short period of time. Uncanny.

Things are pretty difficult here in Australia at the moment. I'm not even sure what I'm going to do with myself, to be honest, so coming all the way over here probably isn't the best idea right now.

Well, I should go. Lots to do, you know. I hope you're well.

Best,

Skye

I re-read her e-mail three times then sat staring at the curser in some kind of a trance. The sudden static buzz of someone turning on the TV in the next room eventually snapped me out of my reverie. Letting out a breath I hadn't realized I'd been holding in, I clicked open Ben's message, my stomach suddenly swimming with a strange, unnamed panic and nervousness.

Greetings Joseph,

I've volunteered in four different countries so far, but my experience in Nepal was probably the best. I wholeheartedly recommend working for this organization; I can't say one negative thing about it. Within three days of landing, I was a veritable fixture in my village, living with a wonderful family who I am still in contact with to this day.

Good luck on your adventure.

Ben Tollen

Well, that seemed to be a good sign. The tension in my shoulders eased as I typed out a missive for the volunteer agency. I thought about re-reading Skye's message before disconnecting for the night, but a moment's reflection told me not to bother. The message had seemed clear enough.

***

I readied myself for a night on the town with the boys. I hadn't seen any of them in over three years and I wasn't quite sure how to present myself. World-weary traveler there for the sole purpose of delighting my acquaintances with endless anecdotes? I doubted I would be keeping them in awe every second; more likely there'd be ten minutes of my travel tales, then right back to the thrilling goings-on of suburban Ontario life.

I met up with Dean first, an old friend I'd known since elementary school. Dean and I had been close growing up, probably the closest friend I'd ever had. We met up at the same intersection where we used to meet when we were kids, roughly the halfway point between our childhood homes and a twenty-five minute walk from the downtown area where we'd be joining another friend.

I could see the smile on Dean's face from fifty feet away. "You motherfucker," he said, gripping me in a bear hug. He was still much larger than I was, and seemed to have put on about fifteen pounds since I'd seen him last.

"How are you, man?" I asked when he finally let go.

"Better than you. What the hell happened to you?" He grabbed my bony waist and squeezed my sides.

"Nothing, what the hell happened to you?" I poked at his rather pronounced gut.

"Wife's cooking," he said proudly, giving his stomach a self-satisfied smack.

Dean had begun an apprenticeship with an electrician right out of high school. Within a few short months he was earning forty-five grand a year. Many in our graduating class had borrowed more than that just to go to university, which Dean was all too quick to point out when he put down half his home's deposit in cash, a cozy two bedroom wartime house not four blocks from where we used to ride our bikes together as kids. He'd married his boss's daughter the previous year. I had yet to meet her.

"We're meeting down at Smiley's," he said as he walked ahead of me, striding eagerly on his longer legs, despite his heavier frame.

We walked into Smiley's, our old hangout, at seven thirty, where tables full of Friday night drinkers were already filling up. The place hadn't changed much; the pool table had a few more stains, the wood flooring had more splinters, and the paint on the walls had a few more distinguishable chips. I looked around trying to remember the good times I had spent in the place. Most of them had been a blur. We went to the bar, ordered a pitcher, and then took a table near the window.

The main drag of what passed for downtown in those parts was a hodgepodge of watering holes, convenience stores, strip clubs, and pizza joints. The ritzier, more well-to-do establishments ran off the main road. Along the main strip were bars with names like 'The Drunken Duck' or 'Pete's Place', and the wine bars and bistros that ran off of it had names like 'Dean Martinis' or 'The Press Club'. The beer was the same no matter where you went; off the drag it just came in a more elaborate glass.

I heard someone call my name from behind. Before I could turn around, I felt clammy hands on my neck; it could only be Andrew, who had the least awareness of personal space of any of my old friends. He squeezed hard enough for me to wince.

"Come here," he bellowed, practically lifting me up out of my seat.

Our awkward exchange finished, he sat down next to me and grabbed my beer glass, finishing it in one long gulp. The waitress leaned over the table to retrieve the empty pitcher, her upper body grazing mine. She gave me a smile as she straightened and sauntered away.

"She wants you," said Andrew, watching her walk away appreciatively. The smoke from his cigarette wrapped him in a thick haze in the dim light of the bar. I noticed his hair was much shorter than I remembered, but his facial features had yet to be affected by Father Time. We were all at that age when adulthood either hits you with a brick, or lightly caresses you with a feather. He was the former. Wearing a suit, with a white shirt unbuttoned down to his chest he scanned the room like he was looking for someone, his large, short neck craning awkwardly. A large silver watch clung to his left wrist.

The bar continued steadily filling up. Small groups of women walked past us, adjusting their miniskirts and strapless tops, their high heels clicking in military unison on the wooden floor. The men strutted over to the bar, the reek of cheap cologne emanating from their crisp, pressed shirts. I was overcome with the urge to get the hell out of there.

The waitress returned with a pitcher and three shots. Dean's cell phone went off and he left the table.

"Wifey," said Andrew, appointing himself group narrator.

"How's that going anyway? He hasn't really mentioned her."

"It was too early, man. She's nice and all, eh. But they don't even know who they are themselves, let alone try to figure someone else out."

Andrew and I finished our tequila shots without Dean. I protested, but it didn't matter. Dean returned and finished his alone, obviously pissed off. It had been like this since as far back as I could remember. When the DJ started playing, we retreated to a further corner of the bar so we could hear ourselves talk. The waitress brought over another round of shots, "On the house," she said with a wink.

"Dude, she wants you," Dean reiterated Andrew's earlier words. As I watched her walk away, she glanced back and smiled coyly. She was cute, with short blonde hair, fair skin and a tiny waist. I thought about mentioning Skye, but couldn't seem to find a way to work her into the conversation.

"Probably just wants a tip," I muttered, taking my shot without waiting for the other two.

A commotion started near the dance floor. Andrew stood up to have a look.

"Something's going on boys," he said, excited at the prospect of a fight.

I sighed. Not much had changed. I watched over Dean's shoulder as the bouncers bounded towards the ruckus, dragging two men out of the bar. Three women in very short skirts trailed after them, yelling obscenities at the waitress as they stumbled out to join their male counterparts.

"Never fucking changes, buddy," Dean said with a smile when he caught me staring absently after the little group.

We left Smiley's at Andrew's orders and walked over to Dean Martinis. Waiting outside, a waitress who had applied geisha-like levels of makeup smiled and told us we had to wait.

"I fucking hate waiting," said Andrew, flipping his cell phone open. He took a few steps away from us.

Dean gave me a look. "Been like this for a while now. He makes good money, and he knows it. Lucky bastard."

"Why are we going here, again?"

"It's where Andrew hangs out now," Dean confided. "He buys the drinks, so I follow where he leads. We don't really hang out that much anymore. He does his thing, I do mine."

The poorly lit bar, designed to make everyone more attractive, was full of well-dressed men and women talking excitedly over the DJ's music. A long, modern-looking bar to the left could have doubled as a NASA control desk. The mixture of perfume and cologne left an unpleasant tang in my mouth as the waitress lead us past occupied tables and up a staircase to the right. Andrew nudged my shoulder and pointed to her ass, smiling as he went for a mock grab, quickly pulling back when she reached the top step.

The waitress returned with our drinks (three martinis, dry, as per Andrew's smug suggestion). Andrew held his glass up; I feigned a smile and followed.

"To Joseph," said Dean, his eyes already having trouble focusing.

"To Joseph and his triumphant return," said Andrew, eyes wandering to the two girls giggling at the table behind us.

The alcohol began to take its toll on all of us and it wasn't long before Andrew had summoned up the courage to invite three young ladies from the dance floor up to our table. We sat on the plush red couch yelling into each other's ears for over an hour, during which time I was able to string together a sentence or two based on what I thought I overheard of the conversations on either side of me. One of the girls, Monica, sat next to me fiddling uncomfortably with the stem of her glass. Our conversation had stopped after she told me she was either a veterinarian, which was a long shot, or possibly a vegetarian.

After another round of drinks was delivered, she followed me to the railing overlooking the bar and tried getting me to talk again.

"So, you've like, been travelling?" she yelled into my ear, her hand resting lightly on my shoulder. "I love travelling. Last year I went on a cruise."

Before I could come up with a suitably inane reply, I caught sight of a small child out of the corner of my eye, just a flash of bright red and brown, but unmistakably a kid. In a goddamn bar. "Can you believe they let her in here?" I said, inclining my head toward the bar where I had spotted her.

"What?" Monica yelled, squinting into the crowd below.

"There!" I yelled, pointing to the red blur as it slipped into a cluster of people at the edge of the dance floor. "Why the hell would they let a kid into the bar?" Even as I said it, I realized how preposterous it sounded, but I wasn't drunk enough to be hallucinating, of that much I was sure.

"I don't see any kid," said Monica, squinting down at the dance floor. "They wouldn't let one in here, silly." She flashed me a grin as she turned to face me. "Anyway, it was the Caribbean."

"The Caribbean?"

"Yes," she gushed. "The cruise. It was so beautiful." She pushed a lock of chestnut hair over her ear and once again looked down towards the crowded floor below. Was she looking for her too? The sweaty energy from below wafted upwards. I looked at Monica and noticed that her heavily padded bra was poking up above the neckline of her dress. I wanted to pull it up for her.

"Never been there," I said, trying not to look down.

Suddenly overwhelmed by the desire to get the hell out of there, to get on a plane going somewhere, anywhere, I excused myself and hastily said goodbye to Monica and the rest of our table. Andrew gave me a pissed off look and Dean's expression was unreadable with the amount of booze he'd had. They tried and failed to harass me into staying for another round of drinks. Down on the dance floor, I pushed my way past the crowd, seeking out the little girl I was sure I'd seen. All I saw wherever I turned were heavily made up, cologne-drenched, sweat glistening bodies pressed uncomfortably close to me. Memories of being trapped in a roomful of bodies in oppressive heat swarmed up, but my slightly booze-addled mind couldn't decide whether it was a dreaming or waking memory.

A waitress scurried past with a tray of drinks. I reached out to get her attention, convinced she could help me find the little girl, but I accidentally ended up grabbing hold of her tray-carrying arm. The half dozen glasses wavered for a second but remained miraculously upright.

"That was close," I yelled into her ear.

"No fucking kidding!" she trilled. Over her shoulder a bouncer was already eyeing me, waiting to make his move.

"Sorry," I mumbled, letting go of her arm. "Did you see a little girl in here? She was just here. Red jogging pants, brown sweater?" What the hell was I on about? The words sounded crazy, but they rushed out of my mouth unbidden nonetheless.

She adjusted her grip on the tray, looked me straight in the eye and said, "There are no fucking kids in here. Why the hell would we let children into a bar?"

Before I could plead my case, she made an about-face and got the bouncer's attention. He surged towards me.

"Hey man, I'm going, I'm going." I took a step backwards in the direction of the door, evidently not quickly enough for the bouncer's liking; he grabbed my shoulder and helped me right along, chucking me outside into the chilly night air.

Chapter 21

The next morning's hangover wasn't nearly as bad as I thought it was going to be. I awoke at nine thirty to get ready for an interview with the one and only volunteer agency that had answered my inquiries. I brought my dad's cordless phone downstairs to the basement. He had grown weary of the whole volunteer thing, like he suspected I wasn't telling him the entire truth about something but didn't have the energy to find out what it was.

After four rings, someone at the volunteer agency picked up. I gave them my name and they pulled up my application.

"I just have a few questions for you, Joseph. I've gone over your application and everything seems fine. Exactly what we're looking for, really."

The interview started with a run-through of my application. Although I started off listening intently, my mind eventually wandered off and I began thinking about Nepal itself. I thought about trekking with Skye and how everyone thought we were crazy to camp, and how we did it anyway. I thought of Kartik in Bahundanda and the friend he lost in the conflict, Choden and her heroic struggle to stay alive, and Jacquie and Trev fleeing their abandoned hotel. I thought of all the nights I'd spent sleeping next to Skye high up in the mountains, the clean air of the countryside, the stars that blanketed the sky every night.

It didn't feel as though I were being interviewed, not really. There was no nervousness about it. I must have said all the right things, because he concluded the interview with, "So, Joseph, I guess all there is to ask is where you'd like to be placed. We try to be very accommodating when it comes to volunteer placements. Many places need volunteers, and not necessarily in the Kathmandu Valley, but all over Nepal. Unfortunately, there are some places that haven't seen a regular volunteer in years."

"Well, I was actually thinking of somewhere small. A good few hours' drive outside of any major city would be good."

"That would be doable, Joseph. Although many of our smaller destinations are actually a good day, or even up to four or five days', walk from the nearest serviceable city."

"That sounds good, too."

"And another thing, Joseph. I'm sure you're aware of the current political situation over here. It's not exactly paradise. Some of the areas that we covered in the past are no longer accessible due to the conflict."

"Yes, I understand that. I'm sure I'll feel perfectly comfortable."

"Right. Well, Joseph, I can tell you right now that we would love to have you over here. Within the next few days I'll contact you via e-mail with some listings of places that are in need of volunteers. I'll also send you some information on what's going on here with regards to the People's War. It's not as bad as you would think, but as in all areas of conflict there are risks involved, as I'm sure you understand."

"Yeah, I understand. But like I said, it didn't seem so bad when I was there not long ago. Granted, I was on the tourist path."

We hung up a few minutes later. As I set the phone down, a feeling of great relief washed over me, like all the tension had flowed out of my body and into the receiver.

Riding this newfound levity, I decided to send Skye another email. I couldn't keep my excitement out of my message, despite the dampener her last email had put on whatever there was (or wasn't) between us.

That night, I broke the news to my father over a beer after dinner.

"So, when do you leave?" he asked.

"I'm not a hundred percent sure how soon I can start the position after I arrive in Nepal, but it seems pretty much automatic. I'm thinking I'll fly out at the end of next week."

"And what about work?"

"Really, dad? They'll find someone else. I'm going crazy there, anyway. Not sure I would've lasted much longer."

"And what about this Skye you're so fond of?"

"Right, that. I had thought of going to Australia, but I just can't right now." I didn't feel compelled to mention the fact that Skye had basically told me not to bother coming to Australia. Maybe I didn't want to believe it myself.

"So, where will you go after this adventure, then?" he asked, taking the last sip of his beer.

I peeled the remainder of the label off my beer. "Can't really say, dad. You know I appreciate everything you and mom do for me, right?" I waited a few seconds before adding, "I've never let you down before, have I?" I wasn't really sure where these questions were coming from, but it felt eerily similar to the night before in the bar when I'd asked Monica and then the waitress about seeing the little girl.

My father sat perfectly still in his chair. I could feel him staring at me, although I had averted my gaze back to the tattered label of my beer bottle. It felt like there were more words stuck in my throat, but I swallowed them down and sat in uneasy silence, waiting for his reply.

Eventually, he said, "No you haven't, kiddo." He got up from his chair and walked over to me. I remained seated, unsure what he was going to do. As he walked past me, his fingers ghosted over my shoulder. "You're a good boy," he murmured.

Chapter 22

Dinner with my mother's boyfriend had been put off for a reason she didn't disclose. I waited for her at my father's desk, staring at the computer screen wondering if I should send Skye another email. What would I say? I had just started to type a forced, awkward greeting when I heard the horn blare twice outside.

"What took you so long?" she asked as I got in the car.

"What?"

"I honked four times Joseph," she said, though not angrily. "Now, I think you should know, Joseph, your father has spoken to me about you." My mother stared straight ahead through the windshield. She hadn't even said hello. "He's worried about you. He says something is different with you."

"Not this again," I muttered under my breath.

"Well, is there?" She finally turned to face me. Her eyes were rimmed with pink. "He said you've only been out once since you've been back."

"Yeah, well, things are different now." Not the best way to start the evening. "People change, they move on."

"What about this Skye you seemed so keen on? Have you been keeping in touch with her?" she asked.

"Yes," I said slowly. "I'd even been thinking of going to Australia to see her, but let's just say it's not such a good idea at the moment."

"Why's that?" she asked, turning the car onto the bridge.

"Does it matter? Let's just drop it, please." Silence filled the car for the next few blocks. My mother stopped at the liquor store to pick up a bottle of red wine. I waited in the car and fiddled with the radio.

The doorbell rang a few minutes after we'd arrived at her apartment. This was it. This was the new guy. "I'll get it," she said. I heard them speaking to each other in hushed voices in the hallway. They seemed to be talking for an inordinately long time. Were they hiding something from me? Where had that thought even come from?

"Joseph," the stranger said, extending his hand to me. "I'm James. Your mother has told me a lot about you. I hear you've been away for quite a long time, and not exactly checking in enough," he said with a forced chuckle. He was taller than me with a belly that had seen one too many hamburgers. His receding hairline accentuated a large forehead. A thin pinkish scar crested above his right eye.

I let him have this one. "It's a pretty crazy world out there." I feigned a smile in return before sitting back down.

"So, you're thinking of volunteering, eh?" he said when we both had a glass of red in hand. "That's something I have always wanted to do."

"There's a computer," I said pointing to my mother's desktop. He looked towards it then back at me, a little quizzical and more than a little irritated. "Plenty of opportunities out there," I added, painfully aware of how pretentious I sounded, but finding myself far past caring.

"Not for me, unfortunately. I've got to be here now," he answered, taking a sip of his wine. "Where are you thinking of heading?" he asked.

"Probably Nepal." I could hear my mother humming in the kitchen. The aroma of her mushroom, spinach and olive lasagna floated through the apartment.

"You've been there before, right?" he asked, his voice strained. I couldn't fathom why. He obviously knew I'd been to Nepal before. My mother surely would have told him. "Pretty crazy with the Maoists over there, eh?"

"I didn't have any problems," I answered. A surge of anger began to well up in the pit of my stomach.

After another sip of wine he cleared his throat and pressed on. "Every place has its problems, but it always seems like the poorer ones get the worst of it, don't they? For the most part, anyway."

"What the hell would you know about it?" Suddenly I was rising from the couch to my feet. How dare this overfed asshole profess to know anything about what was going on in Nepal, or anywhere outside his pathetically small suburban orbit, for that matter? I stormed into the kitchen and slammed my glass down into the sink. Droplets of wine splashed up onto the counter. "I'm leaving, mom." I planted a swift, angry kiss on her cheek before she could respond.

"What? Joseph? What's going on?" Her voice raised in confusion as I backed out of the kitchen. She followed me to the front door. James still hadn't moved from his seat in the living room.

"Look, I'm sorry, I just can't do this." I had my jacket on and the door opened before she grabbed my hand, her fingernails digging in slightly.

"Joseph," she said, her voice shockingly soft in comparison to the grip she had on my hand. Tears were welling up in her eyes and she looked up at me. "What happened to you? Something is not right, sweetheart. I don't know what it is, but... I love you, and I know you. Something has happened to you."

I pulled her into a hug before she could say anything else. Maybe she was right. "I'm going to walk home. I love you, too." I kissed her wet cheek then turned and shut the door behind me.

The outside air was damp. A thick humidity had settled over the city, warning of thundershowers. The sun had already set and now dark voluminous clouds drifted lazily overhead. The street-lights flickered on. Night had begun. The street itself was empty of life except for a fenced in dog across the street. I could see its shiny wet nose poking through the gaps in the wood that needed paint. I could hear its heavy breathing as it pawed at the earth underneath. A warm gust of wind kicked up and the garbage on the street shot into the air. My shirt pushed against my chest as the first sound of distant thunder murmured unapologetically.

I stood on the sidewalk, motionless. Out of my left eye a streak of heat lightning flashed. What was I doing? Looking up at my mother's apartment I thought about going back, but then I saw the shadow of a large man appear in the doorway. It remained there as if looking out from behind the curtain, and then the hallway light went off. James was taking control.

I peered down the lifeless street at the blinking stoplight. It was a very long walk to my father's house and I contemplated a bus, but then I started thinking about my mother and why I had just stormed out of her house. That was not in my usual character. Had I just simply passed James off without giving him any real chance? Why would I do that? Why did I get so angry? The haloed street lamps yellowed the pavement under my feet as I walked. Stride after stride I paced towards the direction of the river, my thoughts on nothing but what I had just done. Near the downtown center I made a left and continued before stopping outside the movie theater. I lit a cigarette and the smoke filled my lungs, heavier now with the moist air. The first droplets of rain began to fall, heavy drops that pelted the sidewalk, wetting large swathes of it in mere seconds. Lightning flashed, a fierce snake-tongue landed nearby. Its sonic boom followed almost instantly.

I noticed I was not alone. A small object ahead of me skipped about playfully, bobbing between the garbage cans and store fronts. I watched it amused, thinking it was a small dog or raccoon chasing a playmate. The rain grew stronger, thicker, the lightning and thunder kept up their onslaught. I followed the object towards the river, my hands in front, shielding my face from the whipping rain. At the river I made a left for the final push towards my father's house. The object kept up, forever in front of me as if leading me home.

***

The hammer slipped. Falling to the floor in slow motion, I watched it make a full rotation before soundlessly hitting the concrete floor. My thumb throbbed, blood rushing to the point of contact. Eyes, many sets of eyes on me, watching to see my reaction. No pain, just vivid images flashing before. White-capped mountains, scraggly peaks, deep green forest. The stench of rotting flesh, decaying foliage, death. Looking up, I'm in my car. A young girl, red jogging pants, dirtied cheeks. Dark mahogany eyes. She's not smiling. Floating over a village, mud-brick homes lining a familiar dirt path. Now I'm floating down a hill past wooden homes. It starts to rain, drops forming on the windshield. I'm running. Someone is chasing after me. In front, the little red-clad girl, darting amongst trees. I toss a look over my shoulder, and now I'm on the ground. I've left her all alone. A man stands above me, watching her run. His booted foot stomps on me once, then twice, then again, but there is no pain. She runs. The trees devour her. The man takes off in her direction. I lay unmoving, the clouds above closing over me.

The car collides with a tree. Metal folding in on itself jolts my head forward. Dazed and sleepy, I get out to inspect the damage. A pretty sizable dent, but still drivable. Smoke rises like incense. Trees in front, blurred by mist. Water below, a small, brown bog holding an old boat, refusing to release it, tilted on its side. A watery grave. I know where I am. Half a mile away is my father's house. I have skated on this pond before, I have fallen over that boat. It's darker now, the afternoon sun disappearing unannounced. My thumb throbs, swollen. Rain. No, not rain; red water. Blood. I swipe at my forehead and feel the warm liquid smear across to my temple.

The remaining sunlight penetrates the clouds, a thousand torch beams leading me into the forest. I'm drawn irresistibly to it. A path is illuminated among the trees, a corridor. Gunshots ring out from far away; I cover my ears and keep walking. The mist is rising. Someone is there, I can hear them. A scream pierces the air. I can see a small red form in the shadows; it's her, the red jogging pants, the dirtied sweater. I try to yell but nothing comes out. A pasty film covers my tongue. The girl is somehow behind me now, pulling at my jacket. I spin around, get dizzy, droplets of blood wicking off my forehead. The earth trembles beneath me, my footing falters, I stumble back and fall over into darkness.

When I wake up, I am covered in mud. My battered thumb throbs more insistently than ever. Stepping back inside the car, I see the clock flashing a dim green six forty-five. I'm late. Somehow I drove my father's car here, although I don't know how.

Chapter 23

"Hey son, you got a minute?" He hadn't called me son in years. It was a term he only used when he wanted to Talk with a capital T. Like when he once found a small baggie of marijuana in my backpack, or the time I was suspended from school for a practical joke that had gone belly-up.

"Um, yeah. Sure." What I really wanted was to get to the computer and see if the volunteer agency had contacted me. It had been a few days since my interview.

"Let's go into the front room." He motioned for me to follow. He took a seat in his armchair. I hung back and leaned against the doorway. "Grab a seat," he said, not quite meeting my eyes.

"I'm in a bit of a rush, dad," I lied.

"This won't take long." I sat down on the couch. I could hear Amy moving about in the kitchen. My father held my passport in his hand. I stared at the worn pages between his fingers. "You know, you gave us quite the fright the other day." His voice was slow, measured. "We had no idea where you'd gone, you know."

"Yeah, I know." I waited for him to interrupt, but he didn't. "I don't know what happened, to be honest. One minute I was at work, and the next thing I knew, I wasn't."

"You know this is yours?" He held my passport, looked down at the tattered booklet, then back to me. I stared at him blankly, not sure what he was getting at. "Amy was in your room the other day, just giving it a once over, and this happened to fall off the shelf in the closet." I wondered where he was going with this. "Well, Amy thought she'd take a quick look at it after it fell. She hasn't travelled the world like you have, you know. She was curious."

"OK," I said slowly, thickly.

"The thing is," he paused for a second, thinking over his next words. "Well, it says here in this thing," he waved the book back and forth, "that you've been to Nepal twice already." I sat motionless, what did he want me to say? "Twice, son." He repeated. I couldn't for the life of me figure out what he was getting at. Did he think I was hiding something from him? I'd told him all about the trek with Skye, hadn't I? What more did he want? I felt a migraine blooming behind my left eye.

"Let me see that." I shot out of the chair faster than I had intended. I tore the booklet from his hands and flipped through the pages: England,

Belgium, Italy, Holland, France, and other European countries I barely remembered, then I saw India and...Nepal. Twice. I stared at the stamps, feeling my father's eyes on me, watching my expression like I was liable to break down or blow up at any moment. I heard Amy's footsteps in the doorway and looked up to meet her eyes. She held my gaze for a second before shuffling back into the kitchen.

"Dad, it's no big deal. It says twice, yeah, but the problem is getting in and out. I told you about India, I bribed my way out of there," I babbled, feeling the blood rush to my face, the migraine spreading to the right side of my forehead.

"I'm not worried about India!" he yelled. "I'm worried about you!"

"You don't have to!" I shouted back. "Things are fucked there, that's all." I felt the anger inside me build to a head. "I had problems everywhere I went, but there are problems everywhere, dad!"

He looked out the window, his face set grimly. "I don't know what to do son," he eventually sighed, like I had deeply disappointed him. "I just want to understand what happened there, what happened to you."

"Nothing happened to me, nothing at all. I want to go back there. I have to go. Something tells me I should do this. Look," I said, pointing to the pictures of the sponsored children on the mantelpiece. "You're doing your part, right? I just want to do mine."

"Have you seen what's happening there? There's a war going on, people are dying! It's not safe!" His anger puffed him up so much he was almost standing. Why was he doing this? Why was he trying to stop me? I remained standing in front of him, clutching my passport in slightly trembling fingers. Silence blanketed the room, neither of us sure what to do next.

"I have to go dad. I need to do my part." The words came out weak and childlike. I guess that's how I felt, standing there in my childhood home under the gaze of the smiling portraits of sponsor kids, feeling utterly helpless in the face of the unbelievable shit they and others like them had to put up with.

I finally sought out my father's eyes, which were now glistening with moisture as he stared out the window vacantly. "I think you've done your part, son."

***

The lush summer foliage is spread wide in the afternoon sun. I can almost smell the maple from inside my room. The treetops sway in a gust wind I cannot hear behind a locked window. There is my mother, the reflected sunlight cutting her image in half, her left hand dabbing tears that had formed an hour earlier. I'm in the back seat, in the middle, one hand resting on a bag that, when I packed it, I was sure was destined for Nepal. Driving towards what I was convinced was the airport, I saw movement out of the corner of my eye in a small patch of forest. Within the low, forested plains of Southern Ontario I swore I saw a dirtied red blur running amongst the thick brush. I asked my father to stop the car. Starting towards the woods, seeking out what I was certain I had seen, I felt my father's arm seize my shoulder. "You don't see her?" I had asked, my voice coming from somewhere deep inside my throat but emerging barely audible from my mouth. The cars on highway 401 blew past like the wind of the Annapurnas.

A robust brunette in a neatly pressed white uniform stops just outside my door. Seeing I'm awake, sitting by the window, she leans into the room and smiles. It's a nice smile, plain and genuine. She's not much older than I am but she holds herself very well, putting her in an entirely different age bracket somehow. We make eye contact before her uniform makes a starchy about-face and the sound of her shoes continue their duet down the linoleum hallway. I turn back once again to the view outside my window. I recall a different view, one filled with green valleys floating amongst thick mountain mist.

I know now that the image I recall is Nepal. Not with Skye, who has not been in touch (and I cannot blame her), but my first days in Nepal, when I first met the little red blur. Someone I tried to help. It took almost two weeks before I was able to remember the name Rinrut. And not long after I was able to recall the other people that I had met there.

My parents and the doctors tried to make contact with Kunjana and the other villagers. They learned the organization I worked with is no longer in Kathmandu (or so I am told), and the entire region of Myagdi, including the village of Takam is now under the complete control of the Maoists (this I can verify). The country's civil war rages on, and, from what I've heard, the fighting has escalated to barbarous proportions.

I know I will go back.

Sometimes at night when I close my eyes I can see Kunjana smiling up at me, her almond eyes sparkling with life, her dirtied cheeks barely containing a joyful smile. Behind her, holding her close stands wise old Debu. I watch him fiddle for a cigarette in his pajama pocket as he lovingly pats Kunjana's shoulder. His warm smile tells me everything will be fine, that I will be fine, and Kunjana will be, too. And the doctors here agree. They say I won't be here very long, which is a good thing, because I am going back.

Acknowledgements

Writing a book can be a very lonely endeavor, but without the help from others some books would never come to be. I am completely indebted to the following people: Yalic Avila, Andrea Blackie, Howard Choy, Adam Claydon-Platt, Damien Donovan, Stephen Douglas, Yumi Lee Miyama, and Penne Thornton.

I would also like to thank my parents, who I am extremely grateful to have. Some children need to be told how to run, and for some it is where, and then others are just meant to be watched. I thank you for this.

www.ingramcontent.com/pod-product-compliance
Lightning Source LLC
Chambersburg PA
CBHW020642260626
47157CB00008B/2866